Nathaniel Hawthorne

True Stories from History and Biography

Nathaniel Hawthorne

True Stories from History and Biography

ISBN/EAN: 9783337389062

Printed in Europe, USA, Canada, Australia, Japan

Cover: Foto ©Andreas Hilbeck / pixelio.de

More available books at **www.hansebooks.com**

FROM

HISTORY AND BIOGRAPHY.

BY

NATHANIEL HAWTHORNE.

BOSTON:
TICKNOR AND FIELDS.
1866.

UNIVERSITY PRESS:
WELCH, BIGELOW, AND COMPANY,
CAMBRIDGE.

PREFACE.

In writing this ponderous tome, the author's desire has been to describe the eminent characters and remarkable events of our annals in such a form and style that the YOUNG may make acquaintance with them of their own accord. For this purpose, while ostensibly relating the adventures of a chair, he has endeavored to keep a distinct and unbroken thread of authentic history. The chair is made to pass from one to another of those personages of whom he thought it most desirable for the young reader to have vivid and familiar ideas, and whose lives and actions would best enable him to give picturesque sketches of the times. On its sturdy oaken legs it trudges diligently from one scene to another, and seems always to thrust itself in the way, with most benign complacency, whenever an historical personage happens to be looking round for a seat.

There is certainly no method by which the shadowy outlines of departed men and women can be made to assume the hues of life more effectually than by connecting their images with the substantial and homely reality of a fireside chair. It causes us to feel at once that these characters of history had a private and familiar existence, and were not wholly contained within that cold array of outward action which we are compelled to receive as the adequate representation of their lives. If this impression can be given, much is accomplished.

Setting aside Grandfather and his auditors, and excepting the adventures of the chair, which form the machinery of the work, nothing in the ensuing pages can be termed fictitious. The author, it is true, has sometimes assumed the license of filling up the outline of history with details for which he has none but imaginative authority, but which, he hopes, do not violate nor give a false coloring to the truth. He believes that, in this respect, his narrative will not be found to convey ideas and impressions of which the reader may hereafter find it necessary to purge his mind.

The author's great doubt is, whether he has succeeded in writing a book which will be readable by the class for whom he intends it. To make a lively and entertaining narrative for children, with such unmalleable material as is presented by the sombre, stern, and rigid characteristics of the Puritans and their descendants, is quite as difficult an attempt as to manufacture delicate playthings out of the granite rocks on which New England is founded.

THE WHOLE HISTORY

OF

GRANDFATHER'S CHAIR.

COMPLETE IN THREE PARTS.

GRANDFATHER'S CHAIR.

PART I.

CHAPTER I.

GRANDFATHER had been sitting in his old arm chair all that pleasant afternoon, while the children were pursuing their various sports far off or near at hand. Sometimes you would have said, "Grandfather is asleep;" but still, even when his eyes were closed, his thoughts were with the young people, playing among the flowers and shrubbery of the garden.

He heard the voice of Laurence, who had taken possession of a heap of decayed branches which the gardener had lopped from the fruit trees, and was building a little hut for his cousin Clara and himself. He heard Clara's gladsome voice, too, as she weeded and watered the flower bed which had been given her for her own. He could have counted every footstep that Charley took, as he trundled his wheelbarrow along the gravel walk. And though Grandfather was old and gray haired, yet his heart leaped with joy whenever little Alice came fluttering, like a butterfly, into the room. She had made each of the children her playmate in turn, and now made Grandfather her playmate too, and thought him the merriest of them all.

At last the children grew weary of their sports; because a summer afternoon is like a long lifetime to the young. So they came into the room together, and clustered round Grandfather's great chair. Little Alice, who was hardly five years old, took the privilege of the youngest, and climbed his knee. It was a pleasant thing to behold that fair and golden-haired child in the lap of the old man, and to think that, different as they were, the hearts of both could be gladdened with the same joys.

"Grandfather," said little Alice, laying her head back upon his arm, "I am very tired now. You must tell me a story to make me go to sleep."

"That is not what story tellers like," answered Grandfather, smiling. "They are better satisfied when they can keep their auditors awake."

"But here are Laurence, and Charley, and I," cried cousin Clara, who was twice as old as little

Alice. "We will all three keep wide awake. And pray, Grandfather, tell us a story about this strange-looking old chair."

Now, the chair in which Grandfather sat was made of oak, which had grown dark with age, but had been rubbed and polished till it shone as bright as mahogany. It was very large and heavy, and had a back that rose high above Grandfather's white head. This back was curiously carved in open work, so as to represent flowers, and foliage, and other devices, which the children had often gazed at, but could never understand what they meant. On the very tip-top of the chair, over the head of Grandfather himself, was a likeness of a lion's head, which had such a savage grin that you would almost expect to hear it growl and snarl.

The children had seen Grandfather sitting in this chair ever since they could remember any thing. Perhaps the younger of them supposed that he and the chair had come into the world together, and that both had always been as old as they were now. At this time, however, it happened to be the fashion for ladies to adorn their drawing rooms with the oldest and oddest chairs that could be found. It seemed to cousin Clara that, if these ladies could have seen Grandfather's old chair, they would have thought it worth all the rest together. She wondered if it were not even older than Grandfather himself, and longed to know all about its history.

"Do, Grandfather, talk to us about this chair," she repeated.

"Well, child," said Grandfather, patting Clara's cheek, "I can tell you a great many stories of my chair. Perhaps your cousin Laurence would like to hear them too. They would teach him something about the history and distinguished people of his country which he has never read in any of his school books."

Cousin Laurence was a boy of twelve, a bright scholar, in whom an early thoughtfulness and sensibility began to show themselves. His young fancy kindled at the idea of knowing all the adventures of this venerable chair. He looked eagerly in Grandfather's face; and even Charley, a bold, brisk, restless little fellow of nine, sat himself down on the carpet, and resolved to be quiet for at least ten minutes, should the story last so long.

Meantime, little Alice was already asleep; so Grandfather, being much pleased with such an attentive audience, began to talk about matters that happened long ago.

CHAPTER II.

But before relating the adventures of the chair, Grandfather found it necessary to speak of the circumstances that caused the first settlement of New England. For it will soon be perceived that the story of this remarkable chair cannot be told without telling a great deal of the history of the country.

So Grandfather talked about the Puritans, as those persons were called who thought it sinful to practise the religious forms and ceremonies which the church of England had borrowed from the Roman Catholics. These Puritans suffered so much persecution in England, that, in 1607, many of them went over to Holland, and lived ten or twelve years at Amsterdam and Leyden. But they feared that, if they continued there much longer, they should cease to be English, and should adopt all the manners, and ideas, and feelings of the Dutch. For this and other reasons, in the year 1620 they embarked on board of the ship Mayflower, and crossed the ocean to the shores of Cape Cod. There they made a settlement, and called it Plymouth, which, though now a part of Massachusetts, was for a long time a colony by itself. And thus was formed the earliest settlement of the Puritans in America.

Meantime, those of the Puritans who remained in England continued to suffer grievous persecution on account of their religious opinions. They began to look around them for some spot where they might worship God, not as the king and bishops thought fit, but according to the dictates of their own consciences. When their brethren had gone from Holland to America, they bethought themselves that they likewise might find refuge from persecution there. Several gentlemen among them purchased a tract of country on the coast of Massachusetts Bay, and obtained a charter from King Charles, which authorized them to make laws for the settlers. In the year 1628 they sent over a few people, with John Endicott at their head, to commence a plantation at Salem. Peter Palfrey, Roger Conant, and one or two more, had built houses there in 1626, and may be considered as the first settlers of that ancient town. Many other Puritans prepared to follow Endicott.

"And now we come to the chair, my dear children," said Grandfather. "This chair is supposed to have been made of an oak tree which grew in the park of the English Earl of Lincoln, between two and three centuries ago. In its younger days it used, probably, to stand in the hall of the earl's castle. Do not you see the coat of arms of the family of Lincoln carved in the open work of the back? But when his daughter, the Lady Arbella, was married to a certain Mr. Johnson, the earl gave her this valuable chair."

"Who was Mr. Johnson?" inquired Clara.

"He was a gentleman of great wealth, who agreed with the Puritans in their religious opinions," answered Grandfather. "And as his belief was the same as theirs, he resolved that he would live and die with them. Accordingly, in the month of April, 1630, he left his pleasant abode and all his comforts in England, and embarked, with the Lady Arbella, on board of a ship bound for America."

As Grandfather was frequently impeded by the questions and observations of his young auditors, we deem it advisable to omit all such prattle as is not essential to the story. We have taken some pains to find out exactly what Grandfather said, and here offer to our readers, as nearly as possible in his own words, the story of

THE LADY ARBELLA.

The ship in which Mr. Johnson and his lady embarked, taking Grandfather's chair along with them, was called the Arbella, in honor of the lady herself. A fleet of ten or twelve vessels, with many hundred passengers, left England about the same time; for a multitude of people, who were discontented with the king's government and oppressed by the bishops, were flocking over to the new world. One of the vessels in the fleet was that same Mayflower which had carried the Puritan Pilgrims to Plymouth. And now, my children, I would have you fancy yourselves in the cabin of the good ship Arbella; because, if you could behold the passengers aboard that vessel, you would feel what a blessing and honor it was for New England to have such settlers. They were the best men and women of their day.

Among the passengers was John Winthrop, who had sold the estate of his forefathers, and was going to prepare a new home for his wife and children in the wilderness. He had the king's charter in his keeping, and was appointed the first governor of Massachusetts. Imagine him a person of grave and benevolent aspect, dressed in a black velvet suit, with a broad ruff around his neck, and a peaked beard upon his chin. There was likewise a minister of the gospel whom the English bishops had forbidden to preach, but who knew that he should have liberty both to preach and pray in the forests of America. He wore a black cloak, called a Geneva cloak, and had a black velvet cap, fitting close to his head, as was the fashion of almost all the Puritan clergymen. In their company came Sir Richard Saltonstall, who had been one of the five first projectors of the new colony. He soon returned to his native country. But his descendants still remain in New England; and the good old family name is as much respected in our days as it was in those of Sir Richard.

Not only these, but several other men of wealth and pious ministers were in the cabin of the Arbella. One had banished himself forever from the old hall where his ancestors had lived for hundreds of years. Another had left his quiet parsonage, in a country town of England. Others had come from the Universities of Oxford or Cambridge, where they had gained great fame for their learning. And here they all were, tossing upon the uncertain and dangerous sea, and bound for a home that was more dangerous than even the sea itself. In the cabin, likewise, sat the Lady Arbella in her chair, with a gentle and sweet expression on her face, but looking too pale and feeble to endure the hardships of the wilderness.

Every morning and evening the Lady Arbella gave up her great chair to one of the ministers, who took his place in it and read passages from the Bible to his companions. And thus, with prayers, and pious conversation, and frequent singing of hymns, which the breezes caught from their lips and scattered far over the desolate waves, they prosecuted their voyage, and sailed into the harbor of Salem in the month of June.

At that period there were but six or eight dwellings in the town ; and these were miserable hovels, with roofs of straw and wooden chimneys. The passengers in the fleet either built huts with bark and branches of trees, or erected tents of cloth till they could provide themselves with better shelter. Many of them went to form a settlement at Charlestown. It was thought fit that the Lady Arbella should tarry in Salem for a time: she was probably received as a guest into the family of John Endicott. He was the chief person in the plantation, and had the only comfortable house which the new comers had beheld since they left England. So now, children, you must imagine Grandfather's chair in the midst of a new scene.

Suppose it a hot summer's day, and the lattice windows of a chamber in Mr. Endicott's house thrown wide open. The Lady Arbella, looking paler than she did on shipboard, is sitting in her chair and thinking mournfully of far-off England. She rises and goes to the window. There, amid patches of garden ground and cornfield, she sees the few wretched hovels of the settlers, with the still ruder wigwams and cloth tents of the passengers who had arrived in the same fleet with herself. Far and near stretches the dismal forest of pine trees, which throw their black shadows over the whole land, and likewise over the heart of this poor lady.

All the inhabitants of the little village are busy. One is clearing a spot on the verge of the forest for his homestead; another is hewing the trunk of a fallen pine tree, in order to build himself a dwelling; a third is hoeing in his field of Indian corn. Here comes a huntsman out of the woods, dragging a bear which he has shot, and shouting to the neighbors to lend him a hand. There goes a man to the sea shore, with a spade and a bucket, to dig a mess of clams, which were a principal article of food with the first settlers. Scattered here and there are two or three dusky figures, clad in mantles of fur, with ornaments of bone hanging from their ears, and the feathers of wild birds in their coal-black hair. They have belts of shell work slung across their shoulders, and are armed with bows and arrows and flint-headed spears. These are an Indian sagamore and his attendants, who have come to gaze at the labors of the white men. And now rises a cry that a pack of wolves have seized a young calf in the pasture; and every man snatches up his gun or pike and runs in chase of the marauding beasts.

Poor Lady Arbella watches all these sights, and feels that this new world is fit only for rough and hardy people. None should be here but those who can struggle with wild beasts and wild men, and can toil in the heat or cold, and can keep their hearts firm against all difficulties and dangers. But she is not one of these. Her gentle and timid spirit sinks within her; and, turning away from the window, she sits down in the great chair and wonders whereabouts in the wilderness her friends will dig her grave.

Mr. Johnson had gone, with Governor Winthrop and most of the other passengers, to Boston, where he intended to build a house for Lady Arbella and himself. Boston was then covered with wild woods, and had fewer inhabitants, even, than Salem. During her husband's absence, poor Lady Arbella felt herself growing ill, and was hardly able to stir from the great chair. Whenever John Endicott noticed her despondency, he doubtless addressed her with words of comfort. "Cheer up, my good lady!" he would say. "In a little time, you will love this rude life of the wilderness as I do." But Endicott's heart was as bold and resolute as iron, and he could not understand why a woman's heart should not be of iron too.

Still, however, he spoke kindly to the lady, and then hastened forth to till his cornfield and set out fruit trees, or to bargain with the Indians for furs, or perchance to oversee the building of a fort. Also, being a magistrate, he had often to punish some idler or evil doer, by ordering him to be set in the stocks or scourged at the whipping post. Often, too, as was the custom of the times, he and Mr. Higginson, the minister of Salem, held long religious talks together. Thus John Endicott was a man of multifarious business, and had no time to look back regretfully to his native land. He felt himself fit for the new world and for the work that he had to do, and set himself resolutely to accomplish it.

What a contrast, my dear children, between this bold, rough, active man, and the gentle Lady Arbella, who was fading away, like a pale English flower, in the shadow of the forest! And now the great chair was often empty, because Lady Arbella grew too weak to arise from bed.

Meantime, her husband had pitched upon a spot for their new home. He returned from Boston to Salem, travelling through the woods on foot, and leaning on his pilgrim's staff. His heart yearned within him; for he was eager to tell his wife of the new home which he had chosen. But when he beheld her pale and hollow cheek, and found how her strength was wasted, he must have known that her appointed home was in a better land. Happy for him then — happy both for him and her — if they remembered that there was a path to heaven, as well from this heathen wilderness as from the Christian land whence they had come. And so, in one short month from her arrival, the gentle Lady Arbella faded away and died. They dug a grave for her in the new soil, where the roots of the pine trees impeded their spades ; and when her bones had rested there nearly two hundred years, and a city had sprung up around them, a church of stone was built upon the spot.

Charley, almost at the commencement of the foregoing narrative, had galloped away, with a prodigious clatter, upon Grandfather's stick, and was not yet returned. So large a boy should have been ashamed to ride upon a stick. But Laurence and Clara had listened attentively, and were affected by this true story of the gentle lady who had come so far to die so soon. Grandfather had supposed that little Alice was asleep ; but towards the close of the story, happening to look down upon her, he saw that her blue eyes were wide open, and fixed earnestly upon his face. The tears had gathered in them, like dew upon a delicate flower ; but when Grandfather ceased to speak, the sunshine of her smile broke forth again.

"O, the lady must have been so glad to get to heaven ! " exclaimed little Alice.

"Grandfather, what became of Mr. Johnson ? " asked Clara.

" His heart appears to have been quite broken," answered Grandfather ; " for he died at Boston within a month after the death of his wife. He was buried in the very same tract of ground where he had intended to build a dwelling for Lady Arbella and himself. Where their house would have stood, there was his grave."

"I never heard any thing so melancholy," said Claia.

"The people loved and respected Mr. Johnson so much," continued Grandfather, "that it was the last request of many of them, when they died, that they might be buried as near as possible to this good man's grave. And so the field became the first burial ground in Boston. When you pass through Tremont Street, along by King's Chapel, you see a burial ground, containing many old grave stones and monuments. That was Mr. Johnson's field."

"How sad is the thought," observed Clara, "that one of the first things which the settlers had to do, when they came to the new world, was to set apart a burial ground!"

"Perhaps," said Laurence, "if they had found no need of burial grounds here, they would have been glad, after a few years, to go back to England."

Grandfather looked at Laurence, to discover whether he knew how profound and true a thing he had said.

CHAPTER III.

Not long after Grandfather had told the story of his great chair, there chanced to be a rainy day. Our friend Charley, after disturbing the household with beat of drum and riotous shouts, races up and down the staircase, overturning of chairs, and much other uproar, began to feel the quiet and confinement within doors intolerable. But as the rain came down in a flood, the little fellow was hopelessly a prisoner, and now stood with sullen aspect at a window, wondering whether the sun itself were not extinguished by so much moisture in the sky.

Charley had already exhausted the less eager activity of the other children; and they had betaken themselves to occupations that did not admit of his companionship. Laurence sat in a recess near the bookcase, reading, not for the first time, the Midsummer Night's Dream. Clara was making a rosary of beads for a little figure of a Sister of Charity, who was to attend the Bunker Hill fair and lend her aid in erecting the monument. Little Alice sat on Grandfather's footstool, with a picture book in her hand ; and, for every picture, the child was telling Grandfather a story. She did not read from the book, (for little Alice had not much skill in reading,) but told the story out of her own heart and mind.

Charley was too big a boy, of course, to care any thing about little Alice's stories, although Grandfather appeared to listen with a good deal of interest. Often, in a young child's ideas and fancies, there is something which it requires the thought of a lifetime to comprehend. But Charley was of opinion that, if a story must be told, it had better be told by Grandfather than little Alice.

"Grandfather, I want to hear more about your chair," said he.

Now, Grandfather remembered that Charley had galloped away upon a stick in the midst of the narrative of poor Lady Arbella, and I know not whether he would have thought it worth while to tell another story merely to gratify such an inattentive auditor as Charley. But Laurence laid down his book and seconded the request. Clara drew her chair nearer to Grandfather ; and little Alice immediately closed her picture book and looked up into his face. Grandfather had not the heart to disappoint them.

He mentioned several persons who had a share in the settlement of our country, and who would be well worthy of remembrance, if we could find room to tell about them all. Among the rest, Grandfather spoke of the famous Hugh Peters, a minister of the gospel, who did much good to the inhabitants of Salem. Mr. Peters afterwards went back to England, and was chaplain to Oliver Cromwell; but Grandfather did not tell the children what became of this upright and zealous man at last. In fact, his auditors were growing impatient to hear more about the history of the chair.

"After the death of Mr. Johnson," said he, "Grandfather's chair came into the possession of Roger Williams. He was a clergyman, who arrived at Salem, and settled there in 1631. Doubtless the good man has spent many a studious hour in this old chair, either penning a sermon or reading some abstruse book of theology, till midnight came upon him unawares. At that period, as there were few lamps or candles to be had, people used to read or work by the light of pitch-pine torches. These supplied the place of the 'midnight oil' to the learned men of New England."

Grandfather went on to talk about Roger Williams, and told the children several particulars, which we have not room to repeat. One incident, however, which was connected with his life, must be related, because it will give the reader an idea of the opinions and feelings of the first settlers of New England. It was as follows:—

THE RED CROSS.

While Roger Williams sat in Grandfather's chair at his humble residence in Salem, John Endicott would often come to visit him. As the clergy had great influence in temporal concerns, the minister and magistrate would talk over the occurrences of the day, and consult how the people might be governed according to scriptural laws.

One thing especially troubled them both. In the old national banner of England, under which her soldiers have fought for hundreds of years, there is a red cross, which has been there ever since the days when England was in subjection to the pope. The cross, though a holy symbol, was abhorred by the Puritans, because they considered it a relic of Popish idolatry. Now, whenever the trainband of Salem was mustered, the soldiers, with Endicott at their head, had no other flag to march under than this same old Papistical banner of England, with the red cross in the midst of it. The banner of the red cross, likewise, was flying on the walls of the fort of Salem; and a similar one was displayed in Boston Harbor, from the fortress on Castle Island.

"I profess, brother Williams," Captain Endicott would say, after they had been talking of this matter, "it distresses a Christian man's heart to see this idolatrous cross flying over our heads. A stranger, beholding it, would think that we had undergone all our hardships and dangers, by sea and in the wilderness, only to get new dominions for the Pope of Rome."

"Truly, good Mr. Endicott," Roger Williams would answer, "you speak as an honest man and Protestant Christian should. For mine own part, were it my business to draw a sword, I should reckon it sinful to fight under such a banner. Neither can I, in my pulpit, ask the blessing of Heaven upon it."

Such, probably, was the way in which Roger Williams and John Endicott used to talk about the banner of the red cross. Endicott, who was a prompt and resolute man, soon determined that Massachusetts, if she could not have a banner of her own, should at least be delivered from that of the Pope of Rome.

Not long afterwards there was a military muster at Salem. Every ablebodied man in the town and neighborhood was there. All were well armed, with steel caps upon their heads, plates of iron upon their breasts and at their backs, and gorgets of steel around their necks. When the sun shone upon these ranks of iron-clad men, they flashed and blazed with a splendor that bedazzled the wild Indians who had come out of the woods to gaze at them. The soldiers had long pikes, swords, and muskets, which were fired with matches, and were almost as heavy as a small cannon.

These men had mostly a stern and rigid aspect. To judge by their looks, you might have supposed that there was as much iron in their hearts as there was upon their heads and breasts. They were all devoted Puritans, and of the same temper as those with whom Oliver Cromwell afterwards overthrew the throne of England. They hated all the relics of Popish superstition as much as Endicott himself; and yet over their heads was displayed the banner of the red cross.

Endicott was the captain of the company. While the soldiers were expecting his orders to begin their exercise, they saw him take the banner in one hand, holding his drawn sword in the other. Probably he addressed them in a speech, and explained how horrible a thing it was, that men, who had fled from Popish idolatry into the wilderness, should be compelled to fight under its symbols here. Perhaps he concluded his address somewhat in the following style : —

" And now, fellow-soldiers, you see this old banner of England. Some of you, I doubt not, may think it treason for a man to lay violent hands upon it But whether or no it be treason to man, I have good assurance in my conscience that it is no treason to God. Wherefore, I have resolved that we will rather be God's soldiers than soldiers of the Pope of Rome; and in that mind I now cut the Papal cross out of this banner."

And so he did. And thus, in a province belonging to the crown of England, a captain was found bold enough to deface the king's banner with his sword.

When Winthrop and the other wise men of Massachusetts heard of it they were disquieted, being afraid that Endicott's act would bring great trouble upon himself and them. An account of the matter was carried to King Charles; but he was then so much engrossed by dissensions with his people that he had no leisure to punish the offender. In other times, it might have cost Endicott his life, and Massachusetts her charter.

"I should like to know, Grandfather," said Laurence, when the story was ended, "whether, when Endicott cut the red cross out of the banner, he meant to imply that Massachusetts was independent of England?"

"A sense of the independence of his adopted country must have been in that bold man's heart," answered Grandfather; "but I doubt whether he had given the matter much consideration except in its religious bearing. However, it was a very re markable affair, and a very strong expression of Puritan character."

Grandfather proceeded to speak further of Roger Williams and of other persons who sat in the great chair, as will be seen in the following chapter.

CHAPTER IV.

" ROGER WILLIAMS," said Grandfather, " did not keep possession of the chair a great while.   His opinions of civil and religious matters differed, in many respects, from those of the rulers and clergymen of Massachusetts.   Now, the wise men of those days believed that the country could not be safe unless all the inhabitants thought and felt alike."

" Does any body believe so in our days, Grandfather ? " asked Laurence.

" Possibly there are some who believe it," said Grandfather ; " but they have not so much power to act upon their belief as the magistrates and ministers had in the days of Roger Williams.   They had the power to deprive this good man of his home, and to send him out from the midst of them in search of a new place of rest.   He was banished in 1634, and went first to Plymouth colony ; but as the people there held the same opinions as those of Massachusetts, he was not suffered to remain among them. However, the wilderness was wide enough ; so

Roger Williams took his staff and travelled into the forest, and made treaties with the Indians, and began a plantation which he called Providence."

" I have been to Providence on the railroad," said Charley. " It is but a two hours' ride."

" Yes, Charley," replied Grandfather ; " but when Roger Williams travelled thither, over hills and valleys, and through the tangled woods, and across swamps and streams, it was a journey of several days. Well, his little plantation is now grown to be a populous city ; and the inhabitants have a great veneration for Roger Williams. His name is familiar in the mouths of all, because they see it on their bank bills. How it would have perplexed this good clergyman if he had been told that he should give his name to the ROGER WILLIAMS BANK ! "

" When he was driven from Massachusetts," said Laurence, " and began his journey into the woods, he must have felt as if he were burying himself forever from the sight and knowledge of men. Yet the whole country has now heard of him, and will remember him forever."

" Yes," answered Grandfather ; " it often happens that the outcasts of one generation are those who are reverenced as the wisest and best of men by the next. The securest fame is that which comes after a man's death. But let us return to our story. When Roger Williams was banished, he appears to have given the chair to Mrs. Anne Hutchinson. At all events, it was in her possession in 1637. She was a very sharpwitted and well-instructed lady, and was so conscious of her own wisdom and abilities that she thought it a pity that the world should not have the benefit of them. She therefore used to hold lectures in Boston once or twice a week, at which most of the women attended. Mrs. Hutchinson presided at these meetings, sitting with great state and dignity in Grandfather's chair."

"Grandfather, was it positively this very chair?" demanded Clara, laying her hand upon its carved elbow.

"Why not, my dear Clara?" said Grandfather. "Well, Mrs. Hutchinson's lectures soon caused a great disturbance; for the ministers of Boston did not think it safe and proper that a woman should publicly instruct the people in religious doctrines. Moreover, she made the matter worse by declaring that the Rev. Mr. Cotton was the only sincerely pious and holy clergyman in New England. Now, the clergy of those days had quite as much share in the government of the country, though indirectly, as the magistrates themselves; so you may imagine what a host of powerful enemies were raised up against Mrs. Hutchinson. A synod was convened; that is to say, an assemblage of all the ministers in Massachusetts. They declared that there were eighty-two erroneous opinions on religious subjects diffused among the people, and that Mrs. Hutchinson's opinions were of the number."

"If they had eighty-two wrong opinions," observed Charley, "I don't see how they could have any right ones."

"Mrs. Hutchinson had many zealous friends and converts," continued Grandfather. "She was favored by young Henry Vane, who had come over from England a year or two before, and had since been chosen governor of the colony, at the age of twenty-four. But Winthrop and most of the other leading men, as well as the ministers, felt an abhorrence of her doctrines. Thus two opposite parties were formed; and so fierce were the dissensions that it was feared the consequence would be civil war and bloodshed. But Winthrop and the ministers being the most powerful, they disarmed and imprisoned Mrs. Hutchinson's adherents. She, like Roger Williams, was banished."

"Dear Grandfather, did they drive the poor woman into the woods?" exclaimed little Alice, who contrived to feel a human interest even in these discords of polemic divinity.

"They did, my darling," replied Grandfather; "and the end of her life was so sad you must not hear it. At her departure, it appears, from the best authorities, that she gave the great chair to her friend Henry Vane. He was a young man of wonderful talents and great learning, who had imbibed the religious opinions of the Puritans, and left England with the intention of spending his life in Massachusetts. The people chose him governor; but the controversy about Mrs. Hutchinson, and other troubles, caused him to leave the country in 1637. You may read the subsequent events of his life in the History of England."

"Yes, Grandfather," cried Laurence; "and we may read them better in Mr. Upham's Biography of Vane. And what a beautiful death he died, long afterwards! beautiful, though it was on a scaffold."

"Many of the most beautiful deaths have been there," said Grandfather. "The enemies of a great and good man can in no other way make him so glorious as by giving him the crown of martyrdom."

In order that the children might fully understand the all-important history of the chair, Grandfather now thought fit to speak of the progress that was made in settling several colonies. The settlement of Plymouth, in 1620, has already been mentioned. In 1635 Mr. Hooker and Mr. Stone, two ministers, went on foot from Massachusetts to Connecticut, through the pathless woods, taking their whole congregation along with them. They founded the town of Hartford. In 1638 Mr. Davenport, a very celebrated minister, went, with other people, and began a plantation at New Haven. In the same year, some persons who had been persecuted in Massachusetts went to the Isle of Rhodes, since called Rhode Island, and settled there. About this time, also, many settlers had gone to Maine, and were living without any regular government. There were likewise settlers near Piscataqua River, in the region which is now called New Hampshire.

Thus, at various points along the coast of New England, there were communities of Englishmen. Though these communities were independent of one another, yet they had a common dependence upon England; and, at so vast a distance from their native home, the inhabitants must all have felt like brethren. They were fitted to become one united people at a future period. Perhaps their feelings of brotherhood were the stronger because different nations had formed settlements to the north and to the south. In Canada and Nova Scotia were colonies of French. On the banks of the Hudson River was a colony of Dutch, who had taken possession of that region many years before, and called it New Netherlands.

Grandfather, for aught I know, might have gone on to speak of Maryland and Virginia; for the good old gentleman really seemed to suppose that the whole surface of the United States was not too broad a foundation to place the four legs of his chair upon. But, happening to glance at Charley, he perceived that this naughty boy was growing impatient and meditating another ride upon a stick. So here, for the present, Grandfather suspended the history of his chair.

CHAPTER V.

THE children had now learned to look upon the chair with an interest which was almost the same as if it were a conscious being, and could remember the many famous people whom it had held within its arms.

Even Charley, lawless as he was, seemed to feel that this venerable chair must not be clambered upon nor overturned, although he had no scruple in taking such liberties with every other chair in the house. Clara treated it with still greater reverence, often taking occasion to smooth its cushion, and to brush the dust from the carved flowers and grotesque figures of its oaken back and arms. Laurence would sometimes sit a whole hour, especially at twilight, gazing at the chair, and, by the spell of his imaginations, summoning up its ancient occupants to appear in it again.

Little Alice evidently employed herself in a similar way; for once, when Grandfather had gone abroad, the child was heard talking with the gentle Lady Arbella, as if she were still sitting in the chair.

So sweet a child as little Alice may fitly talk with angels, such as the Lady Arbella had long since become.

Grandfather was soon importuned for more stories about the chair. He had no difficulty in relating them; for it really seemed as if every person noted in our early history had, on some occasion or other, found repose within its comfortable arms. If Grandfather took pride in any thing, it was in being the possessor of such an honorable and historic elbow chair.

"I know not precisely who next got possession of the chair after Governor Vane went back to England," said Grandfather. "But there is reason to believe that President Dunster sat in it, when he held the first commencement at Harvard College. You have often heard, children, how careful our forefathers were to give their young people a good education. They had scarcely cut down trees enough to make room for their own dwellings before they began to think of establishing a college. Their principal object was, to rear up pious and learned ministers; and hence old writers call Harvard College a school of the prophets."

"Is the college a school of the prophets now?" asked Charley.

"It is a long while since I took my degree, Charley. You must ask some of the recent graduates," answered Grandfather. " As I was telling you, President Dunster sat in Grandfather's chair in 1642, when he conferred the degree of bachelor of arts on nine young men. They were the first in America who had received that honor. And now, my dear auditors, I must confess that there are contradictory statements and some uncertainty about the adventures of the chair for a period of almost ten years. Some say that it was occupied by your own ancestor, William Hawthorne, first speaker of the house of representatives. I have nearly satisfied myself, however, that, during most of this questionable period, it was literally the chair of state. It gives me much pleasure to imagine that several successive governors of Massachusetts sat in it at the council board."

" But, Grandfather," interposed Charley, who was a matter-of-fact little person, " what reason have you to imagine so ? "

" Pray do imagine it, Grandfather," said Laurence.

" With Charley's permission, I will," replied Grandfather, smiling. " Let us consider it settled, therefore, that Winthrop, Bellingham, Dudley, and Endicott, each of them, when chosen governor, took his seat in our great chair on election day. In this chair, likewise, did those excellent governors preside while holding consultations with the chief councillors of the province, who were styled assistants. The governor sat in this chair, too, whenever messages were brought to him from the chamber of representatives."

And here Grandfather took occasion to talk rather tediously about the nature and forms of government that established themselves, almost spontaneously, in Massachusetts and the other New England colonies. Democracies were the natural growth of the new world. As to Massachusetts, it was at first intended that the colony should be governed by a council in London. But in a little while the people had the whole power in their own hands, and chose annually the governor, the councillors, and the representatives. The people of Old England had never enjoyed any thing like the liberties and privileges which the set-tlers of New England now possessed. And they did not adopt these modes of government after long study, but in simplicity, as if there were no other way for people to be ruled.

" But, Laurence," continued Grandfather, " when you want instruction on these points, you must seek it in Mr. Bancroft's History. I am merely telling the history of a chair. To proceed. The period during which the governors sat in our chair was not very full of striking incidents. The province was now established on a secure foundation ; but it did not increase so rapidly as at first, because the Puritans were no longer driven from England by persecution. However, there was still a quiet and natural growth.

The legislature incorporated towns, and made new purchases of lands from the Indians. A very memorable event took place in 1643. The colonies of Massachusetts, Plymouth, Connecticut, and New Haven formed a union, for the purpose of assisting each other in difficulties, for mutual defence against their enemies. They called themselves the United Colonies of New England."

"Were they under a government like that of the United States?" inquired Laurence.

"No," replied Grandfather; "the different colonies did not compose one nation together; it was merely a confederacy among the governments. It somewhat resembled the league of the Amphictyons, which you remember in Grecian history. But to return to our chair. In 1644 it was highly honored; for Governor Endicott sat in it when he gave audience to an ambassador from the French governor of Acadia, or Nova Scotia. A treaty of peace between Massachusetts and the French colony was then signed."

"Did England allow Massachusetts to make war and peace with foreign countries?" asked Laurence.

"Massachusetts and the whole of New England was then almost independent of the mother country," said Grandfather. "There was now a civil war in England; and the king, as you may well suppose, had his hands full at home, and could pay but little attention to these remote colonies. When the Parliament got the power into their hands, they likewise had enough to do in keeping down the Cavaliers. Thus New England, like a young and hardy lad whose father and mother neglect it, was left to take care of itself. In 1646 King Charles was beheaded. Oliver Cromwell then became Protector of England; and as he was a Puritan himself, and had risen by the valor of the English Puritans, he showed himself a loving and indulgent father to the Puritan colonies in America."

Grandfather might have continued to talk in this dull manner nobody knows how long; but suspecting that Charley would find the subject rather dry, he looked sidewise at that vivacious little fellow, and saw him give an involuntary yawn. Whereupon Grandfather proceeded with the history of the chair, and related a very entertaining incident, which will be found in the next chapter.

CHAPTER VI.

"According to the most authentic records, my dear children," said Grandfather, "the chair, about this time, had the misfortune to break its leg. It was probably on account of this accident that it ceased to be the seat of the governors of Massachusetts; for, assuredly, it would have been ominous of evil to the commonwealth if the chair of state had tottered upon three legs. Being therefore sold at auction, — alas! what a vicissitude for a chair that had figured in such high company! — our venerable friend was knocked down to a certain Captain John Hull. This old gentleman, on carefully examining the maimed chair, discovered that its broken leg might be clamped with iron and made as serviceable as ever."

"Here is the very leg that was broken!" exclaimed Charley, throwing himself down on the floor to look at it. "And here are the iron clamps. How well it was mended!"

When they had all sufficiently examined the

broken leg, Grandfather told them a story about Captain John Hull and

THE PINE-TREE SHILLINGS.

The Captain John Hull aforesaid was the mint-master of Massachusetts, and coined all the money that was made there. This was a new line of business; for, in the earlier days of the colony, the current coinage consisted of gold and silver money of England, Portugal, and Spain. These coins being scarce, the people were often forced to barter their commodities instead of selling them.

For instance, if a man wanted to buy a coat, he perhaps exchanged a bear skin for it. If he wished for a barrel of molasses, he might purchase it with a pile of pine boards. Musket bullets were used instead of farthings. The Indians had a sort of money, called wampum, which was made of clam shells; and this strange sort of specie was likewise taken in payment of debts by the English settlers. Bank bills had never been heard of. There was not money enough of any kind, in many parts of the country, to pay the salaries of the ministers; so that they sometimes had to take quintals of fish, bushels of corn, or cords of wood, instead of silver or gold.

As the people grew more numerous, and their trade one with another increased, the want of current money was still more sensibly felt. To supply the demand, the general court passed a law for establishing a coinage of shillings, sixpences, and threepences. Captain John Hull was appointed to manufacture this money, and was to have about one shilling out of every twenty to pay him for the trouble of making them.

Hereupon all the old silver in the colony was handed over to Captain John Hull. The battered silver cans and tankards, I suppose, and silver buckles, and broken spoons, and silver buttons of worn-out coats, and silver hilts of swords that had figured at court, — all such curious old articles were doubtless thrown into the melting pot together. But by far the greater part of the silver consisted of bullion from the mines of South America, which the English buccaneers — who were little better than pirates — had taken from the Spaniards, and brought to Massachusetts.

All this old and new silver being melted down and coined, the result was an immense amount of splendid shillings, sixpences, and threepences. Each had the date, 1652, on the one side, and the figure of a pine tree on the other. Hence they were called pine-tree shillings. And for every twenty shillings that he coined, you will remember, Captain John Hull was entitled to put one shilling into his own pocket.

The magistrates soon began to suspect that the

mintmaster would have the best of the bargain. They offered him a large sum of money if he would but give up that twentieth shilling which he was continually dropping into his own pocket. But Captain Hull declared himself perfectly satisfied with the shilling. And well he might be; for so diligently did he labor, that, in a few years, his pockets, his money bags, and his strong box were overflowing with pine-tree shillings. This was probably the case when he came into possession of Grandfather's chair; and, as he had worked so hard at the mint, it was certainly proper that he should have a comfortable chair to rest himself in.

When the mintmaster had grown very rich, a young man, Samuel Sewell by name, came a-courting to his only daughter. His daughter — whose name I do not know, but we will call her Betsey — was a fine, hearty damsel, by no means so slender as some young ladies of our own days. On the contrary, having always fed heartily on pumpkin pies, doughnuts, Indian puddings, and other Puritan dainties, she was as round and plump as a pudding herself. With this round, rosy Miss Betsey did Samuel Sewell fall in love. As he was a young man of good character, industrious in his business, and a member of the church, the mintmaster very readily gave his consent.

" Yes, you may take her," said he, in his rough way; " and you'll find her a heavy burden enough! "

On the wedding day, we may suppose that honest John Hull dressed himself in a plum-colored coat, all the buttons of which were made of pine-tree shillings. The buttons of his waistcoat were six-pences; and the knees of his smallclothes were buttoned with silver threepences. Thus attired, he sat with great dignity in Grandfather's chair; and, being a portly old gentleman, he completely filled it from elbow to elbow. On the opposite side of the room, between her bridemaids, sat Miss Betsey. She was blushing with all her might, and looked like a full-blown peony, or a great red apple.

There, too, was the bridegroom, dressed in a fine purple coat and gold lace waistcoat, with as much other finery as the Puritan laws and customs would allow him to put on. His hair was cropped close to his head, because Governor Endicott had forbidden any man to wear it below the ears. But he was a very personable young man; and so thought the bridemaids and Miss Betsey herself.

The mintmaster also was pleased with his new son-in-law; especially as he had courted Miss Betsey out of pure love, and had said nothing at all about her portion. So, when the marriage ceremony was over, Captain Hull whispered a word to two of his men servants, who immediately went out, and soon returned, lugging in a large pair of scales. They were such a pair as wholesale merchants use for weighing bulky commodities; and quite a bulky commodity was now to be weighed in them.

"Daughter Betsey," said the mintmaster, "get into one side of these scales."

Miss Betsey — or Mrs. Sewell, as we must now call her — did as she was bid, like a dutiful child, without any question of the why and wherefore. But what her father could mean, unless to make her husband pay for her by the pound, (in which case she would have been a dear bargain,) she had not the least idea.

"And now," said honest John Hull to the servants, "bring that box hither."

The box to which the mintmaster pointed was a huge, square, iron bound, oaken chest; it was big enough, my children, for all four of you to play at hide-and-seek in. The servants tugged with might and main, but could not lift this enormous receptacle, and were finally obliged to drag it across the floor. Captain Hull then took a key from his girdle, unlocked the chest, and lifted its ponderous lid. Behold! it was full to the brim of bright pine-tree shillings, fresh from the mint; and Samuel Sewell began to think that his father-in-law had got possession of all the money in the Massachusetts treasury. But it was only the mintmaster's honest share of the coinage.

Then the servants, at Captain Hull's command, heaped double handfuls of shillings into one side of the scales, while Betsey remained in the other. Jingle,

jingle, went the shillings, as handful after handful was thrown in, till, plump and ponderous as she was, they fairly weighed the young lady from the floor.

"There, son Sewell!" cried the honest mintmaster, resuming his seat in Grandfather's chair, "take these shillings for my daughter's portion. Use her kindly, and thank Heaven for her. It is not every wife that's worth her weight in silver!"

The children laughed heartily at this legend, and would hardly be convinced but that Grandfather had made it out of his own head. He assured them faithfully, however, that he had found it in the pages of a grave historian, and had merely tried to tell it in a somewhat funnier style. As for Samuel Sewell, he afterwards became chief justice of Massachusetts.

"Well, Grandfather," remarked Clara, "if wedding portions nowadays were paid as Miss Betsey's was, young ladies would not pride themselves upon an airy figure, as many of them do."

CHAPTER VII.

When his little audience next assembled round
the chair, Grandfather gave them a doleful history of
the Quaker persecution, which began in 1656, and
raged for about three years in Massachusetts.

He told them how, in the first place, twelve of the
converts of George Fox, the first Quaker in the world,
had come over from England. They seemed to be im-
pelled by an earnest love for the souls of men, and a
pure desire to make known what they considered a
revelation from Heaven. But the rulers looked upon
them as plotting the downfall of all government and
religion. They were banished from the colony. In
a little while, however, not only the first twelve had
returned, but a multitude of other Quakers had come
to rebuke the rulers and to preach against the priests
and steeple houses.

Grandfather described the hatred and scorn with
which these enthusiasts were received. They were
thrown into dungeons; they were beaten with many
stripes, women as well as men; they were driven

forth into the wilderness, and left to the tender mercies of wild beasts and Indians. The children were amazed to hear that the more the Quakers were scourged, and imprisoned, and banished, the more did the sect increase, both by the influx of strangers and by converts from among the Puritans. But Grandfather told them that God had put something into the soul of man, which always turned the cruelties of the persecutor to nought.

He went on to relate, that, in 1659, two Quakers, named William Robinson and Marmaduke Stephenson, were hanged at Boston. A woman had been sentenced to die with them, but was reprieved on condition of her leaving the colony. Her name was Mary Dyer. In the year 1660 she returned to Boston, although she knew death awaited her there ; and, if Grandfather had been correctly informed, an incident had then taken place which connects her with our story. This Mary Dyer had entered the mint-master's dwelling, clothed in sackcloth and ashes, and seated herself in our great chair with a sort of dignity and state. Then she proceeded to deliver what she called a message from Heaven ; but in the midst of it they dragged her to prison.

" And was she executed ? " asked Laurence.

" She was," said Grandfather.

" Grandfather," cried Charley, clinching his fist, " I would have fought for that poor Quaker woman ! "

"Ah, but if a sword had been drawn for her," said Laurence, "it would have taken away all the beauty of her death."

It seemed as if hardly any of the preceding stories had thrown such an interest around Grandfather's chair as did the fact that the poor, persecuted, wandering Quaker woman had rested in it for a moment. The children were so much excited that Grandfather found it necessary to bring his account of the persecution to a close.

"In 1660, the same year in which Mary Dyer was executed," said he, "Charles II. was restored to the throne of his fathers. This king had many vices; but he would not permit blood to be shed, under pretence of religion, in any part of his dominions. The Quakers in England told him what had been done to their brethren in Massachusetts; and he sent orders to Governor Endicott to forbear all such proceedings in future. And so ended the Quaker persecution — one of the most mournful passages in the history of our forefathers."

Grandfather then told his auditors, that, shortly after the above incident, the great chair had been given by the mintmaster to the Rev. Mr. John Eliot. He was the first minister of Roxbury. But besides attending to his pastoral duties there, he learned the language of the red men, and often went into the woods to preach to them. So earnestly did he labor for their conversion that he has always been called the apostle to the Indians. The mention of this holy man suggested to Grandfather the propriety of giving a brief sketch of the history of the Indians, so far as they were connected with the English colonists.

A short period before the arrival of the first Pilgrims at Plymouth there had been a very grievous plague among the red men; and the sages and ministers of that day were inclined to the opinion that Providence had sent this mortality in order to make room for the settlement of the English. But I know not why we should suppose that an Indian's life is less precious, in the eye of Heaven, than that of a white man. Be that as it may, death had certainly been very busy with the savage tribes.

In many places the English found the wigwams deserted and the cornfields growing to waste, with none to harvest the grain. There were heaps of earth also, which, being dug open, proved to be Indian graves, containing bows and flint-headed spears and arrows; for the Indians buried the dead warrior's weapons along with him. In some spots there were skulls and other human bones lying unburied. In 1633, and the year afterwards, the small pox broke out among the Massachusetts Indians, multitudes of whom died by this terrible disease of the old world. These misfortunes made them far less powerful than they had formerly been.

For nearly half a century after the arrival of the English the red men showed themselves generally inclined to peace and amity. They often made submission when they might have made successful war. The Plymouth settlers, led by the famous Captain Miles Standish, slew some of them, in 1623, without any very evident necessity for so doing. In 1636, and the following year, there was the most dreadful war that had yet occurred between the Indians and the English. The Connecticut settlers, assisted by a celebrated Indian chief named Uncas, bore the brunt of this war, with but little aid from Massachusetts. Many hundreds of the hostile Indians were slain or burned in their wigwams. Sassacus, their sachem, fled to another tribe, after his own people were defeated; but he was murdered by them, and his head was sent to his English enemies.

From that period down to the time of King Philip's war, which will be mentioned hereafter, there was not much trouble with the Indians. But the colonists were always on their guard, and kept their weapons ready for the conflict.

"I have sometimes doubted," said Grandfather, when he had told these things to the children, — "I have sometimes doubted whether there was more than a single man, among our forefathers, who realized that an Indian possesses a mind, and a heart, and an immortal soul. That single man was John Eliot. All the rest of the early settlers seemed to think that the Indians were an inferior race of beings, whom the Creator had merely allowed to keep possession of this beautiful country till the white men should be in want of it."

"Did the pious men of those days never try to make Christians of them?" asked Laurence.

"Sometimes, it is true," answered Grandfather, "the magistrates and ministers would talk about civilizing and converting the red people. But, at the bottom of their hearts, they would have had almost as much expectation of civilizing the wild bear of the woods and making him fit for paradise. They felt no faith in the success of any such attempts, because they had no love for the poor Indians. Now, Eliot was full of love for them; and therefore so full of faith and hope that he spent the labor of a lifetime in their behalf."

"I would have conquered them first, and then converted them," said Charley.

"Ah, Charley, there spoke the very spirit of our forefathers!" replied Grandfather. "But Mr. Eliot had a better spirit. He looked upon them as his brethren. He persuaded as many of them as he could to leave off their idle and wandering habits, and to build houses, and cultivate the earth, as the English did. He established schools among them, and taught many of the Indians how to read. He taught them, likewise, how to pray. Hence they were called 'praying Indians.' Finally, having spent the best years of his life for their good, Mr. Eliot resolved to spend the remainder in doing them a yet greater benefit."

"I know what that was!" cried Laurence.

"He sat down in his study," continued Grandfather, "and began a translation of the Bible into the Indian tongue. It was while he was engaged in this pious work that the mintmaster gave him our great chair. His toil needed it and deserved it."

"O, Grandfather, tell us all about that Indian Bible!" exclaimed Laurence. "I have seen it in the library of the Athenæum; and the tears came into my eyes to think that there were no Indians left to read it."

CHAPTER VIII.

As Grandfather was a great admirer of the apostle
Eliot, he was glad to comply with the earnest request
which Laurence had made at the close of the last
chapter. So he proceeded to describe how good Mr.
Eliot labored, while he was at work upon

THE INDIAN BIBLE.

My dear children, what a task would you think it,
even with a long lifetime before you, were you bid-
den to copy every chapter, and verse, and word in
yonder family Bible! Would not this be a heavy
toil? But if the task were, not to write off the
English Bible, but to learn a language utterly unlike
all other tongues, — a language which hitherto had
never been learned, except by the Indians them-
selves, from their mothers' lips, — a language never
written, and the strange words of which seemed in-
expressible by letters, — if the task were, first to
learn this new variety of speech, and then to translate

the Bible into it, and to do it so carefully that not one idea throughout the holy book should be changed, — what would induce you to undertake this toil? Yet this was what the apostle Eliot did.

It was a mighty work for a man, now growing old, to take upon himself. And what earthly reward could he expect from it? None; no reward on earth. But he believed that the red men were the descendants of those lost tribes of Israel of whom history has been able to tell us nothing for thousands of years. He hoped that God had sent the English across the ocean, Gentiles as they were, to enlighten this benighted portion of his once chosen race. And when he should be summoned hence, he trusted to meet blessed spirits in another world, whose bliss would have been earned by his patient toil in translating the word of God. This hope and trust were far dearer to him than any thing that earth could offer.

Sometimes, while thus at work, he was visited by learned men, who desired to know what literary undertaking Mr. Eliot had in hand. They, like himself, had been bred in the studious cloisters of a university, and were supposed to possess all the erudition which mankind has hoarded up from age to age. Greek and Latin were as familiar to them as the babble of their childhood. Hebrew was like their mother tongue. They had grown gray in study; their eyes were bleared with poring over print and manuscript by the light of the midnight lamp.

And yet, how much had they left unlearned! Mr. Eliot would put into their hands some of the pages which he had been writing; and behold! the gray-headed men stammered over the long, strange words, like a little child in his first attempts to read. Then would the apostle call to him an Indian boy, one of his scholars, and show him the manuscript which had so puzzled the learned Englishmen.

"Read this, my child," said he; "these are some brethren of mine, who would fain hear the sound of thy native tongue."

Then would the Indian boy cast his eyes over the mysterious page, and read it so skilfully that it sounded like wild music. It seemed as if the forest leaves were singing in the ears of his auditors, and as if the roar of distant streams were poured through the young Indian's voice. Such were the sounds amid which the language of the red man had been formed; and they were still heard to echo in it.

The lesson being over, Mr. Eliot would give the Indian boy an apple or a cake, and bid him leap forth into the open air which his free nature loved. The apostle was kind to children, and even shared in their sports sometimes. And when his visitors had bidden him farewell, the good man turned patiently to his toil again.

No other Englishman had ever understood the Indian character so well, nor possessed so great an influence over the New England tribes, as the apostle did. His advice and assistance must often have been valuable to his countrymen in their transactions with the Indians. Occasionally, perhaps, the governor and some of the councillors came to visit Mr. Eliot. Perchance they were seeking some method to circumvent the forest people. They inquired, it may be, how they could obtain possession of such and such a tract of their rich land. Or they talked of making the Indians their servants; as if God had destined them for perpetual bondage to the more powerful white man.

Perhaps, too, some warlike captain, dressed in his buff coat, with a corslet beneath it, accompanied the governor and councillors. Laying his hand upon his sword hilt, he would declare, that the only method of dealing with the red men was to meet them with the sword drawn and the musket presented.

But the apostle resisted both the craft of the politician and the fierceness of the warrior.

" Treat these sons of the forest as men and brethren," he would say ; " and let us endeavor to make them Christians. Their forefathers were of that chosen race whom God delivered from Egyptian bondage. Perchance he has destined us to deliver the children from the more cruel bondage of ignorance and idolatry. Chiefly for this end, it may be, we were directed across the ocean."

When these other visitors were gone, Mr. Eliot bent himself again over the half-written page. He dared hardly relax a moment from his toil. He felt that, in the book which he was translating, there was a deep human as well as heavenly wisdom, which would of itself suffice to civilize and refine the savage tribes. Let the Bible be diffused among them, and all earthly good would follow. But how slight a consideration was this, when he reflected that the eternal welfare of a whole race of men depended upon his accomplishment of the task which he had set himself! What if his hands should be palsied? What if his mind should lose its vigor? What if death should come upon him ere the work were done? Then must the red man wander in the dark wilderness of heathenism forever.

Impelled by such thoughts as these, he sat writing in the great chair when the pleasant summer breeze came in through his open casement; and also when the fire of forest logs sent up its blaze and smoke, through the broad stone chimney, into the wintry air. Before the earliest bird sang in the morning the apostle's lamp was kindled; and, at midnight, his weary head was not yet upon its pillow. And at length, leaning back in the great chair, he could say to himself, with a holy triumph, "The work is finished!"

It was finished. Here was a Bible for the Indians.

Those long-lost descendants of the ten tribes of Israel would now learn the history of their forefathers. That grace which the ancient Israelites had forfeited was offered anew to their children.

There is no impiety in believing that, when his long life was over, the apostle of the Indians was welcomed to the celestial abodes by the prophets of ancient days and by those earliest apostles and evangelists who had drawn their inspiration from the immediate presence of the Savior. They first had preached truth and salvation to the world. And Eliot, separated from them by many centuries, yet full of the same spirit, had borne the like message to the new world of the west. Since the first days of Christianity, there has been no man more worthy to be numbered in the brotherhood of the apostles than Eliot.

"My heart is not satisfied to think," observed Laurence, "that Mr. Eliot's labors have done no good except to a few Indians of his own time. Doubtless he would not have regretted his toil, if it were the means of saving but a single soul. But it is a grievous thing to me that he should have toiled so hard to translate the Bible, and now the language and the people are gone! The Indian Bible itself is almost the only relic of both."

"Laurence," said his Grandfather, "if ever you should doubt that man is capable of disinterested zeal for his brother's good, then remember how the apostle Eliot toiled. And if you should feel your own self-interest pressing upon your heart too closely, then think of Eliot's Indian Bible. It is good for the world that such a man has lived and left this emblem of his life."

The tears gushed into the eyes of Laurence, and he acknowledged that Eliot had not toiled in vain. Little Alice put up her arms to Grandfather, and drew down his white head beside her own golden locks.

"Grandfather," whispered she, "I want to kiss good Mr. Eliot!"

And, doubtless, good Mr. Eliot would gladly receive the kiss of so sweet a child as little Alice, and would think it a portion of his reward in heaven.

Grandfather now observed that Dr. Francis had written a very beautiful Life of Eliot, which he advised Laurence to peruse. He then spoke of King Philip's war, which began in 1675, and terminated with the death of King Philip, in the following year. Philip was a proud, fierce Indian, whom Mr. Eliot had vainly endeavored to convert to the Christian faith.

" It must have been a great anguish to the apostle," continued Grandfather, " to hear of mutual slaughter and outrage between his own countrymen and those for whom he felt the affection of a father. A few of the praying Indians joined the followers of King Philip. A greater number fought on the side of the English. In the course of the war, the little community of red people whom Mr. Eliot had begun to civilize was scattered, and probably never was restored to a flourishing condition. But his zeal did not grow cold; and only about five years before his death he took great pains in preparing a new edition of the Indian Bible."

" I do wish, Grandfather," cried Charley, " you would tell us all about the battles in King Philip's war."

" O, no ! " exclaimed Clara. " Who wants to hear about tomahawks and scalping knives ? "

" No, Charley," replied Grandfather, " I have no time to spare in talking about battles. You must be content with knowing that it was the bloodiest war that the Indians had ever waged against the white men; and that, at its close, the English set King Philip's head upon a pole."

" Who was the captain of the English ? " asked Charley.

" Their most noted captain was Benjamin Church —a very famous warrior," said Grandfather. " But I assure you, Charley, that neither Captain Church, nor any of the officers and soldiers who fought in King Philip's war, did any thing a thousandth part so glorious as Mr. Eliot did when he translated the Bible for the Indians."

" Let Laurence be the apostle," said Charley to himself, " and I will be the captain."

CHAPTER IX.

The children were now accustomed to assemble round Grandfather's chair at all their unocupied moments; and often it was a striking picture to behold the whiteheaded old sire, with this flowery wreath of young people around him. When he talked to them, it was the past speaking to the present, or rather to the future — for the children were of a generation which had not become actual. Their part in life, thus far, was only to be happy and to draw knowledge from a thousand sources. As yet, it was not their time to do.

Sometimes, as Grandfather gazed at their fair, unworldly countenances, a mist of tears bedimmed his spectacles. He almost regretted that it was necessary for them to know any thing of the past or to provide aught for the future. He could have wished that they might be always the happy, youthful creatures who had hitherto sported around his chair without inquiring whether it had a history. It grieved him to think that his little Alice, who was a flower bud fresh from paradise, must open her leaves to the rough breezes of the world, or ever open them in any clime. So sweet a child she was, that it seemed fit her infancy should be immortal.

But such repinings were merely flitting shadows across the old man's heart. He had faith enough to believe, and wisdom enough to know, that the bloom of the flower would be even holier and happier than its bud. Even within himself (though Grandfather was now at that period of life when the veil of mortality is apt to hang heavily over the soul, still, in his inmost being) he was conscious of something that he would not have exchanged for the best happiness of childhood. It was a bliss to which every sort of earthly experience — all that he had enjoyed, or suffered, or seen, or heard, or acted, with the broodings of his soul upon the whole — had contributed somewhat. In the same manner must a bliss, of which now they could have no conception, grow up within these children, and form a part of their sustenance for immortality.

So Grandfather, with renewed cheerfulness, continued his history of the chair, trusting that a profounder wisdom than his own would extract, from these flowers and weeds of Time, a fragrance that might last beyond all time.

At this period of the story Grandfather threw a glance backward as far as the year 1660. He spoke of the ill-concealed reluctance with which the Puritans in America had acknowledged the sway of Charles II. on his restoration to his father's throne. When death had stricken Oliver Cromwell, that mighty protector had no sincerer mourners than in New England. The new king had been more than a year upon the throne before his accession was proclaimed in Boston; although the neglect to perform the ceremony might have subjected the rulers to the charge of treason.

During the reign of Charles II., however, the American colonies had but little reason to complain of harsh or tyrannical treatment. But when Charles died, in 1685, and was succeeded by his brother James, the patriarchs of New England began to tremble. King James was a bigoted Roman Catholic, and was known to be of an arbitrary temper. It was feared by all Protestants, and chiefly by the Puritans, that he would assume despotic power and attempt to establish Popery throughout his dominions. Our forefathers felt that they had no security either for their religion or their liberties.

The result proved that they had reason for their apprehensions. King James caused the charters of all the American colonies to be taken away. The old charter of Massachusetts, which the people regarded as a holy thing and as the foundation of all their liberties, was declared void. The colonists were now no longer freemen ; they were entirely dependent on the king's pleasure. At first, in 1685, King James appointed Joseph Dudley, a native of Massachusetts, to be President of New England. But soon afterwards Sir Edmund Andros, an officer of the English army, arrived, with a commission to be governor general of New England and New York.

The king had given such powers to Sir Edmund Andros that there was now no liberty, nor scarcely any law, in the colonies over which he ruled. The inhabitants were not allowed to choose representatives, and consequently had no voice whatever in the government, nor control over the measures that were adopted. The councillors with whom the governor consulted on matters of state were appointed by himself. This sort of government was no better than an absolute despotism.

"The people suffered much wrong while Sir Edmund Andros ruled over them," continued Grandfather ; "and they were apprehensive of much more. He had brought some soldiers with him from England, who took possession of the old fortress on Castle Island and of the fortification on Fort Hill. Sometimes it was rumored that a general massacre of the inhabitants was to be perpetrated by these soldiers. There were reports, too, that all the ministers were to be slain or imprisoned."

"For what?" inquired Charley.

" Because they were the leaders of the people, Charley," said Grandfather. " A minister was a more formidable man than a general in those days. Well, while these things were going on in America, King James had so misgoverned the people of England that they sent over to Holland for the Prince of Orange. He had married the king's daughter, and was therefore considered to have a claim to the crown. On his arrival in England, the Prince of Orange was proclaimed king, by the name of William III. Poor old King James made his escape to France."

Grandfather told how, at the first intelligence of the landing of the Prince of Orange in England, the people of Massachusetts rose in their strength and overthrew the government of Sir Edmund Andros. He, with Joseph Dudley, Edmund Randolph, and his other principal adherents, was thrown into prison. Old Simon Bradstreet, who had been governor when King James took away the charter, was called by the people to govern them again.

" Governor Bradstreet was a venerable old man, nearly ninety years of age," said Grandfather. " He came over with the first settlers, and had been the intimate companion of all those excellent and famous men who laid the foundation of our country. They were all gone before him to the grave ; and Bradstreet was the last of the Puritans."

Grandfather paused a moment and smiled, as if he had something very interesting to tell his auditors. He then proceeded : —

"And now, Laurence, — now, Clara, — now, Charley, — now, my dear little Alice, — what chair do you think had been placed in the council chamber, for old Governor Bradstreet to take his seat in ? Would you believe that it was this very chair in which Grandfather now sits, and of which he is telling you the history ? "

" I am glad to hear it, with all my heart ! " cried Charley, after a shout of delight. " I thought Grandfather had quite forgotten the chair."

" It was a solemn and affecting sight," said Grandfather, " when this venerable patriarch, with his white beard flowing down upon his breast, took his seat in his chair of state. Within his remembrance, and even since his mature age, the site where now stood the populous town had been a wild and forest-covered peninsula. The province, now so fertile and spotted with thriving villages, had been a desert wilderness. He was surrounded by a shouting multitude, most of whom had been born in the country which he had helped to found. They were of one generation, and he of another. As the old man looked upon them, and beheld new faces every where, he must have felt that it was now time for him to go, whither his brethren had gone before him."

"Were the former governors all dead and gone?"
asked Laurence.

"All of them," replied Grandfather. "Winthrop
had been dead forty years. Endicott died, a very
old man, in 1665. Sir Henry Vane was beheaded, in
London, at the beginning of the reign of Charles II.
And Haynes, Dudley, Bellingham, and Leverett, who
had all been governors of Massachusetts, were now
likewise in their graves. Old Simon Bradstreet was
the sole representative of that departed brotherhood.
There was no other public man remaining to connect
the ancient system of government and manners with
the new system which was about to take its place.
The era of the Puritans was now completed."

"I am sorry for it!" observed Laurence; "for
though they were so stern, yet it seems to me that
there was something warm and real about them. I
think, Grandfather, that each of these old governors
should have his statue set up in our State House,
sculptured out of the hardest of New England
granite."

"It would not be amiss, Laurence," said Grand-
father; "but perhaps clay, or some other perishable
material, might suffice for some of their successors.
But let us go back to our chair. It was occupied by
Governor Bradstreet from April, 1689, until May,
1692. Sir William Phipps then arrived in Boston
with a new charter from King William and a com-
mission to be governor."

CHAPTER X.

"And what became of the chair?" inquired Clara.

"The outward aspect of our chair," replied Grandfather, "was now somewhat the worse for its long and arduous services. It was considered hardly magnificent enough to be allowed to keep its place in the council chamber of Massachusetts. In fact, it was banished as an article of useless lumber. But Sir William Phipps happened to see it, and, being much pleased with its construction, resolved to take the good old chair into his private mansion. Accordingly, with his own gubernatorial hands, he repaired one of its arms, which had been slightly damaged."

"Why, Grandfather, here is the very arm!" interrupted Charley, in great wonderment. "And did Sir William Phipps put in these screws with his own hands? I am sure he did it beautifully! But how came a governor to know how to mend a chair?"

"I will tell you a story about the early life of Sir William Phipps," said Grandfather. "You will then perceive that he well knew how to use his hands."

So Grandfather related the wonderful and true tale of

THE SUNKEN TREASURE.

Picture to yourselves, my dear children, a handsome, old-fashioned room, with a large, open cupboard at one end, in which is displayed a magnificent gold cup, with some other splendid articles of gold and silver plate. In another part of the room, opposite to a tall looking glass, stands our beloved chair, newly polished, and adorned with a gorgeous cushion of crimson velvet tufted with gold.

In the chair sits a man of strong and sturdy frame, whose face has been roughened by northern tempests and blackened by the burning sun of the West Indies. He wears an immense periwig, flowing down over his shoulders. His coat has a wide embroidery of golden foliage; and his waistcoat, likewise, is all flowered over and bedizened with gold. His red, rough hands, which have done many a good day's work with the hammer and adze, are half covered by the delicate lace ruffles at his wrists. On a table lies his silver-hilted sword; and in a corner of the room stands his gold-headed cane, made of a beautifully polished West India wood.

Somewhat such an aspect as this did Sir William Phipps present when he sat in Grandfather's chair, after the king had appointed him governor of Massachusetts. Truly there was need that the old chair should be varnished and decorated with a crimson cushion, in order to make it suitable for such a magnificent looking personage.

But Sir William Phipps had not always worn a gold-embroidered coat, nor always sat so much at his ease as he did in Grandfather's chair. He was a poor man's son, and was born in the Province of Maine, where he used to tend sheep upon the hills in his boyhood and youth. Until he had grown to be a man, he did not even know how to read and write. Tired of tending sheep, he next apprenticed himself to a ship carpenter, and spent about four years in hewing the crooked limbs of oak trees into knees for vessels.

In 1673, when he was twenty-two years old, he came to Boston, and soon afterwards was married to a widow lady, who had property enough to set him up in business. It was not long, however, before he lost all the money that he had acquired by his marriage and became a poor man again. Still he was not discouraged. He often told his wife that, some time or other, he should be very rich, and would build a " fair brick house " in the Green Lane of Boston.

Do not suppose, children, that he had been to a fortune teller to inquire his destiny. It was his own energy and spirit of enterprise, and his resolution to

lead an industrious life, that made him look forward
with so much confidence to better days.

Several years passed away, and William Phipps
had not yet gained the riches which he promised to
himself.   During this time he had begun to follow the
sea for a living.   In the year 1684 he happened to
hear of a Spanish ship which had been cast away
near the Bahama Islands, and which was supposed to
contain a great deal of gold and silver.   Phipps
went to the place in a small vessel, hoping that he
should be able to recover some of the treasure from
the wreck.   He did not succeed, however, in fishing
up gold and silver enough to pay the expenses of his
voyage.

But, before he returned, he was told of another
Spanish ship, or galleon, which had been cast away
near Porto de la Plata.   She had now lain as much
as fifty years beneath the waves.   This old ship had
been ladened with immense wealth; and, hitherto,
nobody had thought of the possibility of recovering
any part of it from the deep sea which was rolling
and tossing it about.   But though it was now an old
story, and the most aged people had almost forgotten
that such a vessel had been wrecked, William Phipps
resolved that the sunken treasure should again be
brought to light.

He went to London and obtained admittance to
King James, who had not yet been driven from his

throne. He told the king of the vast wealth that was lying at the bottom of the sea. King James listened with attention, and thought this a fine opportunity to fill his treasury with Spanish gold. He appointed William Phipps to be captain of a vessel, called the Rose Algier, carrying eighteen guns and ninety-five men. So now he was Captain Phipps of the English navy.

Captain Phipps sailed from England in the Rose Algier, and cruised for nearly two years in the West Indies, endeavoring to find the wreck of the Spanish ship. But the sea is so wide and deep, that it is no easy matter to discover the exact spot where a sunken vessel lies. The prospect of success seemed very small; and most people would have thought that Captain Phipps was as far from having money enough to build a " fair brick house " as he was while he tended sheep.

The seamen of the Rose Algier became discouraged, and gave up all hope of making their fortunes by discovering the Spanish wreck. They wanted to compel Captain Phipps to turn pirate. There was a much better prospect, they thought, of growing rich by plundering vessels which still sailed in the sea than by seeking for a ship that had lain beneath the waves full half a century. They broke out in open mutiny; but were finally mastered by Phipps, and compelled to obey his orders. It would have been dangerous, however, to continue much longer at sea with such a crew of mutinous sailors; and, besides, the Rose Algier was leaky and unseaworthy. So Captain Phipps judged it best to return to England.

Before leaving the West Indies, he met with a Spaniard, an old man, who remembered the wreck of the Spanish ship, and gave him directions how to find the very spot. It was on a reef of rocks, a few leagues from Porto de la Plata.

On his arrival in England, therefore, Captain Phipps solicited the king to let him have another vessel and send him back again to the West Indies. But King James, who had probably expected that the Rose Algier would return laden with gold, refused to have any thing more to do with the affair. Phipps might never have been able to renew the search if the Duke of Albemarle and some other noblemen had not lent their assistance. They fitted out a ship, and gave the command to Captain Phipps. He sailed from England, and arrived safely at Porto de la Plata, where he took an adze and assisted his men to build a large boat.

The boat was intended for the purpose of going closer to the reef of rocks than a large vessel could safely venture. When it was finished, the captain sent several men in it to examine the spot where the Spanish ship was said to have been wrecked. They were accompanied by some Indians, who were skilful divers, and could go down a great way into the depths of the sea.

The boat's crew proceeded to the reef of rocks, and rowed round and round it a great many times. They gazed down into the water, which was so transparent that it seemed as if they could have seen the gold and silver at the bottom, had there been any of those precious metals there. Nothing, however, could they see ; nothing more valuable than a curious sea shrub, which was growing beneath the water, in a crevice of the reef of rocks. It flaunted to and fro with the swell and reflux of the waves, and looked as bright and beautiful as if its leaves were gold.

" We won't go back empty handed," cried an English sailor ; and then he spoke to one of the Indian divers. " Dive down and bring me that pretty sea shrub there. That's the only treasure we shall find."

Down plunged the diver, and soon rose dripping from the water, holding the sea shrub in his hand. But he had learned some news at the bottom of the sea.

" There are some ship's guns," said he, the moment he had drawn breath, " some great cannon, among the rocks, near where the shrub was growing."

No sooner had he spoken than the English sailors knew that they had found the very spot where the Spanish galleon had been wrecked so many years before. The other Indian divers immediately plunged over the boat's side and swam headlong down, groping among the rocks and sunken cannon. In a few moments one of them rose above the water with a heavy lump of silver in his arms. The single lump was worth more than a thousand dollars. The sailors took it into the boat, and then rowed back as speedily as they could, being in haste to inform Captain Phipps of their good luck.

But, confidently as the captain had hoped to find the Spanish wreck, yet, now that it was really found, the news seemed too good to be true. He could not believe it till the sailors showed him the lump of silver.

"Thanks be to God!" then cries Captain Phipps. "We shall every man of us make our fortunes!"

Hereupon the captain and all the crew set to work, with iron rakes and great hooks and lines, fishing for gold and silver at the bottom of the sea. Up came the treasure in abundance. Now they beheld a table of solid silver, once the property of an old Spanish grandee. Now they found a sacramental vessel, which had been destined as a gift to some Catholic church. Now they drew up a golden cup, fit for the King of Spain to drink his wine out of. Perhaps the bony hand of its former owner had been grasping the precious cup, and was drawn up along with it. Now their rakes or fishing lines were loaded with masses of silver bullion. There were also precious stones among the treasure, glittering and sparkling, so that it is a wonder how their radiance could have been concealed.

There is something sad and terrible in the idea of snatching all this wealth from the devouring ocean, which had possessed it for such a length of years. It seems as if men had no right to make themselves rich with it. It ought to have been left with the skeletons of the ancient Spaniards, who had been drowned when the ship was wrecked, and whose bones were now scattered among the gold and silver.

But Captain Phipps and his crew were troubled with no such thoughts as these. After a day or two they lighted on another part of the wreck, where they found a great many bags of silver dollars. But nobody could have guessed that these were money bags. By remaining so long in the salt water, they had become covered over with a crust which had the appearance of stone, so that it was necessary to break them in pieces with hammers and axes. When this was done, a stream of silver dollars gushed out upon the deck of the vessel.

The whole value of the recovered treasure, plate, bullion, precious stones, and all, was estimated at more than two millions of dollars. It was dangerous even to look at such a vast amount of wealth. A sea captain, who had assisted Phipps in the enterprise, utterly lost his reason at the sight of it. He died two years afterwards, still raving about the treasures that lie at the bottom of the sea. It would have been better for this man if he had left the skeletons of the shipwrecked Spaniards in quiet possession of their wealth.

Captain Phipps and his men continued to fish up plate, bullion, and dollars, as plentifully as ever, till their provisions grew short. Then, as they could not feed upon gold and silver any more than old King Midas could, they found it necessary to go in search of better sustenance. Phipps resolved to return to England. He arrived there in 1687, and was received with great joy by the Duke of Albemarle and other English lords who had fitted out the vessel. Well they might rejoice; for they took by far the greater part of the treasure to themselves.

The captain's share, however, was enough to make him comfortable for the rest of his days. It also enabled him to fulfil his promise to his wife, by building a " fair brick house " in the Green Lane of Boston. The Duke of Albemarle sent Mrs. Phipps a magnificent gold cup, worth at least five thousand dollars. Before Captain Phipps left London, King James made him a knight; so that, instead of the obscure ship carpenter who had formerly dwelt among them the inhabitants of Boston welcomed him on his return as the rich and famous Sir William Phipps.

CHAPTER XI.

"Sir William Phipps," continued Grandfather, "was too active and adventurous a man to sit still in the quiet enjoyment of his good fortune. In the year 1690 he went on a military expedition against the French colonies in America, conquered the whole province of Acadia, and returned to Boston with a great deal of plunder."

"Why, Grandfather, he was the greatest man that ever sat in the chair!" cried Charley.

"Ask Laurence what he thinks," replied Grandfather, with a smile. "Well, in the same year, Sir William took command of an expedition against Quebec, but did not succeed in capturing the city. In 1692, being then in London, King William III. appointed him governor of Massachusetts. And now, my dear children, having followed Sir William Phipps through all his adventures and hardships till we find him comfortably seated in Grandfather's chair, we will here bid him farewell. May he be as happy in ruling a people as he was while he tended sheep!"

Charley, whose fancy had been greatly taken by the adventurous disposition of Sir William Phipps, was eager to know how he had acted and what happened to him while he held the office of governor. But Grandfather had made up his mind to tell no more stories for the present.

"Possibly, one of these days, I may go on with the adventures of the chair," said he. "But its history becomes very obscure just at this point; and I must search into some old books and manuscripts before proceeding farther. Besides, it is now a good time to pause in our narrative; because the new charter, which Sir William Phipps brought over from England, formed a very important epoch in the history of the province."

"Really, Grandfather," observed Laurence, "this seems to be the most remarkable chair in the world. Its history cannot be told without intertwining it with the lives of distinguished men and the great events that have befallen the country."

"True, Laurence," replied Grandfather, smiling; "we must write a book with some such title as this — MEMOIRS OF MY OWN TIMES, BY GRANDFATHER'S CHAIR."

"That would be beautiful!" exclaimed Laurence, clapping his hands.

"But, after all," continued Grandfather, "any other old chair, if it possessed memory and a hand

to write its recollections, could record stranger stories
than any that I have told you. From generation to
generation, a chair sits familiarly in the midst of hu-
man interests, and is witness to the most secret and
confidential intercourse that mortal man can hold
with his fellow. The human heart may best be read
in the fireside chair. And as to external events,
Grief and Joy keep a continual vicissitude around it
and within it. Now we see the glad face and glow-
ing form of Joy, sitting merrily in the old chair, and
throwing a warm firelight radiance over all the house-
hold. Now, while we thought not of it, the dark-
clad mourner, Grief, has stolen into the place of Joy,
but not to retain it long. The imagination can hardly
grasp so wide a subject as is embraced in the experi-
ence of a family chair."

"It makes my breath flutter, my heart thrill, to
think of it," said Laurence. "Yes, a family chair
must have a deeper history than a chair of state."

"O, yes!" cried Clara, expressing a woman's feel-
ing on the point in question; "the history of a country
is not nearly so interesting as that of a single family
parte."

beardhe history of a country is more easily told,"
geous father. "So, if we proceed with our nd,
have she chair, I shall still confine myself very
Sir Willith public events." IER'S

andfather now rose and quit

room, while the children remained gazing at the chair.
Laurence, so vivid was his conception of past times,
would hardly have deemed it strange if its former
occupants, one after another, had resumed the seat
which they had each left vacant such a dim length of
years ago.

First, the gentle and lovely Lady Arbella would
have been seen in the old chair, almost sinking out
of its arms for very weakness ; then Roger Williams,
in his cloak and band, earnest, energetic, and benevo-
lent ; then the figure of Anne Hutchinson, with the
like gesture as when she presided at the assemblages
of women ; then the dark, intellectual face of Vane,
"young in years, but in sage counsel old." Next
would have appeared the successive governors, Win-
throp, Dudley, Bellingham, and Endicott, who sat
in the chair while it was a chair of state. Then
its ample seat would have been pressed by the com-
fortable, rotund corporation of the honest mint-
master. Then the half-frenzied shape of Mary Dyer,
the persecuted Quaker woman, clad in sackcloth and
ashes, would have rested in it for a moment. Then
the holy, apostolic form of Eliot would have sanctified
it. Then would have arisen, like the shade of de-
parted Puritanism, the venerable dignity of the white-
bearded Governor Bradstreet. Lastly, on the gor-
geous crimson cushion of Grandfather's chair, would
have shone the purple and golden magnificence of
Sir William Phipps.

But all these, with the other historic personages, in the midst of whom the chair had so often stood, had passed, both in substance and shadow, from the scene of ages. Yet here stood the chair, with the old Lincoln coat of arms, and the oaken flowers and foliage, and the fierce lion's head at the summit, the whole, apparently, in as perfect preservation as when it had first been placed in the Earl of Lincoln's hall. And what vast changes of society and of nations had been wrought by sudden convulsions or by slow degrees since that era!

"This chair had stood firm when the thrones of kings were overturned!" thought Laurence. "Its oaken frame has proved stronger than many frames of government!"

More the thoughtful and imaginative boy might have mused; but now a large yellow cat, a great favorite with all the children, leaped in at the open window. Perceiving that Grandfather's chair was empty, and having often before experienced its comforts, puss laid herself quietly down upon the cushion. Laurence, Clara, Charley, and little Alice all laughed at the idea of such a successor to the worthies of old times.

"Pussy," said little Alice, putting out her hand, into which the cat laid a velvet paw, "you look very wise. Do tell us a story about GRANDFATHER'S CHAIR!"

GRANDFATHER'S CHAIR.

PART II.

CHAPTER I.

"O GRANDFATHER, dear Grandfather," cried little Alice, "pray tell us some more stories about your chair!"

How long a time had fled since the children had felt any curiosity to hear the sequel of this venerable chair's adventures! Summer was now past and gone, and the better part of autumn likewise. Dreary, chill November was howling out of doors, and vexing the atmosphere with sudden showers of wintry rain, or sometimes with gusts of snow, that rattled like small pebbles against the windows.

When the weather began to grow cool, Grandfather's chair had been removed from the summer parlor into a smaller and snugger room. It now stood by the side of a bright, blazing, wood fire. Grandfather loved a wood fire far better than a grate of glowing anthracite, or than the dull heat of an invisible furnace, which seems to think that it has done its duty in merely warming the house. But the wood fire is a kindly, cheerful, sociable spirit, sympathizing with mankind, and knowing that to create warmth is but one of the good offices which are expected from it. Therefore it dances on the hearth, and laughs broadly through the room, and plays a thousand antics, and throws a joyous glow over all the faces that encircle it.

In the twilight of the evening the fire grew brighter and more cheerful. And thus perhaps, there was something in Grandfather's heart that cheered him most with its warmth and comfort in the gathering twilight of old age. He had been gazing at the red embers as intently as if his past life were all pictured there, or as if it were a prospect of the future world, when little Alice's voice aroused him.

"Dear Grandfather," repeated the little girl, more earnestly, "do talk to us again about your chair."

Laurence, and Clara, and Charley, and little Alice had been attracted to other objects for two or three months past. They had sported in the gladsome sunshine of the present, and so had forgotten the shadowy region of the past, in the midst of which stood Grandfather's chair. But now, in the autumnal twilight, illuminated by the flickering blaze of the wood fire, they looked at the old chair, and thought that it had never before worn such an interesting aspect. There it stood in the venerable majesty of more than two hundred years. The light from the hearth quivered upon the flowers and foliage that were wrought into its oaken back; and the lion's head at the summit seemed almost to move its jaws and shake its mane.

"Does little Alice speak for all of you?" asked Grandfather. "Do you wish me to go on with the adventures of the chair?"

"O, yes, yes, Grandfather!" cried Clara. "The dear old chair! How strange that we should have forgotten it so long!"

"O, pray begin, Grandfather," said Laurence; "for I think, when we talk about old times, it should be in the early evening, before the candles are lighted. The shapes of the famous persons who once sat in the chair will be more apt to come back, and be seen among us, in this glimmer and pleasant gloom, than they would in the vulgar daylight. And, besides, we can make pictures of all that you tell us among the glowing embers and white ashes."

Our friend Charley, too, thought the evening the best time to hear Grandfather's stories, because he could not then be playing out of doors. So, finding his young auditors unanimous in their petition, the good old gentleman took up the narrative of the historic chair at the point where he had dropped it.

CHAPTER II.

"You recollect, my dear children," said Grandfather, "that we took leave of the chair in 1692, while it was occupied by Sir William Phipps. This fortunate treasure seeker, you will remember, had come over from England, with King William's commission, to be governor of Massachusetts. Within the limits of this province were now included the old colony of Plymouth and the territories of Maine and Nova Scotia. Sir William Phipps had likewise brought a new charter from the king, which served instead of a constitution, and set forth the method in which the province was to be governed."

"Did the new charter allow the people all their former liberties?" inquired Laurence.

"No," replied Grandfather. "Under the first charter, the people had been the source of all power. Winthrop, Endicott, Bradstreet, and the rest of them had been governors by the choice of the people, without any interference of the king. But henceforth the governor was to hold his station solely by the king's appointment and during his pleasure; and the same was the case with the lieutenant governor and some other high officers. The people, however, were still allowed to choose representatives; and the governor's council was chosen by the general court."

"Would the inhabitants have elected Sir William Phipps," asked Laurence, "if the choice of governor had been left to them?"

"He might probably have been a successful candidate," answered Grandfather; "for his adventures and military enterprises had gained him a sort of renown, which always goes a great way with the people. And he had many popular characteristics, being a kind, warmhearted man, not ashamed of his low origin, nor haughty in his present elevation. Soon after his arrival, he proved that he did not blush to recognize his former associates."

"How was that?" inquired Charley.

"He made a grand festival at his new brick house," said Grandfather, "and invited all the ship carpenters of Boston to be his guests. At the head of the table, in our great chair, sat Sir William Phipps himself, treating these hardhanded men as his brethren, cracking jokes with them and talking familiarly about old times. I know not whether he wore his embroidered dress; but I rather choose to imagine that he had on a suit of rough clothes, such as he used to labor in while he was Phipps the ship carpenter."

"An aristocrat need not be ashamed of the trade," observed Laurence; "for the Czar Peter the Great once served an apprenticeship to it."

"Did Sir William Phipps make as good a governor as he was a ship carpenter?" asked Charley.

"History says but little about his merits as a ship carpenter," answered Grandfather; "but, as a governor, a great deal of fault was found with him. Almost as soon as he assumed the government, he became engaged in a very frightful business, which might have perplexed a wiser and better cultivated head than his. This was the witchcraft delusion."

And here Grandfather gave his auditors such details of this melancholy affair as he thought it fit for them to know. They shuddered to hear that a frenzy, which led to the death of many innocent persons, had originated in the wicked arts of a few children. They belonged to the Rev. Mr. Parris, minister of Salem. These children complained of being pinched and pricked with pins, and otherwise tormented by the shapes of men and women, who were supposed to have power to haunt them invisibly, both in darkness and daylight. Often in the midst of their family and friends the children would pretend to be seized with strange convulsions, and would cry out that the witches were afflicting them.

These stories spread abroad, and caused great tumult and alarm. From the foundation of New England, it had been the custom of the inhabitants, in all matters of doubt and difficulty, to look to their ministers for counsel. So they did now; but, unfortunately, the ministers and wise men were more deluded than the illiterate people. Cotton Mather, a very learned and eminent clergyman, believed that the whole country was full of witches and wizards, who had given up their hopes of heaven, and signed a covenant with the evil one.

Nobody could be certain that his nearest neighbor or most intimate friend was not guilty of this imaginary crime. The number of those who pretended to be afflicted by witchcraft grew daily more numerous; and they bore testimony against many of the best and worthiest people. A minister, named George Burroughs, was among the accused. In the months of August and September, 1692, he and nineteen other innocent men and women were put to death. The place of execution was a high hill, on the outskirts of Salem; so that many of the sufferers, as they stood beneath the gallows, could discern their own habitations in the town.

The martyrdom of these guiltless persons seemed only to increase the madness. The afflicted now grew bolder in their accusations. Many people of rank and wealth were either thrown into prison or compelled to flee for their lives. Among these were two sons of old Simon Bradstreet, the last of the Puritan governors. Mr. Willard, a pious minister of Boston, was cried out upon as a wizard in open court. Mrs. Hale, the wife of the minister of Beverly, was likewise accused. Philip English, a rich merchant of Salem, found it necessary to take flight, leaving his property and business in confusion. But a short time afterwards, the Salem people were glad to invite him back.

"The boldest thing that the accusers did," continued Grandfather, "was to cry out against the governor's own beloved wife. Yes, the lady of Sir William Phipps was accused of being a witch and of flying through the air to attend witch meetings. When the governor heard this he probably trembled, so that our great chair shook beneath him."

"Dear Grandfather," cried little Alice, clinging closer to his knee, "is it true that witches ever come in the nighttime to frighten little children?"

"No, no, dear little Alice," replied Grandfather. "Even if there were any witches, they would flee away from the presence of a purehearted child. But there are none; and our forefathers soon became convinced that they had been led into a terrible delusion. All the prisoners on account of witchcraft were set free. But the innocent dead could not be restored to life; and the hill where they were executed will always remind people of the saddest and most humiliating passage in our history "

Grandfather then said that the next remarkable event, while Sir William Phipps remained in the chair, was the arrival at Boston of an English fleet in 1693. It brought an army which was intended for the conquest of Canada. But a malignant disease, more fatal than the small pox, broke out among the soldiers and sailors, and destroyed the greater part of them. The infection spread into the town of Boston, and made much havoc there. This dreadful sickness caused the governor, and Sir Francis Wheeler, who was commander of the British forces, to give up all thoughts of attacking Canada.

"Soon after this," said Grandfather, "Sir William Phipps quarrelled with the captain of an English frigate, and also with the collector of Boston. Being a man of violent temper, he gave each of them a sound beating with his cane."

"He was a bold fellow," observed Charley, who was himself somewhat addicted to a similar mode of settling disputes.

"More bold than wise," replied Grandfather; "for complaints were carried to the king, and Sir William Phipps was summoned to England to make the best answer he could. Accordingly he went to London, where, in 1695, he was seized with a malignant fever, of which he died. Had he lived longer, he would probably have gone again in search of sunken treasure. He had heard of a Spanish ship, which was cast away in 1502, during the lifetime of Columbus. Bovadilla, Roldan, and many other Spaniards were lost in her, together with the immense wealth of which they had robbed the South American kings."

" Why, Grandfather!" exclaimed Laurence, " what magnificent ideas the governor had! Only think of recovering all that old treasure which had lain almost two centuries under the sea! Methinks Sir William Phipps ought to have been buried in the ocean when he died, so that he might have gone down among the sunken ships and cargoes of treasure which he was always dreaming about in his lifetime."

" He was buried in one of the crowded cemeteries of London," said Grandfather. " As he left no children, his estate was inherited by his nephew, from whom is descended the present marquis of Normanby. The noble marquis is not aware, perhaps, that the prosperity of his family originated in the successful enterprise of a New England ship carpenter."

CHAPTER III.

"At the death of Sir William Phipps," proceeded Grandfather, "our chair was bequeathed to Mr. Ezekiel Cheever, a famous schoolmaster in Boston. This old gentleman came from London in 1637, and had been teaching school ever since; so that there were now aged men, grandfathers like myself, to whom Master Cheever had taught their alphabet. He was a person of venerable aspect, and wore a long, white beard."

"Was the chair placed in his school?" asked Charley.

"Yes, in his school," answered Grandfather; "and we may safely say that it had never before been regarded with such awful reverence — no, not even when the old governors of Massachusetts sat in it. Even you, Charley, my boy, would have felt some respect for the chair if you had seen it occupied by this famous schoolmaster."

And here Grandfather endeavored to give his auditors an idea how matters were managed in schools above a hundred years ago. As this will probably be an interesting subject to our readers, we shall make a separate sketch of it, and call it

THE OLD-FASHIONED SCHOOL.

Now, imagine yourselves, my children, in Master Ezekiel Cheever's school room. It is a large, dingy room, with a sanded floor, and is lighted by windows that turn on hinges and have little diamond-shaped panes of glass. The scholars sit on long benches, with desks before them. At one end of the room is a great fireplace, so very spacious that there is room enough for three or four boys to stand in each of the chimney corners. This was the good old fashion of fireplaces when there was wood enough in the forests to keep people warm without their digging into the bowels of the earth for coal.

It is a winter's day when we take our peep into the school room. See what great logs of wood have been rolled into the fireplace, and what a broad, bright blaze goes leaping up the chimney! And every few moments a vast cloud of smoke is puffed into the room, which sails slowly over the heads of the scholars, until it gradually settles upon the walls and ceiling. They are blackened with the smoke of many years already.

Next look at our old historic chair! It is placed,

you perceive, in the most comfortable part of the
room, where the generous glow of the fire is suffi-
ciently felt without being too intensely hot.   How
stately the old chair looks, as if it remembered its
many famous occupants, but yet were conscious that
a greater man is sitting in it now!   Do you see the
venerable schoolmaster, severe in aspect, with a black
skullcap on his head, like an ancient Puritan, and the
snow of his white beard drifting down to his very
girdle?   What boy would dare to play, or whisper,
or even glance aside from his book, while Master
Cheever is on the lookout behind his spectacles?
For such offenders, if any such there be, a rod of
birch is hanging over the fireplace, and a heavy ferule
lies on the master's desk.

And now school is begun.   What a murmur of
multitudinous tongues, like the whispering leaves of
a wind-stirred oak, as the scholars con over their va-
rious tasks!   Buzz! buzz! buzz!   Amid just such a
murmur has Master Cheever spent above sixty years;
and long habit has made it as pleasant to him as the
hum of a beehive when the insects are busy in the
sunshine.

Now a class in Latin is called to recite.   Forth
steps a row of queer-looking little fellows, wearing
square-skirted coats and smallclothes, with buttons at
the knee.   They look like so many grandfathers in
their second childhood.   These lads are to be sent to

Cambridge and educated for the learned professions. Old Master Cheever has lived so long, and seen so many generations of schoolboys grow up to be men, that now he can almost prophesy what sort of a man each boy will be. One urchin shall hereafter be a doctor, and administer pills and potions, and stalk gravely through life, perfumed with assafœtida. Another shall wrangle at the bar, and fight his way to wealth and honors, and, in his declining age, shall be a worshipful member of his majesty's council. A third — and he is the master's favorite — shall be a worthy successor to the old Puritan ministers now in their graves; he shall preach with great unction and effect, and leave volumes of sermons, in print and manuscript, for the benefit of future generations.

But, as they are merely schoolboys now, their business is to construe Virgil. Poor Virgil! whose verses, which he took so much pains to polish, have been misscanned, and misparsed, and misinterpreted by so many generations of idle schoolboys. There, sit down, ye Latinists. Two or three of you, I fear, are doomed to feel the master's ferule.

Next comes a class in arithmetic. These boys are to be the merchants, shopkeepers, and mechanics of a future period. Hitherto they have traded only in marbles and apples. Hereafter some will send vessels to England for broadcloths and all sorts of manufactured wares, and to the West Indies for sugar, and rum, and coffee. Others will stand behind counters, and measure tape, and ribbon, and cambric by the yard. Others will upheave the blacksmith's hammer, or drive the plane over the carpenter's bench, or take the lapstone and the awl and learn the trade of shoemaking. Many will follow the sea, and become bold, rough sea captains.

This class of boys, in short, must supply the world with those active, skilful hands, and clear, sagacious heads, without which the affairs of life would be thrown into confusion by the theories of studious and visionary men. Wherefore, teach them their multiplication table, good Master Cheever, and whip them well when they deserve it; for much of the country's welfare depends on these boys.

But, alas! while we have been thinking of other matters, Master Cheever's watchful eye has caught two boys at play. Now we shall see awful times. The two malefactors are summoned before the master's chair, wherein he sits with the terror of a judge upon his brow. Our old chair is now a judgment seat. Ah, Master Cheever has taken down that terrible birch rod! Short is the trial—the sentence quickly passed — and now the judge prepares to execute it in person. Thwack! thwack! thwack! In these good old times, a schoolmaster's blows were well laid on.

See, the birch rod has lost several of its twigs, and

will hardly serve for another execution. Mercy on us, what a bellowing the urchins make! My ears are almost deafened, though the clamor comes through the far length of a hundred and fifty years. There, go to your seats, poor boys; and do not cry, sweet little Alice, for they have ceased to feel the pain a long time since.

And thus the forenoon passes away. Now it is twelve o'clock. The master looks at his great silver watch, and then, with tiresome deliberation, puts the ferule into his desk. The little multitude await the word of dismissal with almost irrepressible impatience.

"You are dismissed," says Master Cheever.

The boys retire, treading softly until they have passed the threshold; but, fairly out of the school room, lo, what a joyous shout! what a scampering and trampling of feet! what a sense of recovered freedom expressed in the merry uproar of all their voices! What care they for the ferule and birch rod now? Were boys created merely to study Latin and arithmetic? No; the better purposes of their being are to sport, to leap, to run, to shout, to slide upon the ice, to snowball.

Happy boys! Enjoy your playtime now, and come again to study and to feel the birch rod and the ferule to-morrow; not till to-morrow, for to-day is Thursday lecture; and, ever since the settlement of Massachusetts, there has been no school on Thursday afternoons. Therefore, sport, boys, while you may ; for the morrow cometh, with the birch rod and the ferule; and after that another morrow, with troubles of its own.

Now the master has set every thing to rights, and is ready to go home to dinner. Yet he goes reluctantly. The old man has spent so much of his life in the smoky, noisy, buzzing school room, that, when he has a holiday, he feels as if his place were lost and himself a stranger in the world. But forth he goes; and there stands our old chair, vacant and solitary, till good Master Cheever resumes his seat in it to-morrow morning.

"Grandfather," said Charley, "I wonder whether the boys did not use to upset the old chair when the schoolmaster was out."

"There is a tradition," replied Grandfather, "that one of its arms was dislocated in some such manner. But I cannot believe that any schoolboy would behave so naughtily."

As it was now later than little Alice's usual bedtime, Grandfather broke off his narrative, promising to talk more about Master Cheever and his scholars some other evening.

CHAPTER IV.

Accordingly, the next evening, Grandfather resumed the history of his beloved chair.

"Master Ezekiel Cheever," said he, "died in 1707, after having taught school about seventy years. It would require a pretty good scholar in arithmetic to tell how many stripes he had inflicted, and how many birch rods he had worn out, during all that time, in his fatherly tenderness for his pupils. Almost all the great men of that period, and for many years back, had been whipped into eminence by Master Cheever. Moreover, he had written a Latin Accidence, which was used in schools more than half a century after his death; so that the good old man, even in his grave, was still the cause of trouble and stripes to idle schoolboys."

Grandfather proceeded to say, that, when Master Cheever died, he bequeathed the chair to the most learned man that was educated at his school, or that had ever been born in America. This was the renowned Cotton Mather, minister of the Old North Church in Boston.

"And author of the Magnalia, Grandfather, which we sometimes see you reading," said Laurence.

"Yes, Laurence," replied Grandfather. "The Magnalia is a strange, pedantic history, in which true events and real personages move before the reader with the dreamy aspect which they wore in Cotton Mather's singular mind. This huge volume however, was written and published before our chair came into his possession. But, as he was the author of more books than there are days in the year, we may conclude that he wrote a great deal while sitting in this chair."

"I am tired of these schoolmasters and learned men," said Charley. "I wish some stirring man, that knew how to do something in the world, like Sir William Phipps, would sit in the chair."

"Such men seldom have leisure to sit quietly in a chair," said Grandfather. "We must make the best of such people as we have."

As Cotton Mather was a very distinguished man, Grandfather took some pains to give the children a lively conception of his character. Over the door of his library were painted these words, BE SHORT —as a warning to visitors that they must not do the world so much harm as needlessly to interrupt this great man's wonderful labors. On entering the room you would probably behold it crowded, and piled, and heaped with books. There were huge, ponderous folios, and quartos, and little duodecimos, in English, Latin, Greek, Hebrew, Chaldaic, and all other languages that either originated at the confusion of Babel or have since come into use.

All these books, no doubt, were tossed about in confusion, thus forming a visible emblem of the manner in which their contents were crowded into Cotton Mather's brain. And in the middle of the room stood a table, on which, besides printed volumes, were strewn manuscript sermons, historical tracts, and political pamphlets, all written in such a queer, blind, crabbed, fantastical hand, that a writing master would have gone raving mad at the sight of them. By this table stood Grandfather's chair, which seemed already to have contracted an air of deep erudition, as if its cushion were stuffed with Latin, Greek, and Hebrew, and other hard matters.

In this chair, from one year's end to another, sat that prodigious bookworm, Cotton Mather, sometimes devouring a great book, and sometimes scribbling one as big. In Grandfather's younger days there used to be a wax figure of him in one of the Boston museums, representing a solemn, dark-visaged person, in a minister's black gown, and with a black-letter volume before him.

"It is difficult, my children," observed Grand-father, "to make you understand such a character as Cotton Mather's, in whom there was so much good, and yet so many failings and frailties. Un-doubtedly he was a pious man. Often he kept fasts ; and once, for three whole days, he allowed himself not a morsel of food, but spent the time in prayer and religious meditation. Many a livelong night did he watch and pray. These fasts and vigils made him meagre and haggard, and probably caused him to appear as if he hardly belonged to the world."

" Was not the witchcraft delusion partly caused by Cotton Mather ? " inquired Laurence.

" He was the chief agent of the mischief," an-swered Grandfather ; " but we will not suppose that he acted otherwise than conscientiously. He believed that there were evil spirits all about the world. Doubtless he imagined that they were hidden in the corners and crevices of his library, and that they peeped out from among the leaves of many of his books, as he turned them over, at midnight. He supposed that these unlovely demons were every where, in the sunshine as well as in the darkness, and that they were hidden in men's hearts, and stole into their most secret thoughts."

Here Grandfather was interrupted by little Alice, who hid her face in his lap, and murmured a wish that he would not talk any more about Cotton Mather and the evil spirits. Grandfather kissed her, and told her that angels were the only spirits whom she had any thing to do with. He then spoke of the public affairs of the period.

A new war between France and England had broken out in 1702, and had been raging ever since. In the course of it, New England suffered much injury from the French and Indians, who often came through the woods from Canada and assaulted the frontier towns. Villages were sometimes burned, and the inhabitants slaughtered, within a day's ride of Boston. The people of New England had a bitter hatred against the French, not only for the mischief which they did with their own hands, but because they incited the Indians to hostility.

The New Englanders knew that they could never dwell in security until the provinces of France should be subdued and brought under the English government. They frequently, in time of war, undertook military expeditions against Acadia and Canada, and sometimes besieged the fortresses by which those territories were defended. But the most earnest wish of their hearts was to take Quebec, and so get possession of the whole Province of Canada. Sir William Phipps had once attempted it, but without success.

Fleets and soldiers were often sent from England to assist the colonists in their warlike undertakings.

In 1710 Port Royal, a fortress of Acadia, was taken
by the English. The next year, in the month of
June, a fleet, commanded by Admiral Sir Hovenden
Walker, arrived in Boston Harbor. On board of this
fleet was the English General Hill, with seven regi-
ments of soldiers, who had been fighting under the
Duke of Marlborough in Flanders. The govern-
ment of Massachusetts was called upon to find pro-
visions for the army and fleet, and to raise more men
to assist in taking Canada.

What with recruiting and drilling of soldiers,
there was now nothing but warlike bustle in the
streets of Boston. The drum and fife, the rattle of
arms, and the shouts of boys were heard from morn-
ing till night. In about a month the fleet set sail,
carrying four regiments from New England and New
York, besides the English soldiers. The whole
army amounted to at least seven thousand men.
They steered for the mouth of the River St. Lawrence.

"Cotton Mather prayed most fervently for their
success," continued Grandfather, "both in his pulpit
and when he kneeled down in the solitude of his
library resting his face on our old chair. But Provi-
dence ordered the result otherwise. In a few weeks
tidings were received that eight or nine of the ves-
sels had been wrecked in the St. Lawrence, and that
above a thousand drowned soldiers had been washed
ashore on the banks of that mighty river. After

this misfortune Sir Hovenden Walker set sail for England; and many pious people began to think it a sin even to wish for the conquest of Canada."

"I would never give it up so," cried Charley.

"Nor did they, as we shall see," replied Grandfather. "However, no more attempts were made during this war, which came to a close in 1713. The people of New England were probably glad of some repose; for their young men had been made soldiers, till many of them were fit for nothing else. And those who remained at home had been heavily taxed to pay for the arms, ammunition, fortifications, and all the other endless expenses of a war. There was great need of the prayers of Cotton Mather and of all pious men, not only on account of the sufferings of the people, but because the old moral and religious character of New England was in danger of being utterly lost."

"How glorious it would have been," remarked Laurence, "if our forefathers could have kept the country unspotted with blood!"

"Yes," said Grandfather; "but there was a stern, warlike spirit in them from the beginning. They seem never to have thought of questioning either the morality or piety of war."

The next event which Grandfather spoke of was one that Cotton Mather, as well as most of the other inhabitants of New England, heartily rejoiced at.

This was the accession of the Elector of Hanover to the throne of England, in 1714, on the death of Queen Anne. Hitherto the people had been in continual dread that the male line of the Stuarts, who were descended from the beheaded King Charles and the banished King James, would be restored to the throne. In that case, as the Stuart family were Roman Catholics, it was supposed that they would attempt to establish their own religion throughout the British dominions. But the Elector of Hanover and all his race were Protestants; so that now the descendants of the old Puritans were relieved from many fears and disquietudes.

"The importance of this event," observed Grandfather, " was a thousand times greater than that of a presidential election in our own days. If the people dislike their president, they may get rid of him in four years; whereas a dynasty of kings may wear the crown for an unlimited period."

The German elector was proclaimed king from the balcony of the town house in Boston, by the title of George I.; while the trumpets sounded, and the people cried amen. That night the town was illuminated; and Cotton Mather threw aside book and pen, and left Grandfather's chair vacant, while he walked hither and thither to witness the rejoicings.

CHAPTER V.

"Cotton Mather," continued Grandfather, "was a bitter enemy to Governor Dudley; and nobody exulted more than he when that crafty politician was removed from the government, and succeeded by Colonel Shute. This took place in 1716. The new governor had been an officer in the renowned Duke of Marlborough's army, and had fought in some of the great battles in Flanders."

"Now I hope," said Charley, "we shall hear of his doing great things."

"I am afraid you will be disappointed, Charley," answered Grandfather. "It is true that Colonel Shute had probably never led so unquiet a life while fighting the French as he did now, while governing this province of Massachusetts Bay. But his troubles consisted almost entirely of dissensions with the legislature. The king had ordered him to lay claim to a fixed salary; but the representatives of the people insisted upon paying him only such sums from year to year as they saw fit."

Grandfather here explained some of the circumstances that made the situation of a colonial governor so difficult and irksome. There was not the same feeling towards the chief magistrate now that had existed while he was chosen by the free suffrages of the people. It was felt that as the king appointed the governor, and as he held his office during the king's pleasure, it would be his great object to please the king. But the people thought that a governor ought to have nothing in view but the best interests of those whom he governed.

" The governor," remarked Grandfather, " had two masters to serve — the king, who appointed him ; and the people, on whom he depended for his pay. Few men in this position would have ingenuity enough to satisfy either party. Colonel Shute, though a good-natured, well-meaning man, succeeded so ill with the people, that, in 1722, he suddenly went away to England and made complaint to King George. In the mean time Lieutenant Governor Dummer directed the affairs of the province, and carried on a long and bloody war with the Indians."

" But where was our chair all this time ? " asked Clara.

" It still remained in Cotton Mather's library," replied Grandfather ; " and I must not omit to tell you an incident which is very much to the honor of this celebrated man. It is the more proper, too, that you should hear it, because it will show you what a terrible calamity the small pox was to our forefathers. The history of the province (and, of course, the history of our chair) would be incomplete without particular mention of it."

Accordingly Grandfather told the children a story, to which, for want of a better title, we shall give that of

THE REJECTED BLESSING.

One day, in 1721, Doctor Cotton Mather sat in his library reading a book that had been published by the Royal Society of London. But every few moments he laid the book upon the table, and leaned back in Grandfather's chair with an aspect of deep care and disquietude. There were certain things which troubled him exceedingly, so that he could hardly fix his thoughts upon what he read.

It was now a gloomy time in Boston. That terrible disease, the small pox, had recently made its appearance in the town. Ever since the first settlement of the country this awful pestilence had come, at intervals, and swept away multitudes of the inhabitants. Whenever it commenced its ravages, nothing seemed to stay its progress until there were no more victims for it to seize upon. Oftentimes hundreds of people at once lay groaning with its agony ; and when it departed, its deep footsteps were always to be traced in many graves.

The people never felt secure from this calamity Sometimes, perhaps, it was brought into the country by a poor sailor, who had caught the infection in foreign parts, and came hither to die and to be the cause of many deaths. Sometimes, no doubt, it followed in the train of the pompous governors when they came over from England. Sometimes the disease lay hidden in the cargoes of ships, among silks, and brocades, and other costly merchandise which was imported for the rich people to wear. And sometimes it started up seemingly of its own accord, and nobody could tell whence it came. The physician, being called to attend the sick person, would look at him, and say, "It is the small pox! Let the patient be carried to the hospital."

And now this dreadful sickness had shown itself again in Boston. Cotton Mather was greatly afflicted for the sake of the whole province. He had children, too, who were exposed to the danger. At that very moment he heard the voice of his youngest son, for whom his heart was moved with apprehension.

"Alas! I fear for that poor child," said Cotton Mather to himself. "What shall I do for my son Samuel?"

Again he attempted to drive away these thoughts by taking up the book which he had been reading. And now, all of a sudden, his attention became fixed The book contained a printed letter that an Italian physician had written upon the very subject about which Cotton Mather was so anxiously meditating. He ran his eye eagerly over the pages ; and, behold! a method was disclosed to him by which the small pox might be robbed of its worst terrors. Such a method was known in Greece. The physicians of Turkey, too, those longbearded Eastern sages, had been acquainted with it for many years. The negroes of Africa, ignorant as they were, had likewise practised it, and thus had shown themselves wiser than the white men.

"Of a truth," ejaculated Cotton Mather, clasping his hands and looking up to heaven, "it was a merciful Providence that brought this book under mine eye. I will procure a consultation of physicians, and see whether this wondrous inoculation may not stay the progress of the destroyer."

So he arose from Grandfather's chair and went out of the library. Near the door he met his son Samuel, who seemed downcast and out of spirits. The boy had heard, probably, that some of his playmates were taken ill with the small pox. But, as his father looked cheerfully at him, Samuel took courage, trusting that either the wisdom of so learned a minister would find some remedy for the danger, or else that his prayers would secure protection from on high.

Meanwhile Cotton Mather took his staff and three-cornered hat and walked about the streets, calling at

the houses of all the physicians in Boston. They
were a very wise fraternity; and their huge wigs,
and black dresses, and solemn visages made their
wisdom appear even profounder than it was. One
after another he acquainted them with the discovery
which he had hit upon.

But the grave and sagacious personages would
scarcely listen to him. The oldest doctor in town
contented himself with remarking that no such thing
as inoculation was mentioned by Galen or Hippoc-
rates; and it was impossible that modern physicians
should be wiser than those old sages. A second held
up his hands in dumb astonishment and horror at
the madness of what Cotton Mather proposed to do.
A third told him, in pretty plain terms, that he knew
not what he was talking about. A fourth requested,
in the name of the whole medical fraternity, that
Cotton Mather would confine his attention to people's
souls, and leave the physicians to take care of their
bodies.

In short, there was but a single doctor among them
all who would grant the poor minister so much as a
patient hearing. This was Doctor Zabdiel Boylston.
He looked into the matter like a man of sense, and
finding, beyond a doubt, that inoculation had rescued
many from death, he resolved to try the experiment
in his own family.

And so he did. But when the other physicians

heard of it they arose in great fury and began a war of words, written, printed, and spoken, against Cotton Mather and Doctor Boylston. To hear them talk, you would have supposed that these two harmless and benevolent men had plotted the ruin of the country.

The people, also, took the alarm. Many, who thought themselves more pious than their neighbors, contended that, if Providence had ordained them to die of the small pox, it was sinful to aim at preventing it. The strangest reports were in circulation. Some said that Doctor Boylston had contrived a method for conveying the gout, rheumatism, sick headache, asthma, and all other diseases from one person to another, and diffusing them through the whole community. Others flatly affirmed that the evil one had got possession of Cotton Mather, and was at the bottom of the whole business.

You must observe, children, that Cotton Mather's fellow-citizens were generally inclined to doubt the wisdom of any measure which he might propose to them. They recollected how he had led them astray in the old witchcraft delusion; and now, if he thought and acted ever so wisely, it was difficult for him to get the credit of it.

The people's wrath grew so hot at his attempt to guard them from the small pox that he could not walk the streets in peace. Whenever the venerable form of the old minister, meagre and haggard with fasts and vigils, was seen approaching, hisses were heard, and shouts of derision, and scornful and bitter laughter. The women snatched away their children from his path, lest he should do them a mischief. Still, however, bending his head meekly, and perhaps stretching out his hands to bless those who reviled him, he pursued his way. But the tears came into his eyes to think how blindly the people rejected the means of safety that were offered them.

Indeed, there were melancholy sights enough in the streets of Boston to draw forth the tears of a compassionate man. Over the door of almost every dwelling a red flag was fluttering in the air. This was the signal that the small pox had entered the house and attacked some member of the family; or perhaps the whole family, old and young, were struggling at once with the pestilence. Friends and relatives, when they met one another in the streets, would hurry onward without a grasp of the hand or scarcely a word of greeting, lest they should catch or communicate the contagion; and often a coffin was borne hastily along.

"Alas! alas!" said Cotton Mather to himself, "what shall be done for this poor, misguided people? O that Providence would open their eyes, and enable them to discern good from evil!"

So furious, however, were the people, that they threatened vengeance against any person who should dare to practise inoculation, though it were only in his own family. This was a hard case for Cotton Mather, who saw no other way to rescue his poor child Samuel from the disease. But he resolved to save him, even if his house should be burned over his head.

"I will not be turned aside," said he. "My townsmen shall see that I have faith in this thing, when I make the experiment on my beloved son, whose life is dearer to me than my own. And when I have saved Samuel, peradventure they will be persuaded to save themselves."

Accordingly Samuel was inoculated; and so was Mr. Walter, a son-in-law of Cotton Mather. Doctor Boylston, likewise, inoculated many persons; and while hundreds died who had caught the contagion from the garments of the sick, almost all were preserved who followed the wise physician's advice.

But the people were not yet convinced of their mistake. One night a destructive little instrument, called a hand grenade, was thrown into Cotton Mather's window, and rolled under Grandfather's chair. It was supposed to be filled with gunpowder, the explosion of which would have blown the poor minister to atoms. But the best informed historians are of opinion that the grenade contained only brimstone and assafœtida, and was meant to plague Cotton Mather with a very evil perfume.

This is no strange thing in human experience. Men who attempt to do the world more good than the world is able entirely to comprehend are almost invariably held in bad odor. But yet, if the wise and good man can wait a while, either the present generation or posterity will do him justice. So it proved in the case which we have been speaking of. In after years, when inoculation was universally practised and thousands were saved from death by it, the people remembered old Cotton Mather, then sleeping in his grave. They acknowledged that the very thing for which they had so reviled and persecuted him was the best and wisest thing he ever did.

"Grandfather, this is not an agreeable story," observed Clara.

"No, Clara," replied Grandfather. "But it is right that you should know what a dark shadow this disease threw over the times of our forefathers. And now, if you wish to learn more about Cotton Mather, you must read his biography, written by Mr. Peabody, of Springfield. You will find it very entertaining and instructive; but perhaps the writer is somewhat too harsh in his judgment of this singular man. He estimates him fairly, indeed, and understands him well; but he unriddles his character rather by acuteness than by sympathy. Now, his life should have been written by one who, knowing all his faults, would nevertheless love him."

So Grandfather made an end of Cotton Mather, telling his auditors that he died in 1728, at the age of sixty-five, and bequeathed the chair to Elisha Cooke. This gentleman was a famous advocate of the people's rights.

The same year William Burnet, a son of the celebrated Bishop Burnet, arrived in Boston with the commission of governor. He was the first that had been appointed since the departure of Colonel Shute. Governor Burnet took up his residence with Mr. Cooke while the Province House was undergoing repairs. During this period he was always complimented with a seat in Grandfather's chair; and so comfortable did he find it, that, on removing to the Province House, he could not bear to leave it behind him. Mr. Cooke, therefore, requested his acceptance of it.

"I should think," said Laurence, "that the people would have petitioned the king always to appoint a native-born New Englander to govern them."

"Undoubtedly it was a grievance," answered Grandfather, "to see men placed in this station who perhaps had neither talents nor virtues to fit them for it, and who certainly could have no natural affection for the country. The king generally bestowed the governorships of the American colonies upon needy noblemen, or hangers on at court, or disbanded officers. The people knew that such persons would be very likely to make the good of the country subservient to the wishes of the king. The legislature, therefore, endeavored to keep as much power as possible in their own hands, by refusing to settle a fixed salary upon the governors. It was thought better to pay them according to their deserts."

" Did Governor Burnet work well for his money?" asked Charley.

Grandfather could not help smiling at the simplicity of Charley's question. Nevertheless, it put the matter in a very plain point of view.

He then described the character of Governor Burnet, representing him as a good scholar, possessed of much ability, and likewise of unspotted integrity. His story affords a striking example how unfortunate it is for a man, who is placed as ruler over a country, to be compelled to aim at any thing but the good of the people. Governor Burnet was so chained down by his instructions from the king that he could not act as he might otherwise have wished. Consequently, his whole term of office was wasted in quarrels with the legislature.

" I am afraid, children," said Grandfather, " that Governor Burnet found but little rest or comfort in our old chair. Here he used to sit, dressed in a coat which was made of rough, shaggy cloth outside, but of smooth velvet within. It was said that his own character resembled that coat; for his outward manner was rough, but his inward disposition soft and kind. It is a pity that such a man could not have been kept free from trouble. But so harassing were his disputes with the representatives of the people that he fell into a fever, of which he died in 1729. The legislature had refused him a salary while alive; but they appropriated money enough to give him a splendid and pompous funeral."

And now Grandfather perceived that little Alice had fallen fast asleep, with her head upon his footstool. Indeed, as Clara observed, she had been sleeping from the time of Sir Hovenden Walker's expedition against Quebec until the death of Governor Burnet — a period of about eighteen years. And yet, after so long a nap, sweet little Alice was a golden-haired child of scarcely five years old.

"It puts me in mind," said Laurence, "of the story of the enchanted princess, who slept many a hundred years, and awoke as young and beautiful as ever."

CHAPTER VI.

A few evenings afterwards, cousin Clara happened to inquire of Grandfather whether the old chair had never been present at a ball. At the same time little Alice brought forward a doll, with whom she had been holding a long conversation.

" See, Grandfather !" cried she. " Did such a pretty lady as this ever sit in your great chair ? "

These questions led Grandfather to talk about the fashions and manners which now began to be introduced from England into the provinces. The simplicity of the good old Puritan times was fast disappearing. This was partly owing to the increasing number and wealth of the inhabitants, and to the additions which they continually received by the arrival and settlement of people from beyond the sea.

Another cause of a pompous and artificial mode of life, among those who could afford it, was, that the example was set by the royal governors. Under the old charter, the governors were the representatives of the people, and therefore their way of living had probably been marked by a popular simplicity. But now, as they represented the person of the king, they thought it necessary to preserve the dignity of their station by the practice of high and gorgeous ceremonials. And, besides, the profitable offices under the government were filled by men who had lived in London, and had there contracted fashionable and luxurious habits of living which they would not now lay aside. The wealthy people of the province imitated them; and thus began a general change in social life.

"So, my dear Clara," said Grandfather, "after our chair had entered the Province House, it must often have been present at balls and festivals; though I cannot give you a description of any particular one. But I doubt not that they were very magnificent; and slaves in gorgeous liveries waited on the guests, and offered them wine in goblets of massive silver."

"Were there slaves in those days!" exclaimed Clara.

"Yes, black slaves and white," replied Grandfather. "Our ancestors not only brought negroes from Africa, but Indians from South America, and white people from Ireland. These last were sold, not for life, but for a certain number of years, in order to pay the expenses of their voyage across the Atlantic. Nothing was more common than to see a lot of likely Irish girls advertised for sale in the newspapers. As for the little negro babies, they were offered to be given away like young kittens."

"Perhaps Alice would have liked one to play with instead of her doll," said Charley, laughing.

But little Alice clasped the waxen doll closer to her bosom.

"Now, as for this pretty doll, my little Alice," said Grandfather, "I wish you could have seen what splendid dresses the ladies wore in those times. They had silks, and satins, and damasks, and brocades, and high headdresses, and all sorts of fine things. And they used to wear hooped petticoats, of such enormous size that it was quite a journey to walk round them."

"And how did the gentlemen dress?" asked Charley.

"With full as much magnificence as the ladies," answered Grandfather. "For their holiday suits they had coats of figured velvet, crimson, green, blue, and all other gay colors, embroidered with gold or silver lace. Their waistcoats, which were five times as large as modern ones, were very splendid. Sometimes the whole waistcoat, which came down almost to the knees, was made of gold brocade."

"Why, the wearer must have shone like a golden image!" said Clara.

"And then," continued Grandfather, "they wore various sorts of periwigs, such as the tie, the spencer, the brigadier, the major, the albemarle, the ramilies, the feather top, and the full bottom. Their three-cornered hats were laced with gold or silver. They had shining buckles at the knees of their smallclothes,

and buckles likewise in their shoes. They wore
swords with beautiful hilts, either of silver, or some-
times of polished steel, inlaid with gold."

"O, I should like to wear a sword!" cried Charley.

"And an embroidered crimson velvet coat," said
Clara, laughing, "and a gold brocade waistcoat down
to your knees!"

"And knee buckles and shoe buckles," said Lau-
rence, laughing also.

"And a periwig," added little Alice, soberly, not
knowing what was the article of dress which she
recommended to our friend Charley.

Grandfather smiled at the idea of Charley's sturdy
little figure in such a grotesque caparison. He then
went on with the history of the chair, and told the
children that, in 1730, King George II. appointed
Jonathan Belcher to be governor of Massachusetts
in place of the deceased Governor Burnet. Mr.
Belcher was a native of the province, but had spent
much of his life in Europe.

The new governor found Grandfather's chair in
the Province House. He was struck with its noble
and stately aspect, but was of opinion that age and
hard services had made it scarcely so fit for courtly
company as when it stood in the Earl of Lincoln's
hall. Wherefore, as Governor Belcher was fond of
splendor, he employed a skilful artist to beautify the
chair. This was done by polishing and varnishing

it, and by gilding the carved work of the elbows, and likewise the oaken flowers of the back. The lion's head now shone like a veritable lump of gold. Finally Governor Belcher gave the chair a cushion of blue damask, with a rich golden fringe.

"Our good old chair being thus glorified," proceeded Grandfather, "it glittered with a great deal more splendor than it had exhibited just a century before, when the Lady Arbella brought it over from England. Most people mistook it for a chair of the latest London fashion. And this may serve for an example, that there is almost always an old and time-worn substance under all the glittering show of new invention."

"Grandfather, I cannot see any of the gilding," remarked Charley, who had been examining the chair very minutely.

"You will not wonder that it has been rubbed off," replied Grandfather, "when you hear all the adventures that have since befallen the chair. Gilded it was; and the handsomest room in the Province House was adorned by it."

There was not much to interest the children in what happened during the years that Governor Belcher remained in the chair. At first, like Colonel Shute and Governor Burnet, he was engaged in disputing with the legislature about his salary. But, as he found it impossible to get a fixed sum, he finally obtained the king's leave to accept whatever the legis-lature chose to give him. And thus the people tri-umphed, after this long contest for the privilege of expending their own money as they saw fit.

The remainder of Governor Belcher's term of office was principally taken up in endeavoring to settle the currency. Honest John Hull's pine-tree shillings had long ago been worn out, or lost, or melted down again; and their place was supplied by bills of paper or parchment, which were nominally valued at three-pence and upwards. The value of these bills kept continually sinking, because the real hard money could not be obtained for them. They were a great deal worse than the old Indian currency of clam shells. These disorders of the circulating medium were a source of endless plague and perplexity to the rulers and legislators, not only in Governor Belcher's days, but for many years before and afterwards.

Finally the people suspected that Governor Bel-cher was secretly endeavoring to establish the Episco-pal mode of worship in the provinces. There was enough of the old Puritan spirit remaining to cause most of the true sons of New England to look with horror upon such an attempt. Great exertions were made to induce the king to remove the governor. Accordingly, in 1740, he was compelled to resign his office, and Grandfather's chair into the bargain, to Mr. Shirley.

CHAPTER VII.

"William Shirley," said Grandfather, "had come from England a few years before, and begun to practise law in Boston. You will think, perhaps, that, as he had been a lawyer, the new governor used to sit in our great chair reading heavy law books from morning till night. On the contrary, he was as stirring and active a governor as Massachusetts ever had. Even Sir William Phipps hardly equalled him. The first year or two of his administration was spent in trying to regulate the currency. But in 1744, after a peace of more than thirty years, war broke out between France and England."

"And I suppose," said Charley, "the governor went to take Canada."

"Not exactly, Charley," said Grandfather; "though you have made a pretty shrewd conjecture. He planned, in 1745, an expedition against Louisburg. This was a fortified city, on the Island of Cape Breton, near Nova Scotia. Its walls were of immense height and strength, and were defended by hundreds of heavy cannon. It was the strongest fortress which the French possessed in America; and if the King of France had guessed Governor Shirley's intentions, he would have sent all the ships he could muster to protect it."

As the siege of Louisburg was one of the most remarkable events that ever the inhabitants of New England were engaged in, Grandfather endeavored to give his auditors a lively idea of the spirit with which they set about it. We shall call his description

THE PROVINCIAL MUSTER.

The expedition against Louisburg first began to be thought of in the month of January. From that time the governor's chair was continually surrounded by councillors, representatives, clergymen, captains, pilots, and all manner of people, with whom he consulted about this wonderful project.

First of all, it was necessary to provide men and arms. The legislature immediately sent out a huge quantity of paper money, with which, as if by magic spell, the governor hoped to get possession of all the old cannon, powder and balls, rusty swords and muskets, and every thing else that would be serviceable in killing Frenchmen. Drums were beaten in all the villages of Massachusetts to enlist soldiers for the service. Messages were sent to the other governors of New England, and to New York and Pennsylvania, entreating them to unite in this crusade against the French. All these provinces agreed to give what assistance they could.

But there was one very important thing to be decided. Who shall be the general of this great army? Peace had continued such an unusual length of time, that there was now less military experience among the colonists than at any former period. The old Puritans had always kept their weapons bright, and were never destitute of warlike captains who were skilful in assault or defence. But the swords of their descendants had grown rusty by disuse. There was nobody in New England that knew any thing about sieges or any other regular fighting. The only persons at all acquainted with warlike business were a few elderly men, who had hunted Indians through the underbrush of the forest in old Governor Dummer's war.

In this dilemma Governor Shirley fixed upon a wealthy merchant, named William Pepperell, who was pretty well known and liked among the people. As to military skill, he had no more of it than his neighbors. But, as the governor urged him very pressingly, Mr. Pepperell consented to shut up his leger, gird on a sword, and assume the title of general.

Meantime what a hubbub was raised by this

scheme ! Rub-a-dub-dub ! rub-a-dub-dub ! The rattle of drums, beaten out of all manner of time, was heard above every other sound.

Nothing now was so valuable as arms, of whatever style and fashion they might be. The bellows blew, and the hammer clanged continually upon the anvil, while the blacksmiths were repairing the broken weapons of other wars. Doubtless some of the soldiers lugged out those enormous, heavy muskets which used to be fired, with rests, in the time of the early Puritans. Great horse pistols, too, were found, which would go off with a bang like a cannon. Old cannon, with touchholes almost as big as their muzzles, were looked upon as inestimable treasures. Pikes which, perhaps, had been handled by Miles Standish's soldiers, now made their appearance again. Many a young man ransacked the garret and brought forth his great-grandfather's sword, corroded with rust and stained with the blood of King Philip's war.

Never had there been such an arming as this, when a people, so long peaceful, rose to the war with the best weapons that they could lay their hands upon. And still the drums were heard — rub-a-dub-dub ! rub-a-dub-dub ! — in all the towns and villages ; and louder and more numerous grew the trampling footsteps of the recruits that marched behind.

And now the army began to gather into Boston. Tall, lanky, awkward fellows came in squads, and companies, and regiments, swaggering along, dressed in their brown homespun clothes and blue yarn stockings. They stooped as if they still had hold of the plough handles, and marched without any time or tune. Hither they came, from the cornfields, from the clearing in the forest, from the blacksmith's forge, from the carpenter's workshop, and from the shoemaker's seat. They were an army of rough faces and sturdy frames. A trained officer of Europe would have laughed at them till his sides had ached. But there was a spirit in their bosoms which is more essential to soldiership than to wear red coats and march in stately ranks to the sound of regular music.

Still was heard the beat of the drum — rub-a-dub-dub! And now a host of three or four thousand men had found their way to Boston. Little quiet was there then! Forth scampered the schoolboys, shouting behind the drums. The whole town, the whole land, was on fire with war.

After the arrival of the troops, they were probably reviewed upon the Common. We may imagine Governor Shirley and General Pepperell riding slowly along the line, while the drummers beat strange old tunes, like psalm tunes, and all the officers and soldiers put on their most warlike looks. It would have been a terrible sight for the Frenchmen, could they but have witnessed it !

At length, on the 24th of March, 1745, the army gave a parting shout, and set sail from Boston in ten or twelve vessels which had been hired by the governor. A few days afterwards an English fleet, commanded by Commodore Peter Warren, sailed also for Louisburg to assist the provincial army. So now, after all this bustle of preparation, the town and province were left in stillness and repose.

But stillness and repose, at such a time of anxious expectation, are hard to bear. The hearts of the old people and women sunk within them when they reflected what perils they had sent their sons, and husbands, and brothers to encounter. The boys loitered heavily to school, missing the rub-a-dub-dub and the trampling march, in the rear of which they had so lately run and shouted. All the ministers prayed earnestly in their pulpits for a blessing on the army of New England. In every family, when the good man lifted up his heart in domestic worship, the burden of his petition was for the safety of those dear ones who were fighting under the walls of Louisburg.

Governor Shirley all this time was probably in an ecstasy of impatience. He could not sit still a moment. He found no quiet, not even in Grandfather's chair; but hurried to and fro, and up and down the staircase of the Province House. Now he mounted to the cupola and looked seaward, straining his eyes to discover if there were a sail upon the horizon. Now he hastened down the stairs, and stood beneath the portal, on the red freestone steps, to receive some mud-bespattered courier, from whom he hoped to hear tidings of the army. A few weeks after the departure of the troops, Commodore Warren sent a small vessel to Boston with two French prisoners. One of them was Monsieur Bouladrie, who had been commander of a battery outside of the walls of Louisburg. The other was the Marquis de la Maison Forte, captain of a French frigate which had been taken by Commodore Warren's fleet. These prisoners assured Governor Shirley that the fortifications of Louisburg were far too strong ever to be stormed by the provincial army.

Day after day and week after week went on. The people grew almost heartsick with anxiety; for the flower of the country was at peril in this adventurous expedition. It was now daybreak on the morning of the 3d of July.

But hark! what sound is this? The hurried clang of a bell! There is the Old North pealing suddenly out! — there the Old South strikes in! — now the peal comes from the church in Brattle Street! — the bells of nine or ten steeples are all flinging their iron voices at once upon the morning breeze! Is it joy, or alarm? There goes the roar of a cannon, too! A royal salute is thundered forth. And now we hear the loud, exulting shout of a multitude assembled in the street. Huzza! huzza! Louisburg has surrendered! Huzza!

"O Grandfather, how glad I should have been to live in those times!" cried Charley. "And what reward did the king give to General Pepperell and Governor Shirley?"

"He made Pepperell a baronet; so that he was now to be called Sir William Pepperell," replied Grandfather. "He likewise appointed both Pepperell and Shirley to be colonels in the royal army. These rewards, and higher ones, were well deserved; for this was the greatest triumph that the English met with in the whole course of that war. General Pepperell became a man of great fame. I have seen a full-length portrait of him, representing him in a splendid scarlet uniform, standing before the walls of Louisburg, while several bombs are falling through the air."

"But did the country gain any real good by the conquest of Louisburg?" asked Laurence. "Or was all the benefit reaped by Pepperell and Shirley?"

"The English Parliament," said Grandfather, "agreed to pay the colonists for all the expenses of the siege. Accordingly, in 1749, two hundred and fifteen chests of Spanish dollars and one hundred casks of copper coin were brought from England to Boston. The whole amount was about a million of dollars. Twenty-seven carts and trucks carried this money from the wharf to the provincial treasury. Was not this a pretty liberal reward ?"

"The mothers of the young men who were killed at the siege of Louisburg would not have thought it so," said Laurence.

"No, Laurence," rejoined Grandfather; "and every warlike achievement involves an amount of physical and moral evil, for which all the gold in the Spanish mines would not be the slightest recompense. But we are to consider that this siege was one of the occasions on which the colonists tested their ability for war, and thus were prepared for the great contest of the revolution. In that point of view, the valor of our forefathers was its own reward."

Grandfather went on to say that the success of the expedition against Louisburg induced Shirley and Pepperell to form a scheme for conquering Canada. This plan, however, was not carried into execution.

In the year 1746 great terror was excited by the arrival of a formidable French fleet upon the coast. It was commanded by the Duke d'Anville, and consisted of forty ships of war, besides vessels with soldiers on board. With this force the French intended to retake Louisburg, and afterwards to ravage the whole of New England. Many people were ready to give up the country for lost.

But the hostile fleet met with so many disasters and losses by storm and shipwreck that the Duke d'Anville is said to have poisoned himself in despair. The officer next in command threw himself upon his sword and perished. Thus deprived of their commanders, the remainder of the ships returned to France. This was as great a deliverance for New England as that which Old England had experienced in the days of Queen Elizabeth, when the Spanish Armada was wrecked upon her coast.

"In 1747," proceeded Grandfather, "Governor Shirley was driven from the Province House, not by a hostile fleet and army, but by a mob of the Boston people. They were so incensed at the conduct of the British Commodore Knowles, who had impressed some of their fellow-citizens, that several thousands of them surrounded the council chamber and threw stones and brickbats into the windows. The governor attempted to pacify them ; but not succeeding, he thought it necessary to leave the town and take refuge within the walls of Castle William. Quiet was not restored until Commodore Knowles had sent back the impressed men. This affair was a flash of spirit that might have warned the English not to venture upon any oppressive measures against their colonial brethren."

Peace being declared between France and England in 1748, the governor had now an opportunity to sit at his ease in Grandfather's chair.   Such repose, however, appears not to have suited his disposition ; for in the following year he went to England, and thence was despatched to France on public business.   Meanwhile, as Shirley had not resigned his office, Lieutenant Governor Phipps acted as chief magistrate in his stead.

CHAPTER VIII.

In the early twilight of Thanksgiving eve came Laurence, and Clara, and Charley, and little Alice hand in hand, and stood in a semicircle round Grandfather's chair. They had been joyous throughout that day of festivity, mingling together in all kinds of play, so that the house had echoed with their airy mirth.

Grandfather, too, had been happy, though not mirthful. He felt that this was to be set down as one of the good Thanksgivings of his life. In truth, all his former Thanksgivings had borne their part in the present one; for his years of infancy, and youth, and manhood, with their blessings and their griefs, had flitted before him while he sat silently in the great chair. Vanished scenes had been pictured in the air. The forms of departed friends had visited him. Voices to be heard no more on earth had sent an echo from the infinite and the eternal. These shadows, if such they were, seemed almost as real to him as what was actually present — as the merry shouts and laughter of the children — as their figures, dancing like sunshine before his eyes.

He felt that the past was not taken from him. The happiness of former days was a possession forever. And there was something in the mingled sorrow of his lifetime that became akin to happiness, after being long treasured in the depths of his heart. There it underwent a change, and grew more precious than pure gold.

And now came the children, somewhat aweary with their wild play, and sought the quiet enjoyment of Grandfather's talk. The good old gentleman rubbed his eyes and smiled round upon them all. He was glad, as most aged people are, to find that he was yet of consequence and could give pleasure to the world. After being so merry all day long, did these children desire to hear his sober talk? O, then, old Grandfather had yet a place to fill among living men — or at least among boys and girls!

"Begin quick, Grandfather," cried little Alice; "for pussy wants to hear you."

And truly our yellow friend, the cat, lay upon the hearth rug, basking in the warmth of the fire, pricking up her ears, and turning her head from the children to Grandfather, and from Grandfather to the children, as if she felt herself very sympathetic with them all. A loud pur, like the singing of a teakettle or the hum of a spinning wheel, testified that she was as comfortable and happy as a cat could be. For puss had feasted; and therefore, like Grandfather and the children, had kept a good Thanksgiving.

"Does pussy want to hear me?" said Grandfather, smiling. "Well, we must please pussy, if we can."

And so he took up the history of the chair from the epoch of the peace of 1748. By one of the provisions of the treaty, Louisburg, which the New Englanders had been at so much pains to take, was restored to the King of France.

The French were afraid that, unless their colonies should be better defended than heretofore, another war might deprive them of the whole. Almost as soon as peace was declared, therefore, they began to build strong fortifications in the interior of North America. It was strange to behold these warlike castles on the banks of solitary lakes, and far in the midst of woods. The Indian, paddling his birch canoe on Lake Champlain, looked up at the high ramparts of Ticonderoga, stone piled on stone, bristling with cannon, and the white flag of France floating above. There were similar fortifications on Lake Ontario, and near the great Falls of Niagara, and at the sources of the Ohio River. And all around these forts and castles lay the eternal forest; and the roll of the drum died away in those deep solitudes.

The truth was, that the French intended to build forts all the way from Canada to Louisiana. They

would then have had a wall of military strength at
the back of the English settlements so as completely
to hem them in. The King of England considered
the building of these forts as a sufficient cause of war,
which was accordingly commenced in 1754.

"Governor Shirley," said Grandfather, "had re-
turned to Boston in 1753. While in Paris he had
married a second wife, a young French girl, and now
brought her to the Province House. But when war
was breaking out it was impossible for such a bustling
man to stay quietly at home, sitting in our old chair,
with his wife and children round about him.   He
therefore obtained a command in the English forces."

"And what did Sir William Pepperell do?" asked
Charley.

"He staid at home," said Grandfather, "and was
general of the militia.   The veteran regiments of the
English army which were now sent across the At-
lantic would have scorned to fight under the orders
of an old American merchant.   And now began
what aged people call the old French war.   It would
be going too far astray from the history of our chair to
tell you one half of the battles that were fought.   I
cannot even allow myself to describe the bloody de-
feat of General Braddock, near the sources of the
Ohio River, in 1755.   But I must not omit to men-
tion, that, when the English general was mortally
wounded and his army routed, the remains of it

were preserved by the skill and valor of GEORGE WASHINGTON."

At the mention of this illustrious name the children started as if a sudden sunlight had gleamed upon the history of their country, now that the great deliverer had arisen above the horizon.

Among all the events of the old French war, Grandfather thought that there was none more interesting than the removal of the inhabitants of Acadia. From the first settlement of this ancient province of the French, in 1604, until the present time, its people could scarcely ever know what kingdom held dominion over them. They were a peaceful race, taking no delight in warfare, and caring nothing for military renown. And yet, in every war, their region was infested with iron-hearted soldiers, both French and English, who fought one another for the privilege of ill treating these poor, harmless Acadians. Sometimes the treaty of peace made them subjects of one king, sometimes of another.

At the peace of 1748 Acadia had been ceded to England. But the French still claimed a large portion of it, and built forts for its defence. In 1755 these forts were taken, and the whole of Acadia was conquered by three thousand men from Massachusetts, under the command of General Winslow. The inhabitants were accused of supplying the French with provisions, and of doing other things that violated their neutrality.

"These accusations were probably true," observed Grandfather; "for the Acadians were descended from the French, and had the same friendly feelings towards them that the people of Massachusetts had for the English. But their punishment was severe. The English determined to tear these poor people from their native homes and scatter them abroad."

The Acadians were about seven thousand in number. A considerable part of them were made prisoners, and transported to the English colonies. All their dwellings and churches were burned, their cattle were killed, and the whole country was laid waste, so that none of them might find shelter or food in their old homes after the departure of the English. One thousand of the prisoners were sent to Massachusetts; and Grandfather allowed his fancy to follow them thither, and tried to give his auditors an idea of their situation.

We shall call this passage the story of

THE ACADIAN EXILES.

A sad day it was for the poor Acadians when the armed soldiers drove them, at the point of the bayonet, down to the sea shore. Very sad were they, likewise, while tossing upon the ocean in the crowded transport vessels. But methinks it must have been sadder still when they were landed on the Long

Wharf, in Boston, and left to themselves on a foreign strand.

Then, probably, they huddled together and looked into one another's faces for the comfort which was not there. Hitherto they had been confined on board of separate vessels, so that they could not tell whether their relatives and friends were prisoners along with them. But now, at least, they could tell that many had been left behind or transported to other regions.

Now a desolate wife might be heard calling for her husband. He, alas! had gone, she knew not whither; or perhaps had fled into the woods of Acadia, and had now returned to weep over the ashes of their dwelling.

An aged widow was crying out in a querulous, lamentable tone for her son, whose affectionate toil had supported her for many a year. He was not in the crowd of exiles; and what could this aged widow do but sink down and die? Young men and maidens, whose hearts had been torn asunder by separation, had hoped, during the voyage, to meet their beloved ones at its close. Now they began to feel that they were separated forever. And perhaps a lonesome little girl, a golden-haired child of five years old, the very picture of our little Alice, was weeping and wailing for her mother, and found not a soul to give her a kind word.

.ne

O, how many broken bonds of affection were here! Country lost — friends lost — their rural wealth of cottage, field, and herds all lost together! Every tie between these poor exiles and the world seemed to be cut off at once. They must have regretted that they had not died before their exile ; for even the English would not have been so pitiless as to deny them graves in their native soil. The dead were happy ; for they were not exiles!

While they thus stood upon the wharf, the curiosity and inquisitiveness of the New England people would naturally lead them into the midst of the poor Acadians. Prying busybodies thrust their heads into the circle wherever two or three of the exiles were conversing together. How puzzled did they look at the outlandish sound of the French tongue! There were seen the New England women, too. They had just come out of their warm, safe homes, where every thing was regular and comfortable, and where their husbands and children would be with them at nightfall. Surely they could pity the wretched wives and mothers of Acadia! Or did the sign of the cross which the Acadians continually made upon their breasts, and which was abhorred by the descendants of the Puritans, — did that sign exclude all pity?

Among the spectators, too, was the noisy brood of Boston schoolboys, who came running, with laughter and shouts, to gaze at this crowd of oddly-dressed foreigners. At first they danced and capered around them, full of merriment and mischief. But the despair of the Acadians soon had its effect upon these thoughtless lads, and melted them into tearful sympathy.

At a little distance from the throng might be seen the wealthy and pompous merchants whose warehouses stood on Long Wharf. It was difficult to touch these rich men's hearts; for they had all the comforts of the world at their command; and when they walked abroad their feelings were seldom moved, except by the roughness of the pavement irritating their gouty toes. Leaning upon their goldheaded canes, they watched the scene with an aspect of composure. But let us hope they distributed some of their superfluous coin among these hapless exiles to purchase food and a night's lodging.

After standing a long time at the end of the wharf, gazing seaward, as if to catch a glimpse of their lost Acadia, the strangers began to stray into the town.

They went, we will suppose, in parties and groups, here a hundred, there a score, there ten, there three or four, who possessed some bond of unity among themselves. Here and there was one, who, utterly desolate, stole away by himself, seeking no companionship.

Whither did they go? I imagine them wandering about the streets, telling the townspeople, in outlandish, unintelligible words, that no earthly affliction ever equalled what had befallen them. Man's brotherhood with man was sufficient to make the

New Englanders understand this language. The strangers wanted food. Some of them sought hospitality at the doors of the stately mansions which then stood in the vicinity of Hanover Street and the North Square. Others were applicants at the humble wooden tenements, where dwelt the petty shopkeepers and mechanics. Pray Heaven that no family in Boston turned one of these poor exiles from their door! It would be a reproach upon New England — a crime worthy of heavy retribution — if the aged women and children, or even the strong men, were allowed to feel the pinch of hunger.

Perhaps some of the Acadians, in their aimless wanderings through the town, found themselves near a large brick edifice, which was fenced in from the street by an iron railing, wrought with fantastic figures. They saw a flight of red freestone steps ascending to a portal, above which was a balcony and balustrade. Misery and desolation give men the right of free passage every where. Let us suppose, then, that they mounted the flight of steps and passed into the Province House. Making their way into one of the apartments, they beheld a richly-clad gentleman, seated in a stately chair, with gilding upon the carved work of its back, and a gilded lion's head at the summit. This was Governor Shirley, meditating upon matters of war and state, in Grandfather's chair!

If such an incident did happen, Shirley, reflecting what a ruin of peaceful and humble hopes had been wrought by the cold policy of the statesman and the iron hand of the warrior, might have drawn a deep moral from it.   It should have taught him that the poor man's hearth is sacred, and that armies and nations have no right to violate it.   It should have made him feel that England's triumph and increased dominion could not compensate to mankind nor atone to Heaven for the ashes of a single Acadian cottage.   But it is not thus that statesmen and warriors moralize.

"Grandfather," cried Laurence, with emotion trembling in his voice, " did iron-hearted War itself ever do so hard and cruel a thing as this before ? "

" You have read in history, Laurence, of whole regions wantonly laid waste," said Grandfather.   " In the removal of the Acadians, the troops were guilty of no cruelty or outrage, except what was inseparable from the measure."

Little Alice, whose eyes had all along been brimming full of tears, now burst forth a-sobbing ; for Grandfather had touched her sympathies more than he intended.

" To think of a whole people homeless in the world ! " said Clara, with moistened eyes.   " There never was any thing so sad ! "

" It was their own fault ! " cried Charley, energetically.   " Why did not they fight for the country where they were born ?   Then, if the worst had happened to them, they could only have been killed and buried there.   They would not have been exiles then."

" Certainly their lot was as hard as death," said

Grandfather. "All that could be done for them in the English provinces was, to send them to the almshouses, or bind them out to taskmasters. And this was the fate of persons who had possessed a comfortable property in their native country. Some of them found means to embark for France ; but though it was the land of their forefathers, it must have been a foreign land to them. Those who remained behind always cherished a belief that the King of France would never make peace with England till his poor Acadians were restored to their country and their homes."

"And did he ? " inquired Clara.

"Alas ! my dear Clara," said Grandfather, "it is improbable that the slightest whisper of the woes of Acadia ever reached the ears of Louis XV. The exiles grew old in the British provinces, and never saw Acadia again. Their descendants remain among us to this day. They have forgotten the language of their ancestors, and probably retain no tradition of their misfortunes. But, methinks, if I were an American poet, I would choose Acadia for the subject of my song."

Since Grandfather first spoke these words, the most famous of American poets has drawn sweet tears from all of us by his beautiful poem of Evangeline.

And now, having thrown a gentle gloom around the Thanksgiving fireside by a story that made the children feel the blessing of a secure and peaceful hearth, Grandfather put off the other events of the old French war till the next evening.

CHAPTER IX.

In the twilight of the succeeding eve, when the red beams of the fire were dancing upon the wall, the children besought Grandfather to tell them what had next happened to the old chair.

"Our chair," said Grandfather, "stood all this time in the Province House. But Governor Shirley had seldom an opportunity to repose within its arms. He was leading his troops through the forest, or sailing in a flat boat on Lake Ontario, or sleeping in his tent, while the awful cataract of Niagara sent its roar through his dreams. At one period, in the early part of the war, Shirley had the chief command of all the king's forces in America."

"Did his young wife go with him to the war?" asked Clara.

"I rather imagine," replied Grandfather, "that she remained in Boston. This lady, I suppose, had our chair all to herself, and used to sit in it during those brief intervals when a young Frenchwoman can be quiet enough to sit in a chair. The people of Massachusetts were never fond of Governor Shirley's young French wife. They had a suspicion that she betrayed the military plans of the English to the generals of the French armies."

" And was it true ? " inquired Clara.

" Probably not," said Grandfather. " But the mere suspicion did Shirley a great deal of harm. Partly, perhaps, for this reason, but much more on account of his inefficiency as a general, he was deprived of his command in 1756, and recalled to England. He never afterwards made any figure in public life."

As Grandfather's chair had no locomotive properties, and did not even run on castors, it cannot be supposed to have marched in person to the old French war. But Grandfather delayed its momentous history while he touched briefly upon some of the bloody battles, sieges, and onslaughts, the tidings of which kept continually coming to the ears of the old inhabitants of Boston. The woods of the north were populous with fighting men. All the Indian tribes uplifted their tomahawks, and took part either with the French or English. The rattle of musketry and roar of cannon disturbed the ancient quiet of the forest, and actually drove the bears and other wild beasts to the more cultivated portion of the country in the vicinity of the seaports. The children felt as if they were transported back to those forgotten times, and that the couriers from the army, with the news of a battle lost or won, might even now be heard galloping through the streets. Grandfather told them about the battle of Lake George in 1755, when the gallant Colonel Williams, a Massachusetts officer, was slain, with many of his countrymen. But General Johnson and General Lyman, with their army, drove back the enemy and mortally wounded the French leader, who was called the Baron Dieskau. A gold watch, pilfered from the poor baron, is still in existence, and still marks each moment of time without complaining of weariness, although its hands have been in motion ever since the hour of battle.

In the first years of the war there were many disasters on the English side. Among these was the loss of Fort Oswego in 1756, and of Fort William Henry in the following year. But the greatest misfortune that befell the English during the whole war was the repulse of General Abercrombie, with his army, from the ramparts of Ticonderoga in 1758. He attempted to storm the walls ; but a terrible conflict ensued, in which more than two thousand Englishmen and New Englanders were killed or wounded. The slain soldiers now lie buried around that ancient fortress. When the plough passes over the soil, it turns up here and there a mouldering bone.

Up to this period, none of the English generals had shown any military talent. Shirley, the Earl of Loudon, and General Abercrombie had each held the chief command at different times; but not one of them had won a single important triumph for the British arms. This ill success was not owing to the want of means; for, in 1758, General Abercrombie had fifty thousand soldiers under his command. But the French general, the famous Marquis de Montcalm, possessed a great genius for war, and had something within him that taught him how battles were to be won.

At length, in 1759, Sir Jeffrey Amherst was appointed commander-in-chief of all the British forces in America. He was a man of ability and a skilful soldier. A plan was now formed for accomplishing that object which had so long been the darling wish of the New Englanders, and which their fathers had so many times attempted. This was the conquest of Canada.

Three separate armies were to enter Canada from different quarters. One of the three, commanded by General Prideaux, was to embark on Lake Ontario and proceed to Montreal. The second, at the head of which was Sir Jeffrey Amherst himself, was destined to reach the River St. Lawrence, by the way of Lake Champlain, and then go down the river to meet the third army. This last, led by General Wolfe, was to enter the St. Lawrence from the sea and ascend the river to Quebec. It is to Wolfe and his army that England owes one of the most splendid triumphs ever written in her history.

Grandfather described the siege of Quebec, and told how Wolfe led his soldiers up a rugged and lofty precipice, that rose from the shore of the river to the plain on which the city stood. This bold adventure was achieved in the darkness of night. At daybreak tidings were carried to the Marquis de Montcalm that the English army was waiting to give him battle on the plains of Abraham. This brave French general ordered his drums to strike up, and immediately marched to encounter Wolfe.

He marched to his own death. The battle was the most fierce and terrible that had ever been fought in America. General Wolfe was at the head of his soldiers, and, while encouraging them onward, received a mortal wound. He reclined against a stone in the agonies of death ; but it seemed as if his spirit could not pass away while the fight yet raged so doubtfully. Suddenly a shout came pealing across the battle field — "They flee! they flee!" and, for a moment, Wolfe lifted his languid head. "Who flee?" he inquired. "The French," replied an officer. "Then I die satisfied!" said Wolfe, and expired in the arms of victory.

"If ever a warrior's death were glorious, Wolfe's was so," said Grandfather ; and his eye kindled, though he was a man of peaceful thoughts and gentle spirit. "His lifeblood streamed to baptize the soil which he had added to the dominion of Britain. His dying breath was mingled with his army's shout of victory."

"O, it was a good death to die!" cried Charley, with glistening eyes. "Was it not a good death, Laurence?"

Laurence made no reply; for his heart burned within him, as the picture of Wolfe, dying on the blood-stained field of victory, arose to his imagination; and yet he had a deep inward consciousness that, after all, there was a truer glory than could thus be won.

"There were other battles in Canada after Wolfe's victory," resumed Grandfather; "but we may consider the old French war as having terminated with this great event. The treaty of peace, however, was not signed until 1763. The terms of the treaty were very disadvantageous to the French; for all Canada, and all Acadia, and the Island of Cape Breton, — in short, all the territories that France and England had been fighting about for nearly a hundred years, — were surrendered to the English."

"So now, at last," said Laurence, "New England had gained her wish. Canada was taken."

"And now there was nobody to fight with but the Indians," said Charley.

Grandfather mentioned two other important events. The first was the great fire of Boston in 1760, when the glare from nearly three hundred buildings, all in flames at once, shone through the windows of the Province House, and threw a fierce lustre upon the gilded foliage and lion's head of our old chair The second event was the proclamation, in the same year, of George III. as King of Great Britain. The blast of the trumpet sounded from the balcony of the Town House, and awoke the echoes far and wide, as if to challenge all mankind to dispute King George's title.

Seven times, as the successive monarchs of Britain ascended the throne, the trumpet peal of proclamation had been heard by those who sat in our venerable chair. But when the next king put on his father's crown, no trumpet peal proclaimed it to New England. Long before that day America had shaken off the royal government.

11

CHAPTER X.

Now that Grandfather had fought through the old
French war, in which our chair made no very dis-
tinguished figure, he thought it high time to tell
the children some of the more private history of that
praiseworthy old piece of furniture.

"In 1757," said Grandfather, "after Shirley had
been summoned to England, Thomas Pownall was
appointed governor of Massachusetts. He was a
gay and fashionable English gentleman, who had
spent much of his life in London, but had a consid-
erable acquaintance with America. The new gov-
ernor appears to have taken no active part in the war
that was going on; although, at one period, he talked
of marching against the enemy at the head of his
company of cadets. But, on the whole, he prob-
ably concluded that it was more befitting a governor
to remain quietly in our chair, reading the newspa-
pers and official documents."

"Did the people like Pownall?" asked Charley.

"They found no fault with him," replied Grandfather. "It was no time to quarrel with the governor when the utmost harmony was required in order to defend the country against the French. But Pownall did not remain long in Massachusetts. In 1759 he was sent to be governor of South Carolina. In thus exchanging one government for another, I suppose he felt no regret, except at the necessity of leaving Grandfather's chair behind him."

"He might have taken it to South Carolina," observed Clara.

"It appears to me," said Laurence, giving the rein to his fancy, "that the fate of this ancient chair was, somehow or other, mysteriously connected with the fortunes of old Massachusetts. If Governor Pownall had put it aboard the vessel in which he sailed for South Carolina, she would probably have lain windbound in Boston Harbor. It was ordained that the chair should not be taken away. Don't you think so, Grandfather?"

"It was kept here for Grandfather and me to sit in together," said little Alice, "and for Grandfather to tell stories about."

"And Grandfather is very glad of such a companion and such a theme," said the old gentleman, with a smile. "Well, Laurence, if our oaken chair, like the wooden palladium of Troy, was connected with the country's fate, yet there appears to have been no supernatural obstacle to its removal from the Province

House. In 1760 Sir Francis Bernard, who had been governor of New Jersey, was appointed to the same office in Massachusetts. He looked at the old chair, and thought it quite too shabby to keep company with a new set of mahogany chairs and an aristocratic sofa which had just arrived from London. He therefore ordered it to be put away in the garret."

The children were loud in their exclamations against this irreverent conduct of Sir Francis Bernard. But Grandfather defended him as well as he could. He observed that it was then thirty years since the chair had been beautified by Governor Belcher. Most of the gilding was worn off by the frequent scourings which it had undergone beneath the hands of a black slave. The damask cushion, once so splendid, was now squeezed out of all shape, and absolutely in tatters, so many were the ponderous gentlemen who had deposited their weight upon it during these thirty years.

Moreover, at a council held by the Earl of Loudon with the governors of New England in 1757, his lordship, in a moment of passion, had kicked over the chair with his military boot. By this unprovoked and unjustifiable act, our venerable friend had suffered a fracture of one of its rungs.

" But," said Grandfather, " our chair, after all, was not destined to spend the remainder of its days in the inglorious obscurity of a garret. Thomas

Hutchinson, lieutenant governor of the province, was told of Sir Francis Bernard's design. This gentleman was more familiar with the history of New England than any other man alive. He knew all the adventures and vicissitudes through which the old chair had passed, and could have told as accurately as your own Grandfather who were the personages that had occupied it. Often, while visiting at the Province House, he had eyed the chair with admiration, and felt a longing desire to become the possessor of it. He now waited upon Sir Francis Bernard, and easily obtained leave to carry it home."

"And I hope," said Clara, "he had it varnished and gilded anew."

"No," answered Grandfather. "What Mr. Hutchinson desired was, to restore the chair as much as possible to its original aspect, such as it had appeared when it was first made out of the Earl of Lincoln's oak tree. For this purpose he ordered it to be well scoured with soap and sand and polished with wax, and then provided it with a substantial leather cushion. When all was completed to his mind, he sat down in the old chair, and began to write his History of Massachusetts."

"O, that was a bright thought in Mr. Hutchinson!" exclaimed Laurence. "And no doubt the dim figures of the former possessors of the chair flitted around him as he wrote, and inspired him with a knowledge of all that they had done and suffered while on earth."

"Why, my dear Laurence," replied Grandfather, smiling, "if Mr. Hutchinson was favored with any such extraordinary inspiration, he made but a poor use of it in his history; for a duller piece of composition never came from any man's pen. However, he was accurate, at least, though far from possessing the brilliancy or philosophy of Mr. Bancroft."

"But if Hutchinson knew the history of the chair," rejoined Laurence, "his heart must have been stirred by it."

"It must, indeed," said Grandfather. "It would be entertaining and instructive, at the present day, to imagine what were Mr. Hutchinson's thoughts as he looked back upon the long vista of events with which this chair was so remarkably connected."

And Grandfather allowed his fancy to shape out an image of Lieutenant Governor Hutchinson, sitting in an evening revery by his fireside, and meditating on the changes that had slowly passed around the chair.

A devoted monarchist, Hutchinson would heave no sigh for the subversion of the original republican government, the purest that the world had seen, with which the colony began its existence. While reverencing the grim and stern old Puritans as the founders of his native land, he would not wish to recall them from their graves, nor to awaken again that king-resisting spirit which he imagined to be laid asleep with them forever. Winthrop, Dudley, Bellingham, Endicott, Leverett, and Bradstreet, — all these had had their day. Ages might come and go; but never again would the people's suffrages place a republican governor in their ancient chair of state.

Coming down to the epoch of the second charter, Hutchinson thought of the ship carpenter Phipps, springing from the lowest of the people and attaining to the loftiest station in the land. But he smiled to perceive that this governor's example would awaken no turbulent ambition in the lower orders; for it was a king's gracious boon alone that made the ship carpenter a ruler. Hutchinson rejoiced to mark the gradual growth of an aristocratic class, to whom the common people, as in duty bound, were learning humbly to resign the honors, emoluments, and authority of state. He saw — or else deceived himself — that, throughout this epoch, the people's disposition to self government had been growing weaker through long disuse, and now existed only as a faint traditionary feeling.

The lieutenant governor's revery had now come down to the period at which he himself was sitting in the historic chair. He endeavored to throw his glance forward over the coming years. There, probably, he saw visions of hereditary rank for himself and other aristocratic colonists. He saw the fertile fields of New England proportioned out among a few great landholders, and descending by entail from generation to generation. He saw the people a race of tenantry, dependent on their lords. He saw stars, garters, coronets, and castles.

"But," added Grandfather, turning to Laurence, "the lieutenant governor's castles were built nowhere but among the red embers of the fire before which he was sitting, And, just as he had constructed a baronial residence for himself and his posterity, the fire rolled down upon the hearth and crumbled it to ashes!"

Grandfather now looked at his watch, which hung within a beautiful little ebony temple, supported by four Ionic columns. He then laid his hand on the golden locks of little Alice, whose head had sunk down upon the arm of our illustrious chair.

"To bed, to bed, dear child!" said he. "Grandfather has put you to sleep already by his stories about these FAMOUS OLD PEOPLE."

GRANDFATHER'S CHAIR.

PART III.

CHAPTER I.

On the evening of New Year's day Grandfather was walking to and fro across the carpet, listening to the rain which beat hard against the curtained windows. The riotous blast shook the casement as if a strong man were striving to force his entrance into the comfortable room. With every puff of the wind the fire leaped upward from the hearth, laughing and rejoicing at the shrieks of the wintry storm.

Meanwhile Grandfather's chair stood in its customary place by the fireside. The bright blaze gleamed upon the fantastic figures of its oaken back, and shone through the open work, so that a complete pattern was thrown upon the opposite side of the room. Sometimes, for a moment or two, the shadow remained immovable, as if it were painted on the wall. Then all at once it began to quiver, and leap, and dance with a frisky motion. Anon, seeming to remember that these antics were unworthy of such a dignified and venerable chair, it suddenly stood still. But soon it began to dance anew.

"Only see how Grandfather's chair is dancing!" cried little Alice.

And she ran to the wall and tried to catch hold of the flickering shadow; for, to children of five years old, a shadow seems almost as real as a substance.

"I wish," said Clara, "Grandfather would sit down in the chair and finish its history."

If the children had been looking at Grandfather, they would have noticed that he paused in his walk across the room when Clara made this remark. The kind old gentleman was ready and willing to resume his stories of departed times. But he had resolved to wait till his auditors should request him to proceed, in order that they might find the instructive history of the chair a pleasure, and not a task.

"Grandfather," said Charley, "I am tired to death of this dismal rain and of hearing the wind roar in the chimney. I have had no good time all day. It would be better to hear stories about the chair than to sit doing nothing and thinking of nothing."

To say the truth, our friend Charley was very much out of humor with the storm, because it had kept him all day within doors, and hindered him from making a trial of a splendid sled, which Grandfather had given him for a New Year's gift. As all sleds, nowadays, must have a name, the one in question had been honored with the title of Grandfather's Chair, which was painted in golden letters on each of the sides. Charley greatly admired the construction of the new vehicle, and felt certain that it would outstrip any other sled that ever dashed adown the long slopes of the Common.

As for Laurence, he happened to be thinking, just at this moment, about the history of the chair. Kind old Grandfather had made him a present of a volume of engraved portraits, representing the features of eminent and famous people of all countries. Among them Laurence found several who had formerly occupied our chair or been connected with its adventures. While Grandfather walked to and fro across the room, the imaginative boy was gazing at the historic chair. He endeavored to summon up the portraits which he had seen in his volume, and to place them, like living figures, in the empty seat.

"The old chair has begun another year of its existence, to-day," said Laurence. "We must make haste, or it will have a new history to be told before we finish the old one."

"Yes, my children," replied Grandfather, with a smile and a sigh, "another year has been added to those of the two centuries and upward which have passed since the Lady Arbella brought this chair over from England. It is three times as old as your Grandfather; but a year makes no impression on its oaken frame, while it bends the old man nearer and nearer to the earth; so let me go on with my stories while I may."

Accordingly Grandfather came to the fireside and seated himself in the venerable chair. The lion's head looked down with a grimly good-natured aspect as the children clustered around the old gentleman's knees. It almost seemed as if a real lion were peeping over the back of the chair, and smiling at the group of auditors with a sort of lion-like complaisance. Little Alice, whose fancy often inspired her with singular ideas, exclaimed that the lion's head was nodding at her, and that it looked as if it were going to open its wide jaws and tell a story.

But as the lion's head appeared to be in no haste to speak, and as there was no record or tradition of its having spoken during the whole existence of the chair, Grandfather did not consider it worth while to wait.

CHAPTER II.

" CHARLEY, my boy," said Grandfather, " do you remember who was the last occupant of the chair? "

" It was Lieutenant Governor Hutchinson," answered Charley. " Sir Francis Bernard, the new governor, had given him the chair instead of putting it away in the garret of the Province House. And when we took leave of Hutchinson he was sitting by his fireside, and thinking of the past adventures of the chair and of what was to come."

" Very well," said Grandfather ; " and you recollect that this was in 1763, or thereabouts, at the close of the old French war. Now, that you may fully comprehend the remaining adventure of the chair, I must make some brief remarks on the situation and character of the New England colonies at this period."

So Grandfather spoke of the earnest loyalty of our fathers during the old French war, and after the conquest of Canada had brought that war to a triumphant close.

The people loved and reverenced the King of

England even more than if the ocean had not rolled its waves between him and them; for, at the distance of three thousand miles, they could not discover his bad qualities and imperfections. Their love was increased by the dangers which they had encountered in order to heighten his glory and extend his dominion. Throughout the war the American colonists had fought side by side with the soldiers of Old England; and nearly thirty thousand young men had laid down their lives for the honor of King George. And the survivors loved him the better because they had done and suffered so much for his sake.

But there were some circumstances that caused America to feel more independent of England than at an earlier period. Canada and Acadia had now become British provinces; and our fathers were no longer afraid of the bands of French and Indians who used to assault them in old times. For a century and a half this had been the great terror of New England. Now the old French soldier was driven from the north forever. And even had it been otherwise, the English colonies were growing so populous and powerful, that they might have felt fully able to protect themselves without any help from England.

There were thoughtful and sagacious men, who began to doubt whether a great country like America would always be content to remain under the government of an island three thousand miles away.

This was the more doubtful, because the English Parliament had long ago made laws which were intended to be very beneficial to England at the expense of America. By these laws the colonists were forbidden to manufacture articles for their own use, or to carry on trade with any nation but the English.

"Now," continued Grandfather, "if King George III. and his counsellors had considered these things wisely, they would have taken another course than they did. But when they saw how rich and populous the colonies had grown, their first thought was how they might make more profit out of them than heretofore. England was enormously in debt at the close of the old French war; and it was pretended that this debt had been contracted for the defence of the American colonies, and that, therefore, a part of it ought to be paid by them."

"Why, this was nonsense!" exclaimed Charley. "Did not our fathers spend their lives, and their money, too, to get Canada for King George?"

"True, they did," said Grandfather; "and they told the English rulers so. But the king and his ministers would not listen to good advice. In 1765 the British Parliament passed a stamp act."

"What was that?" inquired Charley.

"The stamp act," replied Grandfather, "was a law by which all deeds, bonds, and other papers of the same kind were ordered to be marked with the king's stamp; and without this mark they were declared illegal and void. Now, in order to get a blank sheet of paper with the king's stamp upon it, people were obliged to pay threepence more than the actual value of the paper. And this extra sum of threepence was a tax, and was to be paid into the king's treasury."

"I am sure threepence was not worth quarrelling about!" remarked Clara.

"It was not for threepence, nor for any amount of money, that America quarrelled with England," replied Grandfather; "it was for a great principle. The colonists were determined not to be taxed except by their own representatives. They said that neither the king and Parliament, nor any other power on earth, had a right to take their money out of their pockets unless they freely gave it. And, rather than pay threepence when it was unjustly demanded, they resolved to sacrifice all the wealth of the country, and their lives along with it. They therefore made a most stubborn resistance to the stamp act."

"That was noble!" exclaimed Laurence. "I understand how it was. If they had quietly paid the tax of threepence, they would have ceased to be freemen, and would have become tributaries of England. And so they contended about a great question of right and wrong, and put every thing at stake for it."

"You are right, Laurence," said Grandfather

" and it was really amazing and terrible to see what
a change came over the aspect of the people the mo-
ment the English Parliament had passed this oppres-
sive act. The former history of our chair, my chil-
dren, has given you some idea of what a harsh, un
yielding, stern set of men the old Puritans were.
For a good many years back, however, it had seemed
as if these characteristics were disappearing. But no
sooner did England offer wrong to the colonies than
the descendants of the early settlers proved that they
had the same kind of temper as their forefathers.
The moment before, New England appeared like a
humble and loyal subject of the crown ; the next
instant she showed the grim, dark features of an old
king-resisting Puritan."

Grandfather spoke briefly of the public measures
that were taken in opposition to the stamp act. As
this law affected all the American colonies alike, it
naturally led them to think of consulting together in
order to procure its repeal. For this purpose the
legislature of Massachusetts proposed that delegates
from every colony should meet in Congress. Ac-
cordingly nine colonies, both northern and southern,
sent delegates to the city of New York.

" And did they consult about going to war with
England ? " asked Charley.

" No, Charley," answered Grandfather ; " a great
deal of talking was yet to be done before England

and America could come to blows. The Congress stated the rights and grievances of the colonists. They sent a humble petition to the king, and a memorial to the Parliament, beseeching that the stamp act might be repealed. This was all that the delegates had it in their power to do."

"They might as well have staid at home, then," said Charley.

"By no means," replied Grandfather. "It was a most important and memorable event, this first coming together of the American people by their representatives from the north and south. If England had been wise, she would have trembled at the first word that was spoken in such an assembly."

These remonstrances and petitions, as Grandfather observed, were the work of grave, thoughtful, and prudent men. Meantime the young and hotheaded people went to work in their own way. It is probable that the petitions of Congress would have had little or no effect on the British statesmen if the violent deeds of the American people had not shown how much excited the people were. LIBERTY TREE was soon heard of in England.

"What was Liberty Tree?" inquired Clara.

"It was an old elm tree," answered Grandfather, "which stood near the corner of Essex Street, opposite the Boylston Market. Under the spreading branches of this great tree the people used to assem-

ble whenever they wished to express their feelings and opinions. Thus, after a while, it seemed as if the liberty of the country was connected with Liberty Tree."

"It was glorious fruit for a tree to bear," remarked Laurence.

"It bore strange fruit, sometimes," said Grandfather. "One morning in August, 1765, two figures were found hanging on the sturdy branches of Liberty Tree. They were dressed in square-skirted coats and smallclothes ; and, as their wigs hung down over their faces, they looked like real men. One was intended to represent the Earl of Bute, who was supposed to have advised the king to tax America. The other was meant for the effigy of Andrew Oliver, a gentleman belonging to one of the most respectable families in Massachusetts."

"What harm had he done ? " inquired Charley.

"The king had appointed him to be distributer of the stamps," answered Grandfather. "Mr. Oliver would have made a great deal of money by this business. But the people frightened him so much by hanging him in effigy, and afterwards by breaking into his house, that he promised to have nothing to do with the stamps. And all the king's friends throughout America were compelled to make the same promise."

CHAPTER III.

"Lieutenant Governor Hutchinson," contin-
ued Grandfather, "now began to be unquiet in our
old chair. He had formerly been much respected
and beloved by the people, and had often proved
himself a friend to their interests. But the time was
come when he could not be a friend to the people
without ceasing to be a friend to the king. It was
pretty generally understood that Hutchinson would
act according to the king's wishes, right or wrong,
like most of the other gentlemen who held offices
under the crown. Besides, as he was brother-in-law
of Andrew Oliver, the people now felt a particular
dislike to him."

"I should think," said Laurence, "as Mr. Hutch-
inson had written the history of our Puritan fore-
fathers, he would have known what the temper of the
people was, and so have taken care not to wrong
them."

"He trusted in the might of the King of England,'
replied Grandfather, "and thought himself safe

under the shelter of the throne. If no dispute had arisen between the king and the people, Hutchinson would have had the character of a wise, good, and patriotic magistrate. But, from the time that he took part against the rights of his country, the people's love and respect were turned to scorn and hatred, and he never had another hour of peace."

In order to show what a fierce and dangerous spirit was now aroused among the inhabitants, Grandfather related a passage from history which we shall call

THE HUTCHINSON MOB.

On the evening of the 26th of August, 1765, a bonfire was kindled in King Street. It flamed high upward, and threw a ruddy light over the front of the Town House, on which was displayed a carved representation of the royal arms. The gilded vane of the cupola glittered in the blaze. The kindling of this bonfire was the well-known signal for the populace of Boston to assemble in the street.

Before the tar barrels, of which the bonfire was made, were half burned out, a great crowd had come together. They were chiefly laborers and seafaring men, together with many young apprentices, and all those idle people about town who are ready for any kind of mischief. Doubtless some schoolboys were among them.

While these rough figures stood round the blazing bonfire, you might hear them speaking bitter words against the high officers of the province. Governor Bernard, Hutchinson, Oliver, Storey, Hallowell, and other men whom King George delighted to honor, were reviled as traitors to the country. Now and then, perhaps, an officer of the crown passed along the street, wearing the gold-laced hat, white wig, and embroidered waistcoat which were the fashion of the day. But when the people beheld him they set up a wild and angry howl; and their faces had an evil aspect, which was made more terrible by the flickering blaze of the bonfire.

"I should like to throw the traitor right into that blaze!" perhaps one fierce rioter would say.

"Yes; and all his brethren too!" another might reply; "and the governor and old Tommy Hutchinson into the hottest of it!"

"And the Earl of Bute along with them!" muttered a third; "and burn the whole pack of them under King George's nose! No matter if it singed him!"

Some such expressions as these, either shouted aloud or muttered under the breath, were doubtless heard in King Street. The mob, meanwhile, were growing fiercer and fiercer, and seemed ready eve to set the town on fire for the sake of burning the k friends out of house and home. And yet, ang

y as

they were, they sometimes broke into a loud roar of laughter, as if mischief and destruction were their sport.

But we must now leave the riotors for a time, and take a peep into the lieutenant governor's splendid mansion. It was a large brick house, decorated with Ionic pilasters, and stood in Garden Court Street, near the North Square.

While the angry mob in King Street were shouting his name, Lieutenant Governor Hutchinson sat quietly in Grandfather's chair, unsuspicious of the evil that was about to fall upon his head. His beloved family were in the room with him. He had thrown off his embroidered coat and powdered wig, and had on a loose-flowing gown and purple-velvet cap. He had likewise laid aside the cares of state and all the thoughts that had wearied and perplexed him throughout the day.

Perhaps, in the enjoyment of his home, he had forgotten all about the stamp act, and scarcely remembered that there was a king, across the ocean, who had resolved to make tributaries of the New Englanders. Possibly, too, he had forgotten his own ambition, and would not have exchanged his situation, at that moment, to be governor, or even a lord.

The wax candles were now lighted, and showed a handsome room, well provided with rich furniture. On the walls hung the pictures of Hutchinson's ancestors who had been eminent men in their day and were honorably remembered in the history of the country. Every object served to mark the residence of a rich, aristocratic gentleman, who held himself high above the common people, and could have nothing to fear from them. In a corner of the room, thrown carelessly upon a chair, were the scarlet robes of the chief justice. This high office, as well as those of lieutenant governor, councillor, and judge of probate, was filled by Hutchinson.

Who or what could disturb the domestic quiet of such a great and powerful personage as now sat in Grandfather's chair?

The lieutenant governor's favorite daughter sat by his side. She leaned on the arm of our great chair, and looked up affectionately into her father's face, rejoicing to perceive that a quiet smile was on his lips. But suddenly a shade came across her countenance. She seemed to listen attentively, as if to catch a distant sound.

"What is the matter, my child?" inquired Hutchinson.

"Father, do not you hear a tumult in the streets?" said she.

The lieutenant governor listened. But his ears were duller than those of his daughter; he could hear nothing more terrible than the sound of a summer breeze, sighing among the tops of the elm trees.

"No, foolish child!" he replied, playfully patting

her cheek. "There is no tumult. Our Boston mobs are satisfied with what mischief they have already done. The king's friends need not tremble."

So Hutchinson resumed his pleasant and peaceful meditations, and again forgot that there were any troubles in the world. But his family were alarmed, and could not help straining their ears to catch the slightest sound. More and more distinctly they heard shouts, and then the trampling of many feet. While they were listening, one of the neighbors rushed breathless into the room.

"A mob! a terrible mob!" cried he. "They have broken into Mr. Storey's house, and into Mr. Hallowell's, and have made themselves drunk with the liquors in his cellar; and now they are coming hither, as wild as so many tigers. Flee, lieutenant governor, for your life! for your life!"

"Father, dear father, make haste!" shrieked his children.

But Hutchinson would not hearken to them. He was an old lawyer; and he could not realize that the people would do any thing so utterly lawless as to assault him in his peaceful home. He was one of King George's chief officers; and it would be an insult and outrage upon the king himself if the lieutenant governor should suffer any wrong.

"Have no fears on my account," said he. "I am perfectly safe. The king's name shall be my protection."

Yet he bade his family retire into one of the neighboring houses. His daughter would have remained; but he forced her away.

The huzzas and riotous uproar of the mob were now heard, close at hand. The sound was terrible, and struck Hutchinson with the same sort of dread as if an enraged wild beast had broken loose and were roaring for its prey. He crept softly to the window. There he beheld an immense concourse of people, filling all the street and rolling onward to his house. It was like a tempestuous flood, that had swelled beyond its bounds and would sweep every thing before it. Hutchinson trembled; he felt, at that moment, that the wrath of the people was a thousand fold more terrible than the wrath of a king.

That was a moment when a loyalist and an aristocrat like Hutchinson might have learned how powerless are kings, nobles, and great men, when the low and humble range themselves against them. King George could do nothing for his servant now. Had King George been there he could have done nothing for himself. If Hutchinson had understood this lesson, and remembered it, he need not, in after years, have been an exile from his native country, nor finally have laid his bones in a distant land.

There was now a rush against the doors of the house. The people sent up a hoarse cry. At this instant the lieutenant governor's daughter, whom he had supposed to be in a place of safety, ran into the room and threw her arms around him. She had returned by a private entrance.

"Father, are you mad?" cried she. "Will the king's name protect you now? Come with me, or they will have your life."

"True," muttered Hutchinson to himself; "what care these roarers for the name of king? I must flee, or they will trample me down on the door of my own dwelling."

Hurrying away, he and his daughter made their escape by the private passage at the moment when the rioters broke into the house. The foremost of them rushed up the staircase, and entered the room which Hutchinson had just quitted. There they beheld our good old chair facing them with quiet dignity, while the lion's head seemed to move its jaws in the unsteady light of their torches. Perhaps the stately aspect of our venerable friend, which had stood firm through a century and a half of trouble, arrested them for an instant. But they were thrust forward by those behind, and the chair lay overthrown.

Then began the work of destruction. The carved and polished mahogany tables were shattered with heavy clubs and hewn to splinters with axes. The marble hearths and mantel pieces were broken. The volumes of Hutchinson's library, so precious to a studious man, were torn out of their covers, and the leaves sent flying out of the windows. Manuscripts, containing secrets of our country's history, which are now lost forever, were scattered to the winds.

The old ancestral portraits, whose fixed countenances looked down on the wild scene, were rent from the walls. The mob triumphed in their downfall and destruction, as if these pictures of Hutchinson's forefathers had committed the same offences as their descendant. A tall looking glass, which had hitherto presented a reflection of the enraged and drunken multitude, was now smashed into a thousand fragments. We gladly dismiss the scene from the mirror of our fancy.

Before morning dawned the walls of the house were all that remained. The interior was a dismal scene of ruin. A shower pattered in at the broken windows; and when Hutchinson and his family returned, they stood shivering in the same room where the last evening had seen them so peaceful and happy.

"Grandfather," said Laurence, indignantly, "if the people acted in this manner, they were not worthy of even so much liberty as the King of England was willing to allow them."

"It was a most unjustifiable act, like many other popular movements at that time," replied Grandfather. "But we must not decide against the justice of the people's cause merely because an excited mob was guilty of outrageous violence. Besides, all these things were done in the first fury of resentment.

Afterwards the people grew more calm, and were more influenced by the counsel of those wise and good men who conducted them safely and gloriously through the revolution."

Little Alice, with tears in her blue eyes, said that she hoped the neighbors had not let Lieutenant Governor Hutchinson and his family be homeless in the street, but had taken them into their houses and been kind to them. Cousin Clara, recollecting the perilous situation of our beloved chair, inquired what had become of it.

"Nothing was heard of our chair for some time afterwards," answered Grandfather. "One day, in September, the same Andrew Oliver, of whom I before told you, was summoned to appear at high noon under Liberty Tree. This was the strangest summons that had ever been heard of; for it was issued in the name of the whole people, who thus took upon themselves the authority of a sovereign power. Mr. Oliver dared not disobey. Accordingly, at the appointed hour he went, much against his will, to Liberty Tree."

Here Charley interposed a remark that poor Mr. Oliver found but little liberty under Liberty Tree. Grandfather assented.

"It was a stormy day," continued he. "The equinoctial gale blew violently, and scattered the yellow leaves of Liberty Tree all along the street. Mr. Oliver's wig was dripping with waterdrops; and he probably looked haggard, disconsolate, and humbled

to the earth.   Beneath the tree, in Grandfather's chair,
— our own venerable chair, — sat Mr. Richard Dana,
a justice of the peace.   He administered an oath to
Mr. Oliver that he would never have any thing to
do with distributing the stamps.   A vast concourse
of people heard the oath, and shouted when it was
taken."

"There is something grand in this," said Laurence.
"I like it, because the people seem to have acted with
thoughtfulness and dignity ; and this proud gentle-
man, one of his majesty's high officers, was made to
feel that King George could not protect him in doing
wrong."

"But it was a sad day for poor Mr. Oliver," ob-
served Grandfather.   "From his youth upward it
had probably been the great principle of his life to
be faithful and obedient to the king.   And now, in
his old age, it must have puzzled and distracted him
to find the sovereign people setting up a claim to his
faith and obedience."

Grandfather closed the evening's conversation by
saying that the discontent of America was so great,
that, in 1766, the British Parliament was compelled
to repeal the stamp act.   The people made great re-
joicings, but took care to keep Liberty Tree well
pruned and free from caterpillars and canker worms.
They foresaw that there might yet be occasion for
them to assemble under its far-projecting shadow.

CHAPTER IV.

THE next evening, Clara, who remembered that
our chair had been left standing in the rain under
Liberty Tree, earnestly besought Grandfather to
tell when and where it had next found shelter.
Perhaps she was afraid that the venerable chair,
by being exposed to the inclemency of a Sep-
tember gale, might get the rheumatism in its aged
joints.

"The chair," said Grandfather, "after the cere-
mony of Mr. Oliver's oath, appears to have been
quite forgotten by the multitude. Indeed, being
much bruised and rather rickety, owing to the violent
treatment it had suffered from the Hutchinson mob,
most people would have thought that its days of use-
fulness were over. Nevertheless, it was conveyed
away under cover of the night and committed to the
care of a skilful joiner. He doctored our old friend
so successfully, that, in the course of a few days, it
made its appearance in the public room of the British
Coffee House, in King Street."

"But why did not Mr. Hutchinson get possession of it again?" inquired Charley.

"I know not," answered Grandfather, "unless he considered it a dishonor and disgrace to the chair to have stood under Liberty Tree. At all events, he suffered it to remain at the British Coffee House, which was the principal hotel in Boston. It could not possibly have found a situation where it would be more in the midst of business and bustle, or would witness more important events, or be occupied by a greater variety of persons."

Grandfather went on to tell the proceedings of the despotic king and ministry of England after the repeal of the stamp act. They could not bear to think that their right to tax America should be disputed by the people. In the year 1767, therefore, they caused Parliament to pass an act for laying a duty on tea and some other articles that were in general use. Nobody could now buy a pound of tea without paying a tax to King George. This scheme was pretty craftily contrived; for the women of America were very fond of tea, and did not like to give up the use of it.

But the people were as much opposed to this new act of Parliament as they had been to the stamp act. England, however, was determined that they should submit. In order to compel their obedience, two regiments, consisting of more than seven hundred British soldiers, were sent to Boston. They arrived

in September, 1768, and were landed on Long
Wharf. Thence they marched to the Common with
loaded muskets, fixed bayonets, and great pomp and
parade. So now, at last, the free town of Boston
was guarded and overawed by redcoats as it had been
in the days of old Sir Edmund Andros.

In the month of November more regiments ar-
rived. There were now four thousand troops in
Boston. The Common was whitened with their
tents. Some of the soldiers were lodged in Faneuil
Hall, which the inhabitants looked upon as a conse-
crated place, because it had been the scene of a great
many meetings in favor of liberty. One regiment
was placed in the Town House, which we now call
the Old State House. The lower floor of this edifice
had hitherto been used by the merchants as an ex-
change. In the upper stories were the chambers of
the judges, the representatives, and the governor's
council. The venerable councillors could not assem-
ble to consult about the welfare of the province
without being challenged by sentinels and passing
among the bayonets of the British soldiers.

Sentinels likewise were posted at the lodgings of
the officers in many parts of the town. When the
inhabitants approached they were greeted by the
sharp question, " Who goes there ? " while the rat-
tle of the soldier's musket was heard as he presented
it against their breasts. There was no quiet even on

the Sabbath day. The pious descendants of the Puritans were shocked by the uproar of military music; the drum, fife, and bugle drowning the holy organ peal and the voices of the singers. It would appear as if the British took every method to insult the feelings of the people.

"Grandfather," cried Charley, impatiently, "the people did not go to fighting half soon enough! These British redcoats ought to have been driven back to their vessels the very moment they landed on Long Wharf."

"Many a hotheaded young man said the same as you do, Charley," answered Grandfather. "But the elder and wiser people saw that the time was not yet come. Meanwhile, let us take another peep at our old chair."

"Ah, it drooped its head, I know," said Charley, "when it saw how the province was disgraced. Its old Puritan friends never would have borne such doings."

"The chair," proceeded Grandfather, "was now continually occupied by some of the high tories, as the king's friends were called, who frequented the British Coffee House. Officers of the Custom House, too, which stood on the opposite side of King Street, often sat in the chair wagging their tongues against John Hancock."

"Why against him?" asked Charley.

"Because he was a great merchant and contended against paying duties to the king," said Grandfather.

" Well, frequently, no doubt, the officers of the British regiments, when not on duty, used to fling themselves into the arms of our venerable chair. Fancy one of them, a red-nosed captain in his scarlet uniform, playing with the hilt of his sword, and making a circle of his brother officers merry with ridiculous jokes at the expense of the poor Yankees. And perhaps he would call for a bottle of wine, or a steaming bowl of punch, and drink confusion to all rebels."

" Our grave old chair must have been scandalized at such scenes," observed Laurence ; " the chair that had been the Lady Arbella's, and which the holy apostle Eliot had consecrated."

" It certainly was little less than sacrilege," replied Grandfather ; " but the time was coming when even the churches, where hallowed pastors had long preached the word of God, were to be torn down or desecrated by the British troops. Some years passed, however, before such things were done."

Grandfather now told his auditors that, in 1769, Sir Francis Bernard went to England after having been governor of Massachusetts ten years. He was a gentleman of many good qualities, an excellent scholar, and a friend to learning. But he was naturally of an arbitrary disposition ; and he had been bred at the University of Oxford, where young men were taught that the divine right of kings was the only thing to be regarded in matters of government. Such ideas were ill adapted to please the people of

Massachusetts. They rejoiced to get rid of Sir Francis Bernard, but liked his successor, Lieutenant Governor Hutchinson, no better than himself.

About this period the people were much incensed at an act committed by a person who held an office in the Custom House. Some lads, or young men, were snowballing his windows. He fired a musket at them, and killed a poor German boy, only eleven years old. This event made a great noise in town and country, and much increased the resentment that was already felt against the servants of the crown.

"Now, children," said Grandfather, "I wish to make you comprehend the position of the British troops in King Street. This is the same which we now call State Street. On the south side of the Town House, or Old State House, was what military men call a court of guard, defended by two brass cannons, which pointed directly at one of the doors of the above edifice. A large party of soldiers were always stationed in the court of guard. The Custom House stood at a little distance down King Street, nearly where the Suffolk Bank now stands, and a sentinel was continually pacing before its front."

"I shall remember this to-morrow," said Charley; "and I will go to State Street, so as to see exactly where the British troops were stationed."

"And before long," observed Grandfather, "I shall have to relate an event which made King Street sadly famous on both sides of the Atlantic. The history of our chair will soon bring us to this melancholy business."

Here Grandfather described the state of things which arose from the ill will that existed between the inhabitants and the redcoats. The old and sober part of the townspeople were very angry at the government for sending soldiers to overawe them. But those grayheaded men were cautious, and kept their thoughts and feelings in their own breasts, without putting themselves in the way of the British bayonets.

The younger people, however, could hardly be kept within such prudent limits. They reddened with wrath at the very sight of a soldier, and would have been willing to come to blows with them at any moment. For it was their opinion that every tap of a British drum within the peninsula of Boston was an insult to the brave old town.

"It was sometimes the case," continued Grandfather, "that affrays happened between such wild young men as these and small parties of the soldiers. No weapons had hitherto been used except fists or cudgels. But when men have loaded muskets in their hands, it is easy to foretell that they will soon be turned against the bosoms of those who provoke their anger."

"Grandfather," said Little Alice, looking fearfully into his face, "your voice sounds as though you were going to tell us something awful!"

CHAPTER V.

Little Alice, by her last remark, proved herself a good judge of what was expressed by the tones of Grandfather's voice. He had given the above description of the enmity between the townspeople and the soldiers in order to prepare the minds of his auditors for a very terrible event. It was one that did more to heighten the quarrel between England and America than any thing that had yet occurred.

Without further preface, Grandfather began the story of

THE BOSTON MASSACRE.

It was now the 3d of March, 1770. The sunset music of the British regiments was heard as usual throughout the town. The shrill fife and rattling drum awoke the echoes in King Street, while the last ray of sunshine was lingering on the cupola of the Town House. And now all the sentinels were posted. One of them marched up and down before the Custom House, treading a short path through the snow, and longing for the time when he would be dismissed to the warm fireside of the guard room. Meanwhile Captain Preston was, perhaps, sitting in our great chair before the hearth of the British Coffee House. In the course of the evening there were two or three slight commotions, which seemed to indicate that trouble was at hand. Small parties of young men stood at the corners of the streets or walked along the narrow pavements. Squads of soldiers who were dismissed from duty passed by them, shoulder to shoulder, with the regular step which they had learned at the drill. Whenever these encounters took place, it appeared to be the object of the young men to treat the soldiers with as much incivility as possible.

"Turn out, you lobsterbacks!" one would say. "Crowd them off the sidewalks!" another would cry. "A redcoat has no right in Boston streets!"

"O, you rebel rascals!" perhaps the soldiers would reply, glaring fiercely at the young men. "Some day or other we'll make our way through Boston streets at the point of the bayonet!"

Once or twice such disputes as these brought on a scuffle; which passed off, however, without attracting much notice. About eight o'clock, for some unknown cause, an alarm bell rang loudly and hurriedly.

At the sound many people ran out of their houses, supposing it to be an alarm of fire. But there were no flames to be seen; nor was there any smell of smoke in the clear, frosty air; so that most of the townsmen went back to their own firesides and sat talking with their wives and children about the calamities of the times. Others who were younger and less prudent remained in the streets; for there seems to have been a presentiment that some strange event was on the eve of taking place.

Later in the evening, not far from nine o'clock, several young men passed by the Town House and walked down King Street. The sentinel was still on his post in front of the Custom House, pacing to and fro; while, as he turned, a gleam of light from some neighboring window glittered on the barrel of his musket. At no great distance were the barracks and the guard house, where his comrades were probably telling stories of battle and bloodshed.

Down towards the Custom House, as I told you, came a party of wild young men. When they drew near the sentinel he halted on his post, and took his musket from his shoulder, ready to present the bayonet at their breasts.

"Who goes there?" he cried, in the gruff, peremptory tones of a soldier's challenge.

The young men, being Boston boys, felt as if they had a right to walk their own streets without being accountable to a British redcoat, even though he challenged them in King George's name. They made some rude answer to the sentinel. There was a dispute, or perhaps a scuffle. Other soldiers heard the noise, and ran hastily from the barracks to assist their comrades. At the same time many of the townspeople rushed into King Street by various avenues, and gathered in a crowd round about the Custom House. It seemed wonderful how such a multitude had started up all of a sudden.

The wrongs and insults which the people had been suffering for many months now kindled them into a rage. They threw snowballs and lumps of ice at the soldiers. As the tumult grew louder it reached the ears of Captain Preston, the officer of the day. He immediately ordered eight soldiers of the main guard to take their muskets and follow him. They marched across the street, forcing their way roughly through the crowd, and pricking the townspeople with their bayonets.

A gentleman (it was Henry Knox, afterwards general of the American artillery) caught Captain Preston's arm.

"For Heaven's sake, sir," exclaimed he, "take heed what you do, or here will be bloodshed."

"Stand aside!" answered Captain Preston, haughtily. "Do not interfere, sir. Leave me to manage the affair."

Arriving at the sentinel's post, Captain Preston drew up his men in a semicircle, with their faces to

the crowd and their rear to the Custom House. When
the people saw the officer and beheld the threatening
attitude with which the soldiers fronted them, their
rage became almost uncontrollable.

" Fire, you lobsterbacks !" bellowed some.

" You dare not fire, you cowardly redcoats !" cried
others.

" Rush upon them !" shouted many voices.
" Drive the rascals to their barracks ! Down with
them ! Down with them ! Let them fire if they
dare !"

Amid the uproar, the soldiers stood glaring at the
people with the fierceness of men whose trade was to
shed blood.

O, what a crisis had now arrived ! Up to this
very moment, the angry feelings between England
and America might have been pacified. England had
but to stretch out the hand of reconciliation, and ac-
knowledge that she had hitherto mistaken her rights,
but would do so no more. Then the ancient
bonds of brotherhood would again have been knit
together as firmly as in old times. The habit of
loyalty, which had grown as strong as instinct, was
not utterly overcome. The perils shared, the vic-
tories won, in the old French war, when the sol-
diers of the colonies fought side by side with their
comrades from beyond the sea, were unforgotten yet.
England was still that beloved country which the

colonists called their home. King George, though he had frowned upon America, was still reverenced as a father.

But should the king's soldiers shed one drop of American blood, then it was a quarrel to the death. Never, never would America rest satisfied until she had torn down the royal authority and trampled it in the dust.

"Fire, if you dare, villains!" hoarsely shouted the people, while the muzzles of the muskets were turned upon them. "You dare not fire!"

They appeared ready to rush upon the levelled bayonets. Captain Preston waved his sword, and uttered a command which could not be distinctly heard amid the uproar of shouts that issued from a hundred throats. But his soldiers deemed that he had spoken the fatal mandate, "Fire!" The flash of their muskets lighted up the street, and the report rang loudly between the edifices. It was said, too, that the figure of a man, with a cloth hanging down over his face, was seen to step into the balcony of the Custom House and discharge a musket at the crowd.

A gush of smoke had overspread the scene. It rose heavily, as if it were loath to reveal the dreadful spectacle beneath it. Eleven of the sons of New England lay stretched upon the street. Some, sorely wounded, were struggling to rise again. Others stirred not nor groaned; for they were past all pain.

Blood was streaming upon the snow ; and that purple stain in the midst of King Street, though it melted away in the next day's sun, was never forgotten nor forgiven by the people.

Grandfather was interrupted by the violent sobs of little Alice. In his earnestness he had neglected to soften down the narrative so that it might not terrify the heart of this unworldly infant. Since Grandfather began the history of our chair, little Alice had listened to many tales of war. But probably the idea had never really impressed itself upon her mind that men have shed the blood of their fellow-creatures. And now that this idea was forcibly presented to her, it affected the sweet child with bewilderment and horror.

"I ought to have remembered our dear little Alice," said Grandfather reproachfully to himself. "O, what a pity! Her heavenly nature has now received its first impression of earthly sin and violence. Well, Clara, take her to bed and comfort her. Heaven grant that she may dream away the recollection of the Boston massacre!"

"Grandfather," said Charley, when Clara and little Alice had retired, "did not the people rush upon the soldiers and take revenge?"

"The town drums beat to arms," replied Grandfather, 'he alarm bells rang, and an immense multitude rushed into King Street. Many of them had weapons in their hands. The British prepared to defend themselves. A whole regiment was drawn up in the street, expecting an attack ; for the townsmen appeared ready to throw themselves upon the bayonets."

"And how did it end?" asked Charley.

"Governor Hutchinson hurried to the spot," said Grandfather, "and besought the people to have patience, promising that strict justice should be done. A day or two afterward the British troops were withdrawn from town and stationed at Castle William. Captain Preston and the eight soldiers were tried for murder. But none of them were found guilty. The judges told the jury that the insults and violence which had been offered to the soldiers justified them in firing at the mob."

"The revolution," observed Laurence, who had said but little during the evening, "was not such a calm, majestic movement as I supposed. I do not love to hear of mobs and broils in the street. These things were unworthy of the people when they had such a great object to accomplish."

"Nevertheless, the world has seen no grander movement than that of our revolution from first to last," said Grandfather. "The people, to a man, were full of a great and noble sentiment. True, there may be much fault to find with their mode of expressing this sentiment ; but they knew no better ;

the necessity was upon them to act out their feelings in the best manner they could. We must forgive what was wrong in their actions, and look into their hearts and minds for the honorable motives that impelled them."

" And I suppose," said Laurence, "there were men who knew how to act worthily of what they felt."

" There were many such," replied Grandfather; " and we will speak of some of them hereafter."

Grandfather here made a pause. That night Charley had a dream about the Boston massacre, and thought that he himself was in the crowd and struck down Captain Preston with a great club. Laurence dreamed that he was sitting in our great chair, at the window of the British Coffee House, and beheld the whole scene which Grandfather had described. It seemed to him, in his dream, that, if the townspeople and the soldiers would but have heard him speak a single word, all the slaughter might have been averted. But there was such an uproar that it drowned his voice.

The next morning the two boys went together to State Street and stood on the very spot where the first blood of the revolution had been shed. The Old State House was still there, presenting almost the same aspect that it had worn on that memorable evening, one and seventy years ago. It is the sole remaining witness of the Boston massacre.

CHAPTER VI.

THE next evening the astral lamp was lighted ear-
lier than usual, because Laurence was very much
engaged in looking over the collection of portraits
which had been his New Year's gift from Grandfather.

Among them he found the features of more than
one famous personage who had been connected with
the adventures of our old chair. Grandfather bade
him draw the table nearer to the fireside ; and they
looked over the portraits together, while Clara and
Charley likewise lent their attention. As for little
Alice, she sat in Grandfather's lap, and seemed to see
the very men alive whose faces were there represented.

Turning over the volume, Laurence came to the
portrait of a stern, grim-looking man, in plain attire,
of much more modern fashion than that of the old
Puritans. But the face might well have befitted one
of those iron-hearted men. Beneath the portrait was
the name of Samuel Adams.

" He was a man of great note in all the doings
that brought about the revolution," said Grandfather.

" His character was such, that it seemed as if one of
the ancient Puritans had been sent back to earth to
animate the people's hearts with the same abhorrence
of tyranny that had distinguished the earliest settlers.
He was as religious as they, as stern and inflexible,
and as deeply imbued with democratic principles.
He, better than any one else, may be taken as a rep-
resentative of the people of New England, and of
the spirit with which they engaged in the revolution-
ary struggle. He was a poor man, and earned his
bread by a humble occupation ; but with his tongue
and pen he made the King of England tremble on
his throne. Remember him, my children, as one of
the strong men of our country."

" Here is one whose looks show a very different
character," observed Laurence, turning to the por-
trait of John Hancock. " I should think, by his
splendid dress and courtly aspect, that he was one
of the king's friends."

" There never was a greater contrast than between
Samuel Adams and John Hancock," said Grandfather.
" Yet they were of the same side in politics, and had
an equal agency in the revolution. Hancock was
born to the inheritance of the largest fortune in New
England. His tastes and habits were aristocratic.
He loved gorgeous attire, a splendid mansion, mag-
nificent furniture, stately festivals, and all that was
glittering and pompous in external things. His

manners were so polished that there stood not a nobleman at the footstool of King George's throne who was a more skilful courtier than John Hancock might have been. Nevertheless, he in his embroidered clothes, and Samuel Adams in his threadbare coat, wrought together in the cause of liberty. Adams acted from pure and rigid principle. Hancock, though he loved his country, yet thought quite as much of his own popularity as he did of the people's rights. It is remarkable that these two men, so very different as I describe them, were the only two exempted from pardon by the king's proclamation."

On the next leaf of the book was the portrait of General Joseph Warren. Charley recognized the name, and said that here was a greater man than either Hancock or Adams.

"Warren was an eloquent and able patriot," replied Grandfather. "He deserves a lasting memory for his zealous efforts in behalf of liberty. No man's voice was more powerful in Faneuil Hall than Joseph Warren's. If his death had not happened so early in the contest, he would probably have gained a high name as a soldier."

The next portrait was a venerable man, who held his thumb under his chin, and, through his spectacles, appeared to be attentively reading a manuscript.

"Here we see the most illustrious Boston boy that ever lived," said Grandfather. "This is Benjamin

Franklin.   But I will not try to compress into a few sentences the character of the sage, who, as a Frenchman expressed it, snatched the lightning from the sky and the sceptre from a tyrant.   Mr. Sparks must help you to the knowledge of Franklin."

The book likewise contained portraits of James Otis and Josiah Quincy.   Both of them, Grandfather observed, were men of wonderful talents and true patriotism.   Their voices were like the stirring tones of a trumpet arousing the country to defend its freedom.   Heaven seemed to have provided a greater number of eloquent men than had appeared at any other period, in order that the people might be fully instructed as to their wrongs and the method of resistance.

" It is marvellous," said Grandfather, " to see how many powerful writers, orators, and soldiers started up just at the time when they were wanted.   There was a man for every kind of work.   It is equally wonderful that men of such different characters were all made to unite in the one object of establishing the freedom and independence of America.   There was an overruling Providence above them."

" Here was another great man," remarked Laurence, pointing to the portrait of John Adams.

" Yes ; an earnest, warm-tempered, honest, and most able man," said Grandfather.   " At the period of which we are now speaking he was a lawyer in

Boston. He was destined in after years to be ruler over the whole American people, whom he contributed so much to form into a nation."

Grandfather here remarked that many a New Englander, who had passed his boyhood and youth in obscurity, afterward attained to a fortune which he never could have foreseen even in his most ambitious dreams. John Adams, the second President of the United States and the equal of crowned kings, was once a schoolmaster and country lawyer. Hancock, the first signer of the Declaration of Independence, served his apprenticeship with a merchant. Samuel Adams, afterwards governor of Massachusetts, was a small tradesman and a tax gatherer. General Warren was a physician, General Lincoln a farmer, and General Knox a bookbinder. General Nathaniel Greene, the best soldier, except Washington, in the revolutionary army, was a Quaker and a blacksmith. All these became illustrious men, and can never be forgotten in American history.

"And any boy who is born in America may look forward to the same things," said our ambitious friend Charley.

After these observations, Grandfather drew the book of portraits towards him, and showed the children several British peers and members of Parliament who had exerted themselves either for or against the rights of America. There were the Earl of Bute,

Mr. Grenville, and Lord North. These were looked upon as deadly enemies to our country.

Among the friends of America was Mr. Pitt, afterward Earl of Chatham, who spent so much of his wondrous eloquence in endeavoring to warn England of the consequences of her injustice. He fell down on the floor of the House of Lords after uttering almost his dying words in defence of our privileges as freemen. There was Edmund Burke, one of the wisest men and greatest orators that ever the world produced. There was Colonel Barré, who had been among our fathers, and knew that they had courage enough to die for their rights. There was Charles James Fox, who never rested until he had silenced our enemies in the House of Commons.

"It is very remarkable to observe how many of the ablest orators in the British Parliament were favorable to America," said Grandfather. "We ought to remember these great Englishmen with gratitude ; for their speeches encouraged our fathers almost as much as those of our own orators in Faneuil Hall and under Liberty Tree. Opinions which might have been received with doubt, if expressed only by a native American, were set down as true, beyond dispute, when they came from the lips of Chatham, Burke, Barré, or Fox."

"But, Grandfather," asked Laurence, "were there no able and eloquent men in this country who took the part of King George ?"

" There were many men of talent who said what they could in defence of the king's tyrannical proceedings," replied Grandfather. " But they had the worst side of the argument, and therefore seldom said any thing worth remembering. Moreover, their hearts were faint and feeble ; for they felt that the people scorned and detested them. They had no friends, no defence, except in the bayonets of the British troops. A blight fell upon all their faculties, because they were contending against the rights of their own native land."

" What were the names of some of them ?" inquired Charley.

" Governor Hutchinson, Chief Justice Oliver, Judge Auchmuty, the Reverend Mather Byles, and several other clergymen, were among the most noted loyalists," answered Grandfather.

" I wish the people had tarred and feathered every man of them ! " cried Charley.

" That wish is very wrong, Charley," said Grandfather. " You must not think that there was no integrity and honor except among those who stood up for the freedom of America. For aught I know, there was quite as much of these qualities on one side as on the other. Do you see nothing admirable in a faithful adherence to an unpopular cause ? Can you not respect that principle of loyalty which made the royalists give up country, friends, fortune, every thing, rather than be false to their king? It was a mistaken principle; but many of them cherished it honorably, and were martyrs to it."

"O, I was wrong!" said Charley, ingenuously. "And I would risk my life rather than one of those good old royalists should be tarred and feathered."

"The time is now come when we may judge fairly of them," continued Grandfather. "Be the good and true men among them honored; for they were as much our countrymen as the patriots were. And, thank Heaven, our country need not be ashamed of her sons, — of most of them at least, — whatever side they took in the revolutionary contest."

Among the portraits was one of King George III. Little Alice clapped her hands, and seemed pleased with the bluff good nature of his physiognomy. But Laurence thought it strange that a man with such a face, indicating hardly a common share of intellect, should have had influence enough on human affairs to convulse the world with war. Grandfather observed that this poor king had always appeared to him one of the most unfortunate persons that ever lived. He was so honest and conscientious, that, if he had been only a private man, his life would probably have been blameless and happy. But his was that worst of fortunes — to be placed in a station far beyond his abilities.

"And so," said Grandfather, "his life, while he

retained what intellect Heaven had gifted him with, was one long mortification. At last he grew crazed with care and trouble. For nearly twenty years the monarch of England was confined as a madman. In his old age, too, God took away his eyesight; so that his royal palace was nothing to him but a dark, lonesome prison house."

CHAPTER VII.

"Our old chair," resumed Grandfather, "did not now stand in the midst of a gay circle of British officers. The troops, as I told you, had been removed to Castle William immediately after the Boston massacre. Still, however, there were many tories, custom-house officers, and Englishmen who used to assemble in the British Coffee House and talk over the affairs of the period. Matters grew worse and worse; and in 1773 the people did a deed which incensed the king and ministry more than any of their former doings."

Grandfather here described the affair, which is known by the name of the Boston Tea Party. The Americans, for some time past, had left off importing tea, on account of the oppressive tax. The East India Company, in London, had a large stock of tea on hand, which they had expected to sell to the Americans, but could find no market for it. But, after a while, the government persuaded this company of merchants to send the tea to America.

"How odd it is," observed Clara, "that the liberties of America should have had any thing to do with a cup of tea!"

Grandfather smiled, and proceeded with his narrative. When the people of Boston heard that several cargoes of tea were coming across the Atlantic, they held a great many meetings at Faneuil Hall, in the Old South Church, and under Liberty Tree. In the midst of their debates, three ships arrived in the harbor with the tea on board. The people spent more than a fortnight in consulting what should be done. At last, on the 16th of December, 1773, they demanded of Governor Hutchinson that he should immediately send the ships back to England.

The governor replied that the ships must not leave the harbor until the custom-house duties upon the tea should be paid. Now, the payment of these duties was the very thing against which the people had set their faces; because it was a tax unjustly imposed upon America by the English government. Therefore, in the dusk of the evening, as soon as Governor Hutchinson's reply was received, an immense crowd hastened to Griffin's Wharf, where the tea ships lay. The place is now called Liverpool Wharf.

"When the crowd reached the wharf," said Grandfather, "they saw that a set of wild-looking figures were already on board of the ships. You would have imagined that the Indian warriors of old times had come back again; for they wore the Indian dress, and had their faces covered with red and black paint, like the Indians when they go to war. These grim figures hoisted the tea chests on the decks of the vessels, broke them open, and threw all the contents into the harbor."

"Grandfather," said little Alice, "I suppose Indians don't love tea; else they would never waste it so."

"They were not real Indians, my child," answered Grandfather. "They were white men in disguise; because a heavy punishment would have been inflicted on them if the king's officers had found who they were. But it was never known. From that day to this, though the matter has been talked of by all the world, nobody can tell the names of those Indian figures. Some people say that there were very famous men among them, who afterwards became governors and generals. Whether this be true, I cannot tell."

When tidings of this bold deed were carried to England, King George was greatly enraged. Parliament immediately passed an act, by which all vessels were forbidden to take in or discharge their cargoes at the Port of Boston. In this way they expected to ruin all the merchants, and starve the poor people, by depriving them of employment. At the same time another act was passed, taking away many rights and privileges which had been granted in the charter of Massachusetts.

Governor Hutchinson, soon afterward, was summoned to England, in order that he might give his advice about the management of American affairs. General Gage, an officer of the old French war, and since commander-in-chief of the British forces in America, was appointed governor in his stead. One of his first acts was to make Salem, instead of Boston, the metropolis of Massachusetts, by summoning the general court to meet there.

According to Grandfather's description, this was the most gloomy time that Massachusetts had ever seen. The people groaned under as heavy a tyranny as in the days of Sir Edmund Andros. Boston looked as if it were afflicted with some dreadful pestilence — so sad were the inhabitants, and so desolate the streets. There was no cheerful hum of business. The merchants shut up their warehouses, and the laboring men stood idle about the wharves. But all America felt interested in the good town of Boston; and contributions were raised, in many places, for the relief of the poor inhabitants.

"Our dear old chair!" exclaimed Clara. "How dismal it must have been now!"

" O," replied Grandfather, " a gay throng of officers had now come back to the British Coffee House ; so that the old chair had no lack of mirthful company. Soon after General Gage became governor a great many troops had arrived, and were encamped upon the Common. Boston was now a garrisoned and fortified town ; for the general had built a battery across the Neck, on the road to Roxbury, and placed guards for its defence. Every thing looked as if a civil war were close at hand."

" Did the people make ready to fight ? " asked Charley.

" A Continental Congress assembled at Philadelphia," said Grandfather, " and proposed such measures as they thought most conducive to the public good. A Provincial Congress was likewise chosen in Massachusetts. They exhorted the people to arm and discipline themselves. A great number of minute men were enrolled. The Americans called them minute men, because they engaged to be ready to fight at a minute's warning. The English officers laughed, and said that the name was a very proper one, because the minute men would run away the minute they saw the enemy. Whether they would fight or run was soon to be proved."

Grandfather told the children that the first open resistance offered to the British troops, in the Province of Massachusetts, was at Salem. Colonel Timothy Pickering, with thirty or forty militia men, prevented the English colonel, Leslie, with four times as many regular soldiers, from taking possession of some military stores. No blood was shed on this occasion; but soon afterward it began to flow.

General Gage sent eight hundred soldiers to Concord, about eighteen miles from Boston, to destroy some ammunition and provisions which the colonists had collected there. They set out on their march in the evening of the 18th of April, 1775. The next morning, the general sent Lord Percy with nine hundred men to strengthen the troops that had gone before. All that day the inhabitants of Boston heard various rumors. Some said that the British were making great slaughter among our countrymen. Others affirmed that every man had turned out with his musket, and that not a single soldier would ever get back to Boston.

"It was after sunset," continued Grandfather, "when the troops, who had marched forth so proudly, were seen entering Charlestown. They were covered with dust, and so hot and weary that their tongues hung out of their mouths. Many of them were faint with wounds. They had not all returned. Nearly three hundred were strown, dead or dying, along the road from Concord. The yeomanry had risen upon the invaders and driven them back."

"Was this the battle of Lexington?" asked Charley.

"Yes," replied Grandfather; "it was so called, because the British, without provocation, had fired upon a party of minute men, near Lexington meeting house, and killed eight of them. That fatal volley, which was fired by order of Major Pitcairn, began the war of the revolution."

About this time, if Grandfather had been correctly informed, our chair disappeared from the British Coffee House. The manner of its departure cannot be satisfactorily ascertained. Perhaps the keeper of the Coffee House turned it out of doors on account of its old-fashioned aspect. Perhaps he sold it as a curiosity. Perhaps it was taken, without leave, by some person who regarded it as public property because it had once figured under Liberty Tree. Or perhaps the old chair, being of a peaceable disposition, had made use of its four oaken legs and run away from the seat of war.

"It would have made a terrible clattering over the pavement," said Charley, laughing.

"Meanwhile," continued Grandfather, "during the mysterious non-appearance of our chair, an army of twenty thousand men had started up and come to the siege of Boston. General Gage and his troops were cooped up within the narrow precincts of the peninsula. On the 17th of June, 1775, the famous battle of Bunker Hill was fought. Here General Warren fell. The British got the victory, indeed, but with the loss of more than a thousand officers and men."

"O Grandfather," cried Charley, "you must tell us about that famous battle."

"No, Charley," said Grandfather, "I am not like other historians. Battles shall not hold a prominent place in the history of our quiet and comfortable old chair. But to-morrow evening, Laurence, Clara, and yourself, and dear little Alice too, shall visit the Diorama of Bunker Hill. There you shall see the whole business, the burning of Charlestown and all, with your own eyes, and hear the cannon and musketry with your own ears."

CHAPTER VIII.

THE next evening but one, when the children had given Grandfather a full account of the Diorama of Bunker Hill, they entreated him not to keep them any longer in suspense about the fate of his chair. The reader will recollect that, at the last accounts, it had trotted away upon its poor old legs nobody knew whither. But, before gratifying their curiosity, Grandfather found it necessary to say something about public events.

The Continental Congress, which was assembled at Philadelphia, was composed of delegates from all the colonies. They had now appointed George Washington, of Virginia, to be commander-in-chief of all the American armies. He was, at that time, a member of Congress; but immediately left Philadelphia, and began his journey to Massachusetts. On the 3d of July, 1775, he arrived at Cambridge, and took command of the troops which were besieging General Gage.

"O Grandfather," exclaimed Laurence, "it makes

my heart throb to think what is coming now. We are to see General Washington himself."

The children crowded around Grandfather and looked earnestly into his face. Even little Alice opened her swegorblue eyes, with her lips apart, and almost held her breath to listen; so instinctive is the reverence of childhood for the father of his country. Grandfather paused a moment; for he felt as if it might be irreverent to introduce the hallowed shade of Washington into a history where an ancient elbow chair occupied the most prominent place. However, he determined to proceed with his narrative, and speak of the hero when it was needful, but with an unambitious simplicity.

So Grandfather told his auditors, that, on General Washington's arrival at Cambridge, his first care was to reconnoitre the British troops with his spyglass, and to examine the condition of his own army. He found that the American troops amounted to about fourteen thousand men. They were extended all round the peninsula of Boston, a space of twelve miles, from the high grounds of Roxbury on the right to Mystic River on the left. Some were living in tents of sailcloth, some in shanties rudely constructed of boards, some in huts of stone or turf, with curious windows and doors of basket work.

In order to be near the centre and oversee the whole of this widestretched army, the commander-in-chief made his head quarters at Cambridge, about half a mile from the colleges. A mansion house, which perhaps had been the country seat of some tory gentleman, was provided for his residence.

"When General Washington first entered this mansion," said Grandfather, " he was ushered up the staircase and shown into a handsome apartment. He sat down in a large chair, which was the most conspicuous object in the room. The noble figure of Washington would have done honor to a throne. As he sat there, with his hand resting on the hilt of his sheathed sword, which was placed between his knees, his whole aspect well befitted the chosen man on whom his country leaned for the defence of her dearest rights. America seemed safe under his protection. His face was grander than any sculptor had ever wrought in marble; none could behold him without awe and reverence. Never before had the lion's head at the summit of the chair looked down upon such a face and form as Washington's."

"Why, Grandfather!" cried Clara, clasping her hands in amazement, "was it really so? Did General Washington sit in our great chair?"

"I knew how it would be," said Laurence; "I foresaw it the moment Grandfather began to speak."

Grandfather smiled. But, turning from the personal and domestic life of the illustrious leader, he spoke of the methods which Washington adopted to win back the metropolis of New England from the British.

The army, when he took command of it, was without any discipline or order. The privates considered themselves as good as their officers; and seldom thought it necessary to obey their commands, unless they understood the why and wherefore. Moreover, they were enlisted for so short a period, that, as soon as they began to be respectable soldiers, it was time to discharge them. Then came new recruits, who had to be taught their duty before they could be of any service. Such was the army with which Washington had to contend against more than twenty veteran British regiments.

Some of the men had no muskets, and almost all were without bayonets. Heavy cannon, for battering the British fortifications, were much wanted. There was but a small quantity of powder and ball, few tools to build intrenchments with, and a great deficiency of provisions and clothes for the soldiers. Yet, in spite of these perplexing difficulties, the eyes of the whole people were fixed on General Washington, expecting him to undertake some great enterprise against the hostile army.

The first thing that he found necessary was, to bring his own men into better order and discipline. It is wonderful how soon he transformed this rough mob of country people into the semblance of a regular army. One of Washington's most invaluable characteristics was, the faculty of bringing order out of confusion. All business with which he had any concern seemed to regulate itself as if by magic. The influence of his mind was like light gleaming through an unshaped world. It was this faculty, more than any other, that made him so fit to ride upon the storm of the revolution when every thing was unfixed and drifting about in a troubled sea.

"Washington had not been long at the head of the army," proceeded Grandfather, "before his soldiers thought as highly of him as if he had led them to a hundred victories. They knew that he was the very man whom the country needed, and the only one who could bring them safely through the great contest against the might of England. They put entire confidence in his courage, wisdom, and integrity."

"And were they not eager to follow him against the British?" asked Charley.

"Doubtless they would have gone whithersoever his sword pointed the way," answered Grandfather; "and Washington was anxious to make a decisive assault upon the enemy. But as the enterprise was very hazardous, he called a council of all the generals in the army. Accordingly, they came from their different posts, and were ushered into the reception room. The commander-in-chief arose from our great chair to greet them."

"What were their names?" asked Charley.

"There was General Artemas Ward," replied Grandfather, "a lawyer by profession. He had commanded the troops before Washington's arrival. Another was General Charles Lee, who had been a colonel in the English army, and was thought to possess vast military science. He came to the council, followed by two or three dogs which were always at his heels. There was General Putnam, too, who was known all over New England by the name of Old Put."

"Was it he who killed the wolf?" inquired Charley.

"The same," said Grandfather; "and he had done good service in the old French war. His occupation was that of a farmer; but he left his plough in the furrow at the news of Lexington battle. Then there was General Gates, who afterward gained great renown at Saratoga, and lost it again at Camden. General Greene, of Rhode Island, was likewise at the council. Washington soon discovered him to be one of the best officers in the army."

When the generals were all assembled, Washington consulted them about a plan for storming the English batteries. But it was their unanimous opinion that so perilous an enterprise ought not to be attempted. The army, therefore, continued to besiege Boston, preventing the enemy from obtaining supplies of provisions, but without taking any immediate measures to get possession of the town. In this manner the summer, autumn, and winter passed away.

"Many a night, doubtless," said Grandfather, "after Washington had been all day on horseback, galloping from one post of the army to another, he used to sit in our great chair, rapt in earnest thought. Had you seen him, you might have supposed that his whole mind was fixed on the blue china tiles which adorned the old-fashioned fireplace. But, in reality, he was meditating how to capture the British army, or drive it out of Boston. Once, when there was a hard frost, he formed a scheme to cross the Charles River on the ice. But the other generals could not be persuaded that there was any prospect of success."

"What were the British doing all this time?" inquired Charley.

"They lay idle in the town," replied Grandfather. "General Gage had been recalled to England, and was succeeded by Sir William Howe. The British army and the inhabitants of Boston were now in great distress. Being shut up in the town so long, they had consumed almost all their provisions and burned up all their fuel. The soldiers tore down the

Old North Church, and used its rotten boards and timbers for firewood. To heighten their distress, the small pox broke out. They probably lost far more men by cold, hunger, and sickness than had been slain at Lexington and Bunker Hill."

"What a dismal time for the poor women and children!" exclaimed Clara.

"At length," continued Grandfather, "in March, 1776, General Washington, who had now a good supply of powder, began a terrible cannonade and bombardment from Dorchester Heights. One of the cannon balls which he fired into the town struck the tower of the Brattle Street Church, where it may still be seen. Sir William Howe made preparations to cross over in boats and drive the Americans from their batteries, but was prevented by a violent gale and storm. General Washington next erected a battery on Nook's Hill, so near the enemy that it was impossible for them to remain in Boston any longer."

"Hurrah! Hurrah!" cried Charley, clapping his hands triumphantly. "I wish I had been there to see how sheepish the Englishmen looked."

And as Grandfather thought that Boston had never witnessed a more interesting period than this, when the royal power was in its death agony, he determined to take a peep into the town and imagine the feelings of those who were quitting it forever.

CHAPTER IX.

"Alas for the poor tories!" said Grandfather. "Until the very last morning after Washington's troops had shown themselves on Nook's Hill, these unfortunate persons could not believe that the audacious rebels, as they called the Americans, would ever prevail against King George's army. But when they saw the British soldiers preparing to embark on board of the ships of war, then they knew that they had lost their country. Could the patriots have known how bitter were their regrets, they would have forgiven them all their evil deeds, and sent a blessing after them as they sailed away from their native shore."

In order to make the children sensible of the pitiable condition of these men, Grandfather singled out Peter Oliver, chief justice of Massachusetts under the crown, and imagined him walking through the streets of Boston on the morning before he left it forever.

This effort of Grandfather's fancy may be called

THE TORY'S FAREWELL.

Old Chief Justice Oliver threw on his red cloak, and placed his three-cornered hat on the top of his white wig. In this garb he intended to go forth and take a parting look at objects that had been familiar to him from his youth. Accordingly, he began his walk in the north part of the town, and soon came to Faneuil Hall. This edifice, the cradle of liberty, had been used by the British officers as a play-house.

"Would that I could see its walls crumble to dust!" thought the chief justice; and, in the bitterness of his heart, he shook his fist at the famous hall. "There began the mischief which now threatens to rend asunder the British empire. The seditious harangues of demagogues in Faneuil Hall have made rebels of a loyal people and deprived me of my country."

He then passed through a narrow avenue and found himself in King Street, almost on the very spot which, six years before, had been reddened by the blood of the Boston massacre. The chief justice stepped cautiously, and shuddered, as if he were afraid that, even now, the gore of his slaughtered countrymen might stain his feet.

Before him rose the Town House, on the front of which were still displayed the royal arms. Within that edifice he had dispensed justice to the people in the days when his name was never mentioned without honor. There, too, was the balcony whence the trumpet had been sounded and the proclamation read to an assembled multitude, whenever a new King of England ascended the throne.

"I remember — I remember," said Chief Justice Oliver to himself, "when his present most sacred majesty was proclaimed. Then how the people shouted! Each man would have poured out his life-blood to keep a hair of King George's head from harm. But now there is scarcely a tongue in all New England that does not imprecate curses on his name. It is ruin and disgrace to love him. Can it be possible that a few fleeting years have wrought such a change?"

It did not occur to the chief justice that nothing but the most grievous tyranny could so soon have changed the people's hearts. Hurrying from the spot, he entered Cornhill, as the lower part of Washington Street was then called. Opposite to the Town House was the waste foundation of the Old North Church. The sacrilegious hands of the British soldiers had torn it down, and kindled their barrack fires with the fragments.

Farther on he passed beneath the tower of the

Old South. The threshold of this sacred edifice was worn by the iron tramp of horses' feet ; for the interior had been used as a riding school and rendezvous for a regiment of dragoons. As the chief justice lingered an instant at the door a trumpet sounded within, and the regiment came clattering forth and galloped down the street. They were proceeding to the place of embarkation.

"Let them go!" thought the chief justice, with somewhat of an old Puritan feeling in his breast. "No good can come of men who desecrate the house of God."

He went on a few steps farther, and paused before the Province House. No range of brick stores had then sprung up to hide the mansion of the royal governors from public view. It had a spacious court yard, bordered with trees, and enclosed with a wrought-iron fence. On the cupola that surmounted the edifice was the gilded figure of an Indian chief, ready to let fly an arrow from his bow. Over the wide front door was a balcony, in which the chief justice had often stood when the governor and high officers of the province showed themselves to the people.

While Chief Justice Oliver gazed sadly at the Province House, before which a sentinel was pacing, the double leaves of the door were thrown open, and Sir William Howe made his appearance. Behind him came a throng of officers, whose steel scabbards clattered against the stones as they hastened down the court yard. Sir William Howe was a dark-complexioned man, stern and haughty in his deportment. He stepped as proudly, in that hour of defeat, as if he were going to receive the submission of the rebel general.

The chief justice bowed and accosted him.

" This is a grievous hour for both of us, Sir William," said he.

"Forward! gentlemen," said Sir William Howe to the officers who attended him; " we have no time to hear lamentations now."

And, coldly bowing, he departed. Thus the chief justice had a foretaste of the mortifications which the exiled New Englanders afterwards suffered from the haughty Britons. They were despised even by that country which they had served more faithfully than their own.

A still heavier trial awaited Chief Justice Oliver, as he passed onward from the Province House. He was recognized by the people in the street. They had long known him as the descendant of an ancient and honorable family. They had seen him sitting in his scarlet robes upon the judgment seat. All his life long, either for the sake of his ancestors or on account of his own dignified station and unspotted character, he had been held in high respect. The old gentry of the province were looked upon almost as noblemen while Massachusetts was under royal government.

But now all hereditary reverence for birth and rank was gone. The inhabitants shouted in derision when they saw the venerable form of the old chief justice. They laid the wrongs of the country and their own sufferings during the siege — their hunger, cold, and sickness — partly to his charge and to that of his brother Andrew and his kinsman Hutchinson. It was by their advice that the king had acted in all the colonial troubles. But the day of recompense was come.

" See the old tory ! " cried the people, with bitter laughter. " He is taking his last look at us. Let him show his white wig among us an hour hence, and we'll give him a coat of tar and feathers ! "

The chief justice, however, knew that he need fear no violence so long as the British troops were in possession of the town. But, alas ! it was a bitter thought that he should leave no loving memory behind him. His forefathers, long after their spirits left the earth, had been honored in the affectionate remembrance of the people. But he, who would henceforth be dead to his native land, would have no epitaph save scornful and vindictive words. The old man wept.

" They curse me — they invoke all kinds of evil

on my head!" thought he, in the midst of his tears. "But, if they could read my heart, they would know that I love New England well. Heaven bless her, and bring her again under the rule of our gracious king! A blessing, too, on these poor, misguided people!"

The chief justice flung out his hands with a gesture, as if he were bestowing a parting benediction on his countrymen. He had now reached the southern portion of the town, and was far within the range of cannon shot from the American batteries. Close beside him was the broad stump of a tree, which appeared to have been recently cut down. Being weary and heavy at heart, he was about to sit down upon the stump.

Suddenly it flashed upon his recollection that this was the stump of Liberty Tree! The British soldiers had cut it down, vainly boasting that they could as easily overthrow the liberties of America. Under its shadowy branches, ten years before, the brother of Chief Justice Oliver had been compelled to acknowledge the supremacy of the people by taking the oath which they prescribed. This tree was connected with all the events that had severed America from England.

"Accursed tree!" cried the chief justice, gnashing his teeth; for anger overcame his sorrow. "Would that thou hadst been left standing till

Hancock, Adams, and every other traitor were hanged upon thy branches! Then fitly mightest thou have been hewn down and cast into the flames."

He turned back, hurried to Long Wharf without looking behind him, embarked with the British troops for Halifax, and never saw his country more. Throughout the remainder of his days Chief Justice Oliver was agitated with those same conflicting emotions that had tortured him while taking his farewell walk through the streets of Boston. Deep love and fierce resentment burned in one flame within his breast. Anathemas struggled with benedictions. He felt as if one breath of his native air would renew his life, yet would have died rather than breathe the same air with rebels. And such likewise were the feelings of the other exiles, a thousand in number, who departed with the British army. Were they not the most unfortunate of men?

"The misfortunes of those exiled tories," observed Laurence, "must have made them think of the poor exiles of Acadia."

"They had a sad time of it, I suppose," said Charley. "But I choose to rejoice with the patriots, rather than be sorrowful with the tories. Grandfather, what did General Washington do now?"

"As the rear of the British army embarked from the wharf," replied Grandfather, "General Washington's troops marched over the Neck, through the fortification gates, and entered Boston in triumph. And now, for the first time since the Pilgrims landed, Massachusetts was free from the dominion of England. May she never again be subjected to foreign rule — never again feel the rod of oppression!"

"Dear Grandfather," asked little Alice, "did General Washington bring our chair back to Boston?"

"I know not how long the chair remained at Cambridge," said Grandfather. "Had it staid there till this time, it could not have found a better or more appropriate shelter. The mansion which General Washington occupied is still standing, and his apartments have since been tenanted by several eminent men. Governor Everett, while a professor in the university, resided there. So at an after period did Mr. Sparks, whose invaluable labors have connected his name with the immortality of Washington. And at this very time a venerable friend and contemporary of your Grandfather, after long pilgrimages beyond the sea, has set up his staff of rest at Washington's head quarters."

"You mean Professor Longfellow, Grandfather," said Laurence. "O, how I should love to see the author of those beautiful VOICES OF THE NIGHT!"

"We will visit him next summer," answered Grandfather, "and take Clara and little Alice with us — and Charley, too, if he will be quiet."

CHAPTER X.

When Grandfather resumed his narrative the next evening, he told the children that he had some difficulty in tracing the movements of the chair during a short period after General Washington's departure from Cambridge.

Within a few months, however, it made its appearance at a shop in Boston, before the door of which was seen a striped pole. In the interior was displayed a stuffed alligator, a rattlesnake's skin, a bundle of Indian arrows, an old-fashioned matchlock gun, a walking stick of Governor Winthrop's, a wig of old Cotton Mather's, and a colored print of the Boston massacre. In short, it was a barber's shop, kept by a Mr. Pierce, who prided himself on having shaved General Washington, Old Put, and many other famous persons.

"This was not a very dignified situation for our venerable chair," continued Grandfather; "but, you know, there is no better place for news than a barber's shop. All the events of the revolutionary war were heard of there sooner than any where else. People used to sit in the chair, reading the newspaper or talking, and waiting to be shaved, while Mr. Pierce, with his scissors and razor, was at work upon the heads or chins of his other customers."

"I am sorry the chair could not betake itself to some more suitable place of refuge," said Laurence. "It was old now, and must have longed for quiet. Besides, after it had held Washington in its arms, it ought not to have been compelled to receive all the world. It should have been put into the pulpit of the Old South Church, or some other consecrated place."

"Perhaps so," answered Grandfather. "But the chair, in the course of its varied existence, had grown so accustomed to general intercourse with society that I doubt whether it would have contented itself in the pulpit of the Old South. There it would have stood solitary, or with no livelier companion than the silent organ, in the opposite gallery, six days out of seven. I incline to think that it had seldom been situated more to its mind than on the sanded floor of the snug little barber's shop."

Then Grandfather amused his children and himself with fancying all the different sorts of people who had occupied our chair while they awaited the leisure of the barber.

There was the old clergyman, such as Dr. Chauncey, wearing a white wig, which the barber took from his head and placed upon a wig block. Half an hour, perhaps, was spent in combing and powdering this reverend appendage to a clerical skull. There, too, were officers of the continental army, who required their hair to be pomatumed and plastered, so as to give them a bold and martial aspect. There, once in a while, was seen the thin, careworn, melancholy visage of an old tory, with a wig that, in times long past, had perhaps figured at a Province House ball. And there, not unfrequently, sat the rough captain of a privateer, just returned from a successful cruise, in which he had captured half a dozen richly-laden vessels belonging to King George's subjects. And sometimes a rosy little schoolboy climbed into our chair, and sat staring, with wide-open eyes, at the alligator, the rattlesnake, and the other curiosities of the barber's shop. His mother had sent him, with sixpence in his hand, to get his glossy curls cropped off. The incidents of the revolution plentifully supplied the barber's customers with topics of conversation. They talked sorrowfully of the death of General Montgomery and the failure of our troops to take Quebec; for the New Englanders were now as anxious to get Canada from the English as they had formerly been to conquer it from the French.

"But very soon," said Grandfather, "came news from Philadelphia, the most important that America had ever heard of. On the 4th of July, 1776, Congress had signed the Declaration of Independence. The thirteen colonies were now free and independent states. Dark as our prospects were, the inhabitants welcomed these glorious tidings, and resolved to perish rather than again bear the yoke of England."

"And I would perish, too!" cried Charley.

"It was a great day — a glorious deed!" said Laurence, coloring high with enthusiasm. "And, Grandfather, I love to think that the sages in Congress showed themselves as bold and true as the soldiers in the field; for it must have required more courage to sign the Declaration of Independence than to fight the enemy in battle."

Grandfather acquiesced in Laurence's view of the matter. He then touched briefly and hastily upon the prominent events of the revolution. The thunder storm of war had now rolled southward, and did not again burst upon Massachusetts, where its first fury had been felt. But she contributed her full share to the success of the contest. Wherever a battle was fought, — whether at Long Island, White Plains, Trenton, Princeton, Brandywine, or Germantown, — some of her brave sons were found slain upon the field.

In October, 1777, General Burgoyne surrendered his army, at Saratoga, to the American general, Gates. The captured troops were sent to Massachusetts. Not long afterwards Doctor Franklin and other American commissioners made a treaty at Paris, by which France bound herself to assist our country-men. The gallant Lafayette was already fighting for our freedom by the side of Washington. In 1778 a French fleet, commanded by Count d'Estaing, spent a considerable time in Boston Harbor. It marks the vicissitudes of human affairs, that the French, our ancient enemies, should come hither as comrades and brethren, and that kindred England should be our foe.

"While the war was raging in the Middle and Southern States," proceeded Grandfather, "Massachusetts had leisure to settle a new constitution of government instead of the royal charter. This was done in 1780. In the same year John Hancock, who had been president of Congress, was chosen governor of the state. He was the first whom the people had elected since the days of old Simon Bradstreet."

" But, Grandfather, who had been governor since the British were driven away?" inquired Laurence. " General Gage and Sir William Howe were the last whom you have told us of."

"There had been no governor for the last four years," replied Grandfather. " Massachusetts had been ruled by the legislature, to whom the people paid obedience of their own accord. It is one of the most remarkable circumstances in our history, that, when the charter government was overthrown by the war, no anarchy nor the slightest confusion ensued. This was a great honor to the people. But now Hancock was proclaimed governor by sound of trumpet; and there was again a settled government."

Grandfather again adverted to the progress of the war. In 1781 General Greene drove the British from the Southern States. In October of the same year General Washington compelled Lord Cornwallis to surrender his army, at Yorktown, in Virginia. This was the last great event of the revolutionary contest. King George and his ministers perceived that all the might of England could not compel America to renew her allegiance to the crown. After a great deal of discussion, a treaty of peace was signed in September, 1783.

"Now, at last," said Grandfather, "after weary years of war, the regiments of Massachusetts returned in peace to their families. Now the stately and dignified leaders, such as General Lincoln and General Knox, with their powdered hair and their uniforms of blue and buff, were seen moving about the streets."

"And little boys ran after them, I suppose," remarked Charley; "and the grown people bowed respectfully."

"They deserved respect; for they were good men

as well as brave," answered Grandfather. " Now, too, the inferior officers and privates came home to seek some peaceful occupation. Their friends remembered them as slender and smooth cheeked young men; but they returned with the erect and rigid mien of disciplined soldiers. Some hobbled on crutches and wooden legs; others had received wounds, which were still rankling in their breasts. Many, alas! had fallen in battle, and perhaps were left unburied on the bloody field."

" The country must have been sick of war," observed Laurence.

" One would have thought so," said Grandfather. " Yet only two or three years elapsed before the folly of some misguided men caused another mustering of soldiers. This affair was called Shays's war, because a Captain Shays was the chief leader of the insurgents."

" O Grandfather, don't let there be another war !" cried little Alice, piteously.

Grandfather comforted his dear little girl by assuring her that there was no great mischief done. Shays's war happened in the latter part of 1786 and the beginning of the following year. Its principal cause was the badness of the times. The State of Massachusetts, in its public capacity, was very much in debt. So likewise were many of the people. An insurrection took place, the object of which seems to have been, to interrupt the course of law and get rid of debts and taxes.

James Bowdoin, a good and able man, was now governor of Massachusetts. He sent General Lincoln, at the head of four thousand men, to put down the insurrection. This general, who had fought through several hard campaigns in the revolution, managed matters like an old soldier, and totally defeated the rebels at the expense of very little blood.

"There is but one more public event to be recorded in the history of our chair," proceeded Grandfather. "In the year 1794 Samuel Adams was elected governor of Massachusetts. I have told you what a distinguished patriot he was, and how much he resembled the stern old Puritans. Could the ancient freemen of Massachusetts who lived in the days of the first charter have arisen from their graves, they would probably have voted for Samuel Adams to be governor."

"Well, Grandfather, I hope he sat in our chair," said Clara.

"He did," replied Grandfather. "He had long been in the habit of visiting the barber's shop, where our venerable chair, philosophically forgetful of its former dignities, had now spent nearly eighteen not uncomfortable years. Such a remarkable piece of furniture, so evidently a relic of long-departed times, could not escape the notice of Samuel Adams. He made minute researches into its history, and ascertained what a succession of excellent and famous people had occupied it."

"How did he find it out?" asked Charley; "for I suppose the chair could not tell its own history."

"There used to be a vast collection of ancient letters and other documents in the tower of the Old South Church," answered Grandfather. "Perhaps the history of our chair was contained among these. At all events, Samuel Adams appears to have been well acquainted with it. When he became governor, he felt that he could have no more honorable seat than that which had been the ancient chair of state. He therefore purchased it for a trifle, and filled it worthily for three years as governor of Massachusetts."

"And what next?" asked Charley.

"That is all," said Grandfather, heaving a sigh; for he could not help being a little sad at the thought that his stories must close here. "Samuel Adams died in 1803, at the age of above threescore and ten. He was a great patriot, but a poor man. At his death he left scarcely property enough to pay the expenses of his funeral. This precious chair, among his other effects, was sold at auction; and your Grandfather, who was then in the strength of his years, became the purchaser."

Laurence, with a mind full of thoughts that

struggled for expression but could find none, looked steadfastly at the chair.

He had now learned all its history, yet was not satisfied.

"O, how I wish that the chair could speak!" cried he. "After its long intercourse with mankind, — after looking upon the world for ages, — what lessons of golden wisdom it might utter! It might teach a private person how to lead a good and happy life, or a statesman how to make his country prosperous."

CHAPTER XI.

Grandfather was struck by Laurence's idea that the historic chair should utter a voice, and thus pour forth the collected wisdom of two centuries. The old gentleman had once possessed no inconsiderable share of fancy; and even now its fading sunshine occasionally glimmered among his more sombre reflections.

As the history of his chair had exhausted all his facts, Grandfather determined to have recourse to fable. So, after warning the children that they must not mistake this story for a true one, he related what we shall call

GRANDFATHER'S DREAM.

Laurence and Clara, where were you last night? Where were you, Charley, and dear little Alice? You had all gone to rest, and left old Grandfather to meditate alone in his great chair. The lamp had grown so dim that its light hardly illuminated the alabaster shade. The wood fire had crumbled into heavy embers, among which the little flames danced, and quivered, and sported about like fairies.

And here sat Grandfather all by himself. He knew that it was bedtime; yet he could not help longing to hear your merry voices, or to hold a comfortable chat with some old friend; because then his pillow would be visited by pleasant dreams. But, as neither children nor friends were at hand, Grandfather leaned back in the great chair and closed his eyes, for the sake of meditating more profoundly.

And, when Grandfather's meditations had grown very profound indeed, he fancied that he heard a sound over his head, as if somebody were preparing to speak.

"Hem!" it said, in a dry, husky tone. "H-e-m! Hem!"

As Grandfather did not know that any person was in the room he started up in great surprise, and peeped hither and thither, behind the chair, and into the recess by the fireside, and at the dark nook yonder near the bookcase. Nobody could he see.

"Poh!" said Grandfather to himself, "I must have been dreaming."

But, just as he was going to resume his seat, Grandfather happened to look at the great chair. The rays of firelight were flickering upon it in such a manner that it really seemed as if its oaken frame were all alive. What! did it not move its elbow? There, too! It certainly lifted one of its ponderous fore legs, as if it had a notion of drawing itself a little nearer to the fire. Meanwhile the lion's head nodded at Grandfather with as polite and sociable a look as a lion's visage, carved in oak, could possibly be expected to assume. Well, this is strange!

"Good evening, my old friend," said the dry and husky voice, now a little clearer than before. "We have been intimately acquainted so long that I think it high time we have a chat together."

Grandfather was looking straight at the lion's head, and could not be mistaken in supposing that it moved its lips. So here the mystery was all explained.

"I was not aware," said Grandfather, with a civil salutation to his oaken companion, "that you possessed the faculty of speech. Otherwise I should often have been glad to converse with such a solid, useful, and substantial if not brilliant member of society."

"O!" replied the ancient chair, in a quiet and easy tone; for it had now cleared its throat of the dust of ages. "I am naturally a silent and incommunicative sort of character. One or twice in the course of a century I unclose my lips. When the gentle Lady Arbella departed this life I uttered a groan. When the honest mintmaster weighed his plump daughter against the pine tree shillings I chuckled audibly at the joke. When old Simon Bradstreet took the place of the tyrant Andros I joined in the general huzza, and capered on my wooden legs for joy. To be sure, the bystanders were so fully occupied with their own feelings that my sympathy was quite unnoticed."

"And have you often held a private chat with your friends?" asked Grandfather.

"Not often," answered the chair. "I once talked with Sir William Phipps, and communicated my ideas about the witchcraft delusion. Cotton Mather had several conversations with me, and derived great benefit from my historical reminiscences. In the days of the stamp act I whispered in the ear of Hutchinson, bidding him to remember what stock his countrymen were descended of, and to think whether the spirit of their forefathers had utterly departed from them. The last man whom I favored with a colloquy was that stout old republican, Samuel Adams."

"And how happens it," inquired Grandfather, "that there is no record nor tradition of your conversational abilities? It is an uncommon thing to meet with a chair that can talk."

"Why, to tell you the truth," said the chair, giving itself a hitch nearer to the hearth, "I am not apt to choose the most suitable moments for unclosing my lips. Sometimes I have inconsiderately begun to speak, when my occupant, lolling back in my arms, was inclined to take an after-dinner nap. Or perhaps the impulse to talk may be felt at midnight, when the lamp burns dim and the fire crumbles into decay, and the studious or thoughtful man finds that his brain is in a mist. Oftenest I have unwisely uttered my wisdom in the ears of sick persons, when the inquietude of fever made them toss about upon my cushion. And so it happens, that though my words make a pretty strong impression at the moment, yet my auditors invariably remember them only as a dream. I should not wonder if you, my excellent friend, were to do the same to-morrow morning."

"Nor I either," thought Grandfather to himself.

However, he thanked this respectable old chair for beginning the conversation, and begged to know whether it had any thing particular to communicate.

"I have been listening attentively to your narrative of my adventures," replied the chair; "and it must be owned that your correctness entitles you to be held up as a pattern to biographers. Nevertheless, there are a few omissions which I should be glad to see supplied. For instance, you make no mention of the good knight Sir Richard Saltonstall, nor of the famous Hugh Peters, nor of those old regicide judges, Whalley, Goffe, and Dixwell. Yet

I have borne the weight of all those distinguished characters at one time or another."

Grandfather promised amendment if ever he should have an opportunity to repeat his narrative. The good old chair, which still seemed to retain a due regard for outward appearance, then reminded him how long a time had passed since it had been provided with a new cushion. It likewise expressed the opinion that the oaken figures on its back would show to much better advantage by the aid of a little varnish.

" And I have had a complaint in this joint," continued the chair, endeavoring to lift one of its legs, " ever since Charley trundled his wheelbarrow against me."

" It shall be attended to," said Grandfather. " And now, venerable chair, I have a favor to solicit. During an existence of more than two centuries you have had a familiar intercourse with men who were esteemed the wisest of their day. Doubtless, with your capacious understanding, you have treasured up many an invaluable lesson of wisdom. You certainly have had time enough to guess the riddle of life. Tell us poor mortals, then, how we may be happy."

The lion's head fixed its eyes thoughtfully upon the fire, and the whole chair assumed an aspect of deep meditation. Finally it beckoned to Grandfather with its elbow, and made a step sideways towards him, as if it had a very important secret to communicate.

" As long as I have stood in the midst of human affairs," said the chair, with a very oracular enunciation, "I have constantly observed that JUSTICE, TRUTH, and LOVE are the chief ingredients of every happy life."

" Justice, Truth, and Love!" exclaimed Grandfather. " We need not exist two centuries to find out that these qualities are essential to our happiness. This is no secret. Every human being is born with the instinctive knowledge of it."

" Ah !" cried the chair, drawing back in surprise. " From what I have observed of the dealings of man with man, and nation with nation, I never should have suspected that they knew this all-important secret. And, with this eternal lesson written in your soul, do you ask me to sift new wisdom for you out of my petty existence of two or three centuries ? "

" But, my dear chair ——— " said Grandfather.

" Not a word more," interrupted the chair ; " here I close my lips for the next hundred years. At the end of that period, if I shall have discovered any new precepts of happiness better than what Heaven has already taught you, they shall assuredly be given to the world."

In the energy of its utterance the oaken chair

seemed to stamp its foot, and trod (we hope unintentionally) upon Grandfather's toe. The old gentleman started, and found that he had been asleep in the great chair, and that his heavy walking stick had fallen down across his foot.

"Grandfather," cried little Alice, clapping her hands, "you must dream a new dream every night about our chair!"

Laurence, and Clara, and Charley said the same. But the good old gentleman shook his head, and declared that here ended the history, real or fabulous, of GRANDFATHER'S CHAIR.

BIOGRAPHICAL STORIES.

<table>
<tr><td>BENJAMIN WEST,
SIR ISAAC NEWTON,
SAMUEL JOHNSON,</td><td>OLIVER CROMWELL,
BENJAMIN FRANKLIN,
QUEEN CHRISTINA.</td></tr>
</table>

This small volume and others of a similar character, from the same hand, have not been composed without a deep sense of responsibility. The author regards children as sacred, and would not, for the world, cast any thing into the fountain of a young heart that might imbitter and pollute its waters. And, even in point of the reputation to be aimed at, juvenile literature is as well worth cultivating as any other. The writer, if he succeed in pleasing his little readers, may hope to be remembered by them till their own old age — a far longer period of literary existence than is generally attained by those who seek immortality from the judgments of full-grown men.

BIOGRAPHICAL STORIES.

CHAPTER I.

WHEN Edward Temple was about eight or nine years old he was afflicted with a disorder of the eyes. It was so severe, and his sight was naturally so delicate, that the surgeon felt some apprehensions lest the boy should become totally blind. He therefore gave strict directions to keep him in a darkened chamber, with a bandage over his eyes. Not a ray of the blessed light of heaven could be suffered to visit the poor lad.

This was a sad thing for Edward. It was just the same as if there were to be no more sunshine, nor moonlight, nor glow of the cheerful fire, nor light of lamps. A night had begun which was to continue perhaps for months — a longer and drearier night than that which voyagers are compelled to endure when their ship is icebound, throughout the winter, in the Arctic Ocean. His dear father and mother, his brother George, and the sweet face of little Emily Robinson must all vanish and leave him in utter darkness and solitude. Their voices and footsteps, it is true, would be heard around him; he would feel his mother's embrace and the kind pressure of all their hands; but still it would seem as if they were a thousand miles away.

And then his studies, — they were to be entirely given up. This was another grievous trial; for Edward's memory hardly went back to the period when he had not known how to read. Many and many a holiday had he spent at his book, poring over its pages until the deepening twilight confused the print and made all the letters run into long words. Then would he press his hands across his eyes and wonder why they pained him so; and when the candles were lighted, what was the reason that they burned so dimly, like the moon in a foggy night? Poor little fellow! So far as his eyes were concerned he was already an old man, and needed a pair of spectacles almost as much as his own grandfather did.

And now, alas! the time was come when even grandfather's spectacles could not have assisted Edward to read. After a few bitter tears, which only pained his eyes the more, the poor boy submitted to the surgeon's orders. His eyes were bandaged, and, with his mother on one side and his little friend

Emily on the other, he was led into a darkened chamber.

"Mother, I shall be very miserable!" said Edward, sobbing.

"O, no, my dear child!" replied his mother, cheerfully. "Your eyesight was a precious gift of Heaven, it is true; but you would do wrong to be miserable for its loss, even if there were no hope of regaining it. There are other enjoyments besides what come to us through our eyes."

"None that are worth having," said Edward.

"Ah, but you will not think so long," rejoined Mrs. Temple, with tenderness. "All of us — your father, and myself, and George, and our sweet Emily — will try to find occupation and amusement for you. We will use all our eyes to make you happy. Will they not be better than a single pair?"

"I will sit by you all day long," said Emily, in her low, sweet voice, putting her hand into that of Edward.

"And so will I, Ned," said George, his elder brother, "school time and all, if my father will permit me."

Edward's brother George was three or four years older than himself — a fine, hardy lad, of a bold and ardent temper. He was the leader of his comrades in all their enterprises and amusements. As to his proficiency at study there was not much to be said. He had sense and ability enough to have made himself a scholar, but found so many pleasanter things to do that he seldom took hold of a book with his whole heart. So fond was George of boisterous sports and exercises that it was really a great token of affection and sympathy when he offered to sit all day long in a dark chamber with his poor brother Edward.

As for little Emily Robinson, she was the daughter of one of Mr. Temple's dearest friends. Ever since her mother went to heaven (which was soon after Emily's birth) the little girl had dwelt in the household where we now find her. Mr. and Mrs. Temple seemed to love her as well as their own children; for they had no daughter except Emily; nor would the boys have known the blessing of a sister had not this gentle stranger come to teach them what it was. If I could show you Emily's face, with her dark hair smoothed away from her forehead, you would be pleased with her look of simplicity and loving kindness, but might think that she was somewhat too grave for a child of seven years old. But you would not love her the less for that.

So brother George and this loving little girl were to be Edward's companions and playmates while he should be kept prisoner in the dark chamber. When the first bitterness of his grief was over he began to feel that there might be some comforts and enjoyments in life even for a boy whose eyes were covered with a bandage.

"I thank you, dear mother," said he, with only a few sobs; "and you, Emily; and you too, George. You will all be very kind to me, I know. And my father, — will not he come and see me every day?"

"Yes, my dear boy," said Mr. Temple; for, though invisible to Edward, he was standing close beside him. "I will spend some hours of every day with you. And as I have often amused you by relating stories and adventures while you had the use of your eyes, I can do the same now that you are unable to read. Will this please you, Edward?"

"O, very much," replied Edward.

"Well, then," said his father, "this evening we will begin the series of Biographical Stories which I promised you some time ago."

CHAPTER II.

WHEN evening came. Mr. Temple found Edward
considerably revived in spirits and disposed to be
resigned to his misfortune. Indeed, the figure of the
boy, as it was dimly seen by the firelight, reclining
in a well-stuffed easy chair, looked so very comforta-
ble that many people might have envied him. When
a man's eyes have grown old with gazing at the ways
of the world, it does not seem such a terrible misfor-
tune to have them bandaged.

Little Emily Robinson sat by Edward's side with
the air of an accomplished nurse. As well as the
duskiness of the chamber would permit she watched
all his motions and each varying expression of his
face, and tried to anticipate her patient's wishes be-
fore his tongue could utter them. Yet it was notice-
able that the child manifested an indescribable awe
and disquietude whenever she fixed her eyes on the
bandage; for, to her simple and affectionate heart, it
seemed as if her dear friend Edward was separated
from her because she could not see his eyes. A

friend's eyes tell us many things which could never be spoken by the tongue.

George, likewise, looked awkward and confused, as stout and healthy boys are accustomed to do in the society of the sick or afflicted. Never having felt pain or sorrow, they are abashed, from not knowing how to sympathize with the sufferings of others.

" Well, my dear Edward," inquired Mrs. Temple, " is your chair quite comfortable? and has your little nurse provided for all your wants? If so, your father is ready to begin his stories."

" O, I am very well now," answered Edward, with a faint smile. " And my ears have not forsaken me, though my eyes are good for nothing. So pray, dear father, begin."

It was Mr. Temple's design to tell the children a series of true stories, the incidents of which should be taken from the childhood and early life of eminent people. Thus he hoped to bring George, and Edward, and Emily into closer acquaintance with the famous persons who have lived in other times by showing that they also had been children once. Although Mr. Temple was scrupulous to relate nothing but what was founded on fact, yet he felt himself at liberty to clothe the incidents of his narrative in a new coloring, so that his auditors might understand them the better.

" My first story," said he, " shall be about a painter of pictures.

"Dear me!" cried Edward, with a sigh. "I am afraid I shall never look at pictures any more."

"We will hope for the best," answered his father. "In the mean time, you must try to see things within your own mind."

Mr. Temple then began the following story:—

BENJAMIN WEST.

Born 1738. Died 1820.

In the year 1738 there came into the world, in the town of Springfield, Pennsylvania, a Quaker infant, from whom his parents and neighbors looked for wonderful things. A famous preacher of the Society of Friends had prophesied about little Ben, and foretold that he would be one of the most remarkable characters that had appeared on the earth since the days of William Penn. On this account the eyes of many people were fixed upon the boy. Some of his ancestors had won great renown in the old wars of England and France; but it was probably expected that Ben would become a preacher, and would convert multitudes to the peaceful doctrines of the Quakers. Friend West and his wife were thought to be very fortunate in having such a son.

Little Ben lived to the ripe age of six years without doing any thing that was worthy to be told in history. But one summer afternoon, in his seventh year, his mother put a fan into his hand and bade him keep the flies away from the face of a little babe who lay fast asleep in the cradle. She then left the room.

The boy waved the fan to and fro and drove away the buzzing flies whenever they had the impertinence to come near the baby's face. When they had all flown out of the window or into distant parts of the room, he bent over the cradle and delighted himself with gazing at the sleeping infant. It was, indeed, a very pretty sight. The little personage in the cradle slumbered peacefully, with its waxen hands under its chin, looking as full of blissful quiet as if angels were singing lullabies in its ear. Indeed, it must have been dreaming about heaven; for, while Ben stooped over the cradle, the little baby smiled.

"How beautiful she looks!" said Ben to himself. "What a pity it is that such a pretty smile should not last forever!"

Now Ben, at this period of his life, had never heard of that wonderful art by which a look, that appears and vanishes in a moment, may be made to last for hundreds of years. But, though nobody had told him of such an art, he may be said to have invented it for himself. On a table near at hand there were pens and paper, and ink of two colors, black and red. The boy seized a pen and sheet of paper, and, kneeling down beside the cradle, began to draw a likeness of the infant.   While he was busied in this manner he heard his mother's step approaching, and hastily tried to conceal the paper.

"Benjamin, my son, what hast thou been doing?" inquired his mother, observing marks of confusion in his face.

At first Ben was unwilling to tell; for he felt as if there might be something wrong in stealing the baby's face and putting it upon a sheet of paper. However, as his mother insisted, he finally put the sketch into her hand, and then hung his head, expecting to be well scolded.   But when the good lady saw what was on the paper, in lines of red and black ink, she uttered a scream of surprise and joy.

"Bless me!" cried she.   "It is a picture of little Sally!"

And then she threw her arms round our friend Benjamin, and kissed him so tenderly that he never afterwards was afraid to show his performances to his mother.

As Ben grew older, he was observed to take vast delight in looking at the hues and forms of Nature. For instance, he was greatly pleased with the blue violets of spring, the wild roses of summer, and the scarlet cardinal flowers of early autumn.   In the decline of the year, when the woods were variegated with all the colors of the rainbow, Ben seemed to desire nothing better than to gaze at them from morn

till night. The purple and golden clouds of sunset
were a joy to him.   And he was continually endeav-
oring to draw the figures of trees, men, mountains,
houses, cattle, geese, ducks, and turkeys, with a
piece of chalk, on barn doors or on the floor.

In these old times the Mohawk Indians were still
numerous in Pennsylvania. Every year a party of
them used to pay a visit to Springfield, because the
wigwams of their ancestors had formerly stood there.
These wild men grew fond of little Ben, and made
him very happy by giving him some of the red
and yellow paint with which they were accustomed
to adorn their faces. His mother, too, presented him
with a piece of indigo. Thus he now had three col-
ors, — red, blue, and yellow, — and could manufac-
ture green by mixing the yellow with the blue. Our
friend Ben was overjoyed, and doubtless showed his
gratitude to the Indians by taking their likenesses in
the strange dresses which they wore, with feathers,
tomahawks, and bows and arrows.

But all this time the young artist had no paint
brushes ; nor were there any to be bought, unless he
had sent to Philadelphia on purpose. However, he
was a very ingenious boy, and resolved to manufac-
ture paint brushes for himself. With this design he
laid hold upon — what do you think ? Why, upon a
respectable old black cat, who was sleeping quietly
by the fireside.

" Puss," said little Ben to the cat, " pray give me some of the fur from the tip of thy tail ? "

Though he addressed the black cat so civilly, yet Ben was determined to have the fur, whether she were willing or not.   Puss, who had no great zeal for the fine arts, would have resisted if she could ; but the boy was armed with his mother's scissors, and very dexterously clipped off fur enough to make a paint brush.   This was of so much use to him that he applied to Madame Puss again and again, until her warm coat of fur had become so thin and ragged that she could hardly keep comfortable through the winter.   Poor thing ! she was forced to creep close into the chimney corner, and eyed Ben with a very rueful physiognomy.   But Ben considered it more necessary that he should have paint brushes than that puss should be warm.

About this period friend West received a visit from Mr. Pennington, a merchant of Philadelphia, who was likewise a member of the Society of Friends.   The visitor, on entering the parlor, was surprised to see it ornamented with drawings of Indian chiefs, and of birds with beautiful plumage, and of the wild flowers of the forest.   Nothing of the kind was ever seen before in the habitation of a Quaker farmer.

" Why, friend West," exclaimed the Philadelphia merchant, " what has possessed thee to cover thy walls with all these pictures ?   Where on earth didst thou get them ? "

Then friend West explained that all these pictures were painted by little Ben, with no better materials than red and yellow ochre and a piece of indigo, and with brushes made of the black cat's fur.

"Verily," said Mr. Pennington, "the boy hath a wonderful faculty. Some of our friends might look upon these matters as vanity; but little Benjamin appears to have been born a painter; and Providence is wiser than we are."

The good merchant patted Benjamin on the head, and evidently considered him a wonderful boy. When his parents saw how much their son's performances were admired, they, no doubt, remembered the prophecy of the old Quaker preacher respecting Ben's future eminence. Yet they could not understand how he was ever to become a very great and useful man merely by making pictures.

One evening, shortly after Mr. Pennington's return to Philadelphia, a package arrived at Springfield, directed to our little friend Ben.

"What can it possibly be?" thought Ben, when it was put into his hands. "Who can have sent me such a great square package as this?"

On taking off the thick brown paper which enveloped it, behold! there was a paint box, with a great many cakes of paint and brushes of various sizes. It was the gift of good Mr. Pennington. There were likewise several squares of canvas such as artists use for painting pictures upon, and, in addition to all these treasures, some beautiful engravings of landscapes. These were the first pictures that Ben had ever seen except those of his own drawing.

What a joyful evening was this for the little artist! At bedtime he put the paint box under his pillow, and got hardly a wink of sleep; for, all night long, his fancy was painting pictures in the darkness. In the morning he hurried to the garret, and was seen no more till the dinner hour; nor did he give himself time to eat more than a mouthful or two of food before he hurried back to the garret again. The next day, and the next, he was just as busy as ever; until at last his mother thought it time to ascertain what he was about. She accordingly followed him to the garret.

On opening the door, the first object that presented itself to her eyes was our friend Benjamin, giving the last touches to a beautiful picture. He had copied portions of two of the engravings, and made one picture out of both, with such admirable skill that it was far more beautiful than the originals. The grass, the trees, the water, the sky, and the houses were all painted in their proper colors. There, too, were the sunshine and the shadow, looking as natural as life.

"My dear child, thou hast done wonders!" cried his mother.

The good lady was in an ecstasy of delight. And

well might she be proud of her boy; for there were touches in this picture which old artists, who had spent a lifetime in the business, need not have been ashamed of. Many a year afterwards, this wonderful production was exhibited at the Royal Academy in London.

When Benjamin was quite a large lad he was sent to school at Philadelphia. Not long after his arrival he had a slight attack of fever, which confined him to his bed. The light, which would otherwise have disturbed him, was excluded from his chamber by means of closed wooden shutters. At first it appeared so totally dark that Ben could not distinguish any object in the room. By degrees, however, his eyes became accustomed to the scanty light.

He was lying on his back, looking up towards the ceiling, when suddenly he beheld the dim apparition of a white cow moving slowly over his head! Ben started, and rubbed his eyes in the greatest amazement.

"What can this mean?" thought he.

The white cow disappeared; and next came several pigs, which trotted along the ceiling and vanished into the darkness of the chamber. So lifelike did these grunters look that Ben almost seemed to hear them squeak.

"Well, this is very strange!" said Ben to himself.

When the people of the house came to see him, Benjamin told them of the marvellous circumstance which had occurred. But they would not believe him.

" Benjamin, thou art surely out of thy senses ! " cried they. " How is it possible that a white cow and a litter of pigs should be visible on the ceiling of a dark chamber ? "

Ben, however, had great confidence in his own eyesight, and was determined to search the mystery to the bottom. For this purpose, when he was again left alone, he got out of bed and examined the window shutters. He soon perceived a small chink in one of them, through which a ray of light found its passage and rested upon the ceiling. Now, the science of optics will inform us that the pictures of the white cow and the pigs, and of other objects out of doors, came into the dark chamber through this narrow chink, and were painted over Benjamin's head. It is greatly to his credit that he discovered the scientific principle of this phenomenon, and by means of it constructed a camera obscura, or magic lantern, out of a hollow box. This was of great advantage to him in drawing landscapes.

Well, time went on, and Benjamin continued to draw and paint pictures until he had now reached the age when it was proper that he should choose a business for life. His father and mother were in considerable perplexity about him. According to the ideas of the Quakers, it is not right for people to spend their lives in occupations that are of no real and sensible advantage to the world. Now, what advantage could the world expect from Benjamin's pictures? This was a difficult question; and, in order to set their minds at rest, his parents determined to consult the preachers and wise men of their society. Accordingly, they all assembled in the meeting house, and discussed the matter from beginning to end.

Finally they came to a very wise decision. It seemed so evident that Providence had created Benjamin to be a painter, and had given him abilities which would be thrown away in any other business, that the Quakers resolved not to oppose his inclination. They even acknowledged that the sight of a beautiful picture might convey instruction ·to the mind and might benefit the heart as much as a good book or a wise discourse. They therefore committed the youth to the direction of God, being well assured that he best knew what was his proper sphere of usefulness. The old men laid their hands upon Benjamin's head and gave him their blessing, and the women kissed him affectionately. All consented that he should go forth into the world and learn to be a painter by studying the best pictures of ancient and modern times.

So our friend Benjamin left the dwelling of his parents, and his native woods and streams, and the good Quakers of Springfield, and the Indians who had given him his first colors; he left all the places and persons whom he had hitherto known, and returned to them no more. He went first to Philadelphia, and afterwards to Europe. Here he was noticed by many great people, but retained all the sobriety and simplicity which he had learned among the Quakers. It is related of him, that, when he was presented at the court of the Prince of Parma, he kept his hat upon his head even while kissing the Prince's hand.

When he was twenty-five years old he went to London and established himself there as an artist. In due course of time he acquired great fame by his pictures, and was made chief painter to King George III. and president of the Royal Academy of Arts. When the Quakers of Pennsylvania heard of his success, they felt that the prophecy of the old preacher as to little Ben's future eminence was now accomplished. It is true, they shook their heads at his pictures of battle and bloodshed, such as the Death of Wolfe, thinking that these terrible scenes should not be held up to the admiration of the world.

But they approved of the great paintings in which he represented the miracles and sufferings of the Redeemer of mankind. King George employed him to adorn a large and beautiful chapel at Windsor Castle with pictures of these sacred subjects. He likewise painted a magnificent picture of Christ Healing the Sick, which he gave to the hospital at Philadelphia. It was exhibited to the public, and produced so much profit that the hospital was enlarged so as to accommodate thirty more patients. If Benjamin West had done no other good deed than this, yet it would have been enough to entitle him to an honorable remembrance forever. At this very day there are thirty poor people in the hospital who owe all their comforts to that same picture.

We shall mention only a single incident more. The picture of Christ Healing the Sick was exhibited at the Royal Academy in London, where it covered a vast space and displayed a multitude of figures as large as life. On the wall, close beside this admirable picture, hung a small and faded landscape. It was the same that little Ben had painted in his father's garret, after receiving the paint box and engravings from good Mr. Pennington.

He lived many years in peace and honor, and died in 1820, at the age of eighty-two. The story of his life is almost as wonderful as a fairy tale; for there are few stranger transformations than that of a little unknown Quaker boy, in the wilds of America, into the most distinguished English painter of his day. Let us each make the best use of our natural abilities as Benjamin West did; and, with the blessing of Providence, we shall arrive at some good end. As for fame, it is but little matter whether we acquire it or not.

"Thank you for the story, my dear father," said Edward, when it was finished. "Do you know that it seems as if I could see things without the help of my eyes? While you were speaking I have seen little Ben, and the baby in its cradle, and the Indians, and the white cow, and the pigs, and kind Mr. Pennington, and all the good old Quakers, almost as plainly as if they were in this very room."

"It is because your attention was not disturbed by outward objects," replied Mr. Temple. "People, when deprived of sight, often have more vivid ideas than those who possess the perfect use of their eyes. I will venture to say that George has not attended to the story quite so closely."

"No, indeed," said George; "but it was a very pretty story for all that. How I should have laughed to see Ben making a paint brush out of the black cat's tail! I intend to try the experiment with Emily's kitten."

"O, no, no, George!" cried Emily, earnestly. "My kitten cannot spare her tail."

Edward being an invalid, it was now time for him to retire to bed. When the family bade him good night he turned his face towards them, looking very loath to part.

"I shall not know when morning comes," said he, sorrowfully. "And besides, I want to hear your voices all the time; for, when nobody is speaking, it seems as if I were alone in a dark world."

"You must have faith, my dear child," replied his mother. "Faith is the soul's eyesight; and when we possess it the world is never dark nor lonely."

CHAPTER III.

The next day Edward began to get accustomed to his new condition of life. Once, indeed, when his parents were out of the way and only Emily was left to take care of him, he could not resist the temptation to thrust aside the bandage and peep at the anxious face of his little nurse. But, in spite of the dimness of the chamber, the experiment caused him so much pain that he felt no inclination to take another look. So, with a deep sigh, he resigned himself to his fate.

"Emily, pray talk to me!" said he, somewhat impatiently.

Now, Emily was a remarkably silent little girl, and did not possess that liveliness of disposition which renders some children such excellent companions. She seldom laughed, and had not the faculty of making many words about small matters. But the love and earnestness of her heart taught her how to amuse poor Edward in his darkness. She put her knitting work into his hands.

" You must learn how to knit," said she.

" What! without using my eyes?" cried Edward.

" I can knit with my eyes shut," replied Emily.

Then with her own little hands she guided Edward's fingers while he set about this new occupation. So awkward were his first attempts that any other little girl would have laughed heartily. But Emily preserved her gravity, and showed the utmost patience in taking up the innumerable stitches which he let down. In the course of an hour or two his progress was quite encouraging.

When evening came, Edward acknowledged that the day had been far less wearisome than he anticipated. But he was glad, nevertheless, when his father and mother, and George and Emily, all took their seats around his chair. He put out his hand to grasp each of their hands, and smiled with a very bright expression upon his lips.

" Now I can see you all with my mind's eye," said he. " And now, father, pray tell us another story."

So Mr Temple began.

SIR ISAAC NEWTON.

Born 1642. Died 1727.

On Christmas day, in the year 1642, Isaac Newton was born at the small village of Woolsthorpe, in

England. Little did his mother think, when she beheld her new-born babe, that he was destined to explain many matters which had been a mystery ever since the creation of the world.

Isaac's father being dead, Mrs. Newton was married again to a clergyman, and went to reside at North Witham. Her son was left to the care of his good old grandmother, who was very kind to him and sent him to school. In his early years Isaac did not appear to be a very bright scholar, but was chiefly remarkable for his ingenuity in all mechanical occupations. He had a set of little tools and saws of various sizes manufactured by himself. With the aid of these Isaac contrived to make many curious articles, at which he worked with so much skill that he seemed to have been born with a saw or chisel in hand.

The neighbors looked with vast admiration at the things which Isaac manufactured. And his old grandmother, I suppose, was never weary of talking about him.

"He'll make a capital workman one of these days," she would probably say. "No fear but what Isaac will do well in the world and be a rich man before he dies."

It is amusing to conjecture what were the anticipations of his grandmother and the neighbors about Isaac's future life. Some of them, perhaps, fancied that he would make beautiful furniture of mahogany, rosewood, or polished oak, inlaid with ivory and ebony and magnificently gilded. And then, doubtless, all the rich people would purchase these fine things to adorn their drawing rooms. Others probably thought that little Isaac was destined to be an architect, and would build splendid mansions for the nobility and gentry, and churches too, with the tallest steeples that had ever been seen in England.

Some of his friends, no doubt, advised Isaac's grandmother to apprentice him to a clockmaker ; for, besides his mechanical skill, the boy seemed to have a taste for mathematics, which would be very useful to him in that profession. And then, in due time, Isaac would set up for himself, and would manufacture curious clocks, like those that contain sets of dancing figures, which issue from the dialplate when the hour is struck ; or like those where a ship sails across the face of the clock, and is seen tossing up and down on the waves as often as the pendulum vibrates.

Indeed, there was some ground for supposing that Isaac would devote himself to the manufacture of clocks ; since he had already made one, of a kind which nobody had ever heard of before. It was set a-going, not by wheels and weights like other clocks, but by the dropping of water. This was an object of great wonderment to all the people round about ;

and it must be confessed that there are few boys, or men either, who could contrive to tell what a clock it is by means of a bowl of water.

Besides the water clock, Isaac made a sundial. Thus his grandmother was never at a loss to know the hour; for the water clock would tell it in the shade, and the dial in the sunshine. The sundial is said to be still in existence at Woolsthorpe, on the corner of the house where Isaac dwelt. If so, it must have marked the passage of every sunny hour that has elapsed since Isaac Newton was a boy. It marked all the famous moments of his life; it marked the hour of his death; and still the sunshine creeps slowly over it, as regularly as when Isaac first set it up.

Yet we must not say that the sundial has lasted longer than its maker; for Isaac Newton will exist long after the dial — yea, and long after the sun itself — shall have crumbled to decay.

Isaac possessed a wonderful faculty of acquiring knowledge by the simplest means. For instance, what method do you suppose he took to find out the strength of the wind? You will never guess how the boy could compel that unseen, inconstant, and ungovernable wonder, the wind, to tell him the measure of his strength. Yet nothing can be more simple. He jumped against the wind; and by the length of his jump he could calculate the force of a gentle breeze, a brisk gale, or a tempest. Thus, even in his boyish sports, he was continually searching out the secrets of philosophy.

Not far from his grandmother's residence there was a windmill which operated on a new plan. Isaac was in the habit of going thither frequently, and would spend whole hours in examining its various parts. While the mill was at rest he pried into its internal machinery. When its broad sails were set in motion by the wind he watched the process by which the millstones were made to revolve and crush the grain that was put into the hopper. After gaining a thorough knowledge of its construction he was observed to be unusually busy with his tools.

It was not long before his grandmother and all the neighborhood knew what Isaac had been about. He had constructed a model of the windmill. Though not so large, I suppose, as one of the box traps which boys set to catch squirrels, yet every part of the mill and its machinery was complete. Its little sails were neatly made of linen, and whirled round very swiftly when the mill was placed in a draught of air. Even a puff of wind from Isaac's mouth or from a a pair of bellows was sufficient to set the sails in motion. And, what was most curious, if a handful of grains of wheat were put into the little hopper, they would soon be converted into snow-white flour.

Isaac's playmates were enchanted with his new

windmill.   They thought that nothing so pretty and so wonderful had ever been seen in the whole world.

"But, Isaac," said one of them, "you have forgotten one thing that belongs to a mill."

"What is that?" asked Isaac; for he supposed that, from the roof of the mill to its foundation, he had forgotten nothing.

"Why, where is the miller?" said his friend.

"That is true — I must look out for one," said Isaac; and he set himself to consider how the deficiency should be supplied.

He might easily have made the miniature figure of a man; but then it would not have been able to move about and perform the duties of a miller.   As Captain Lemuel Gulliver had not yet discovered the Island of Liliput, Isaac did not know that there were little men in the world whose size was just suited to his windmill.   It so happened, however, that a mouse had just been caught in the trap; and, as no other miller could be found, Mr. Mouse was appointed to that important office.   The new miller made a very respectable appearance in his dark-gray coat.   To be sure, he had not a very good character for honesty, and was suspected of sometimes stealing a portion of the grain which was given him to grind.   But perhaps some two-legged millers are quite as dishonest as this small quadruped.

As Isaac grew older, it was found that he had far

more important matters in his mind than the manufacture of toys like the little windmill. All day long, if left to himself, he was either absorbed in thought or engaged in some book of mathematics or natural philosophy. At night, I think it probable, he looked up with reverential curiosity to the stars, and wondered whether they were worlds like our own, and how great was their distance from the earth, and what was the power that kept them in their courses. Perhaps, even so early in life, Isaac Newton felt a presentiment that he should be able, hereafter, to answer all these questions.

When Isaac was fourteen years old, his mother's second husband being now dead, she wished her son to leave school and assist her in managing the farm at Woolsthorpe. For a year or two, therefore, he tried to turn his attention to farming. But his mind was so bent on becoming a scholar that his mother sent him back to school, and afterwards to the University of Cambridge.

I have now finished my anecdotes of Isaac Newton's boyhood. My story would be far too long were I to mention all the splendid discoveries which he made after he came to be a man. He was the first that found out the nature of light; for, before his day, nobody could tell what the sunshine was composed of. You remember, I suppose, the story of an apple's falling on his head, and thus leading him to discover the force of gravitation, which keeps the heavenly bodies in their courses. When he had once got hold of this idea, he never permitted his mind to rest until he had searched out all the laws by which the planets are guided through the sky. This he did as thoroughly as if he had gone up among the stars and tracked them in their orbits. The boy had found out the mechanism of a windmill; the man explained to his fellow-men the mechanism of the universe.

While making these researches he was accustomed to spend night after night in a lofty tower, gazing at the heavenly bodies through a telescope. His mind was lifted far above the things of this world. He may be said, indeed, to have spent the greater part of his life in worlds that lie thousands and millions of miles away; for where the thoughts and the heart are, there is our true existence.

Did you never hear the story of Newton and his little dog Diamond? One day, when he was fifty years old, and had been hard at work more than twenty years studying the theory of light, he went out of his chamber, leaving his little dog asleep before the fire. On the table lay a heap of manuscript papers, containing all the discoveries which Newton had made during those twenty years. When his master was gone, up rose little Diamond, jumped upon the table, and overthrew the lighted candle. The papers immediately caught fire.

Just as the destruction was completed Newton opened the chamber door, and perceived that the labors of twenty years were reduced to a heap of ashes. There stood little Diamond, the author of all the mischief. Almost any other man would have sentenced the dog to immediate death. But Newton patted him on the head with his usual kindness, although grief was at his heart.

"O Diamond, Diamond," exclaimed he, "thou little knowest the mischief thou hast done!"

This incident affected his health and spirits for some time afterwards; but, from his conduct towards the little dog, you may judge what was the sweetness of his temper.

Newton lived to be a very old man, and acquired great renown, and was made a member of parliament, and received the honor of knighthood from the king. But he cared little for earthly fame and honors, and felt no pride in the vastness of his knowledge. All that he had learned only made him feel how little he knew in comparison to what remained to be known.

"I seem to myself like a child," observed he, "playing on the sea shore, and picking up here and there a curious shell or a pretty pebble, while the boundless ocean of Truth lies undiscovered before me."

At last, in 1727, when he was fourscore and five years old, Sir Isaac Newton died — or rather, he ceased to live on earth. We may be permitted to believe that he is still searching out the infinite wisdom and goodness of the Creator as earnestly, and with even more success than while his spirit animated a mortal body. He has left a fame behind him which will be as endurable as if his name were written in letters of light formed by the stars upon the midnight sky.

"I love to hear about mechanical contrivances, such as the water clock and the little windmill," remarked George. "I suppose, if Sir Isaac Newton had only thought of it, he might have found out the steam engine, and railroads, and all the other famous inventions that have come into use since his day."

"Very possibly he might," replied Mr. Temple; "and no doubt a great many people would think it more useful to manufacture steam engines than to search out the system of the universe. Other great astronomers besides Newton have been endowed with mechanical genius. There was David Rittenhouse, an American, — he made a perfect little water mill when he was only seven or eight years old. But this sort of ingenuity is but a mere trifle in comparison with the other talents of such men."

" It must have been beautiful," said Edward, " to spend whole nights in a high tower as Newton did, gazing at the stars, and the comets, and the meteors.

But what would Newton have done had he been blind? or if his eyes had been no better than mine?"

"Why, even then, my dear child," observed Mrs. Temple, "he would have found out some way of enlightening his mind and of elevating his soul. But come; little Emily is waiting to bid you good night. You must go to sleep and dream of seeing all our faces."

"But how sad it will be when I awake!" murmured Edward.

CHAPTER IV.

In the course of the next day the harmony of our little family was disturbed by something like a quarrel between George and Edward.

The former, though he loved his brother dearly, had found it quite too great a sacrifice of his own enjoyments to spend all his play time in a darkened chamber. Edward, on the other hand, was inclined to be despotic. He felt as if his bandaged eyes entitled him to demand that every body who enjoyed the blessing of sight should contribute to his comfort and amusement. He therefore insisted that George, instead of going out to play at football, should join with himself and Emily in a game of questions and answers.

George resolutely refused, and ran out of the house. He did not revisit Edward's chamber till the evening, when he stole in, looking confused, yet somewhat sullen, and sat down beside his father's chair. It was evident, by a motion of Edward's head and a slight trembling of his lips, that he was aware of George's entrance, though his footsteps had been almost inaudible. Emily, with her serious and earnest little face, looked from one to the other, as if she longed to be a messenger of peace between them.

Mr. Temple, without seeming to notice any of these circumstances, began a story.

SAMUEL JOHNSON.

Born 1709. Died 1784.

"Sam," said Mr. Michael Johnson, of Lichfield, one morning, "I am very feeble and ailing to-day. You must go to Uttoxeter in my stead, and tend the book stall in the market-place there."

This was spoken above a hundred years ago, by an elderly man, who had once been a thriving bookseller at Lichfield, in England. Being now in reduced circumstances, he was forced to go every market day and sell books at a stall, in the neighboring village of Uttoxeter.

His son, to whom Mr. Johnson spoke, was a great boy, of very singular aspect. He had an intelligent face ; but it was seamed and distorted by a scrofulous humor, which affected his eyes so badly that sometimes he was almost blind. Owing to the same cause his head would often shake with a tremulous motion as if he were afflicted with the palsy. When Sam was an infant, the famous Queen Anne had tried to cure him of this disease by laying her royal hands upon his head. But though the touch of a king or queen was supposed to be a certain remedy for scrofula, it produced no good effect upon Sam Johnson.

At the time which we speak of the poor lad was not very well dressed, and wore shoes from which his toes peeped out; for his old father had barely the means of supporting his wife and children. But, poor as the family were, young Sam Johnson had as much pride as any nobleman's son in England. The fact was, he felt conscious of uncommon sense and ability, which, in his own opinion, entitled him to great respect from the world. Perhaps he would have been glad if grown people had treated him as reverentially as his schoolfellows did. Three of them were accustomed to come for him every morning; and while he sat upon the back of one, the two others supported him on each side; and thus he rode to school in triumph.

Being a personage of so much importance, Sam could not bear the idea of standing all day in Uttoxeter market offering books to the rude and ignorant country people. Doubtless he felt the more reluctant on account of his shabby clothes, and the disorder of his eyes, and the tremulous motion of his head.

When Mr. Michael Johnson spoke Sam pouted and made an indistinct grumbling in his throat; then he looked his old father in the face and answered him loudly and deliberately.

"Sir," said he, "I will not go to Uttoxeter market!"

Mr. Johnson had seen a great deal of the lad's obstinacy ever since his birth; and while Sam was younger, the old gentleman had probably used the rod whenever occasion seemed to require. But he was now too feeble and too much out of spirits to contend with this stubborn and violent-tempered boy. He therefore gave up the point at once, and prepared to go to Uttoxeter himself.

"Well, Sam," said Mr. Johnson, as he took his hat and staff, "if for the sake of your foolish pride you can suffer your poor sick father to stand all day in the noise and confusion of the market when he ought to be in his bed, I have no more to say. But you will think of this, Sam, when I am dead and gone."

So the poor old man (perhaps with a tear in his eye, but certainly with sorrow in his heart) set forth towards Uttoxeter. The grayhaired, feeble, melancholy Michael Johnson! How sad a thing it was that he should be forced to go, in his sickness, and toil for the support of an ungrateful son who was too proud to do any thing for his father, or his mother, or himself! Sam looked after Mr. Johnson with a sullen countenance till he was out of sight.

But when the old man's figure, as he went stooping along the street, was no more to be seen, the boy's heart began to smite him. He had a vivid imagination, and it tormented him with the image of his father standing in the market-place of Uttoxeter and offering his books to the noisy crowd around him. Sam seemed to behold him arranging his literary merchandise upon the stall in such a way as was best calculated to attract notice. Here was Addison's Spectator, a long row of little volumes; here was Pope's translation of the Iliad and Odyssey; here were Dryden's poems, or those of Prior. Here, likewise, were Gulliver's Travels, and a variety of little gilt-covered children's books, such as Tom Thumb, Jack the Giant Queller, Mother Goose's Melodies, and others which our great-grand parents used to read in their childhood. And here were sermons for the pious, and pamphlets for the politicians, and ballads, some merry and some dismal ones, for the country people to sing.

Sam, in imagination, saw his father offer these books, pamphlets, and ballads, now to the rude yeomen who perhaps could not read a word; now to the country squires, who cared for nothing but to hunt hares and foxes; now to the children, who chose to spend their coppers for sugar plums or gingerbread rather than for picture books. And if Mr. Johnson should sell a book to man, woman, or child, it would cost him an hour's talk to get a profit of only sixpence.

"My poor father!" thought Sam to himself. "How his head will ache! and how heavy his heart will be! I am almost sorry that I did not do as he bade me."

Then the boy went to his mother, who was busy about the house. She did not know of what had passed between Mr. Johnson and Sam.

"Mother," said he, "did you think father seemed very ill to-day?"

"Yes, Sam," answered his mother, turning with a flushed face from the fire, where she was cooking their scanty dinner. "Your father did look very ill; and it is a pity he did not send you to Uttoxeter in his stead. You are a great boy now, and would rejoice, I am sure, to do something for your poor father, who has done so much for you."

The lad made no reply. But again his imagination set to work and conjured up another picture of poor Michael Johnson. He was standing in the hot sunshine of the market-place, and looking so weary, sick, and disconsolate, that the eyes of all the crowd were drawn to him. "Had this old man no son," the people would say among themselves, "who might have taken his place at the book stall while the father kept his bed?" And perhaps, — but this was a terrible thought for Sam! — perhaps his father would faint away and fall down in the market-place, with his gray hair in the dust and his venerable face as deathlike as that of a corpse. And there would be the bystanders gazing earnestly at Mr. Johnson, and whispering, "Is he dead? Is he dead?"

And Sam shuddered as he repeated to himself, "Is he dead?"

"O, I have been a cruel son!" thought he, within his own heart. "God forgive me! God forgive me!"

But God could not yet forgive him; for he was not truly penitent. Had he been so, he would have hastened away that very moment to Uttoxeter, and have fallen at his father's feet, even in the midst of the crowded market-place. There he would have confessed his fault, and besought Mr. Johnson to go home and leave the rest of the day's work to him. But such was Sam's pride and natural stubbornness that he could not bring himself to this humiliation. Yet he ought to have done so, for his own sake, for his father's sake, and for God's sake.

After sunset old Michael Johnson came slowly home and sat down in his customary chair. He said nothing to Sam; nor do I know that a single word ever passed between them on the subject of the son's disobedience. In a few years his father died, and left Sam to fight his way through the world by himself. It would make our story much too long were I to tell you even a few of the remarkable events of Sam's life. Moreover, there is the less need of this, because many books have been written about that poor boy, and the fame that he acquired, and all that he did or talked of doing after he came to be a man.

But one thing I must not neglect to say.   From his boyhood upward until the latest day of his life he never forgot the story of Uttoxeter market.   Often when he was a scholar of the University of Oxford, or master of an academy at Edial, or a writer for the London booksellers, — in all his poverty and toil and in all his success, — while he was walking the streets without a shilling to buy food, or when the greatest men of England were proud to feast him at their table, — still that heavy and remorseful thought came back to him, " I was cruel to my poor father in his illness!"   Many and many a time, awake or in his dreams, he seemed to see old Michael Johnson standing in the dust and confusion of the market-place and pressing his withered hand to his forehead as if it ached.

Alas! my dear children, it is a sad thing to have such a thought as this to bear us company through life.

Though the story was but half finished, yet, as it was longer than usual, Mr. Temple here made a short pause.   He perceived that Emily was in tears, and Edward turned his half-veiled face towards the speaker with an air of great earnestness and interest. As for George, he had withdrawn into the dusky shadow behind his father's chair.

CHAPTER V.

In a few moments Mr. Temple resumed the story, as follows:—

SAMUEL JOHNSON.

CONTINUED.

Well, my children, fifty years had passed away since young Sam Johnson had shown himself so hard-hearted towards his father. It was now market day in the village of Uttoxeter.

In the street of the village you might see cattle dealers with cows and oxen for sale, and pig drovers with herds of squeaking swine, and farmers with cartloads of cabbages, turnips, onions, and all other produce of the soil. Now and then a farmer's red-faced wife trotted along on horseback, with butter and cheese in two large panniers. The people of the village, with country squires, and other visitors from the neighborhood, walked hither and thither, trading, jesting, quarrelling, and making just such a bustle as their fathers and grandfathers had made half a century before.

In one part of the street there was a puppet show, with a ridiculous merryandrew, who kept both grown people and children in a roar of laughter. On the opposite side was the old stone church of Uttoxeter, with ivy climbing up its walls and partly obscuring its Gothic windows.

There was a clock in the gray tower of the ancient church, and the hands on the dialplate had now almost reached the hour of noon. At this busiest hour of the market a strange old gentleman was seen making his way among the crowd. He was very tall and bulky, and wore a brown coat and smallclothes, with black worsted stockings and buckled shoes. On his head was a three-cornered hat, beneath which a bushy gray wig thrust itself out, all in disorder. The old gentleman elbowed the people aside, and forced his way through the midst of them with a singular kind of gait, rolling his body hither and thither, so that he needed twice as much room as any other person there.

"Make way, sir!" he would cry out, in a loud, harsh voice, when somebody happened to interrupt his progress. "Sir, you intrude your person into the public thoroughfare!"

"What a queer old fellow this is!" muttered the people among themselves, hardly knowing whether to laugh or to be angry.

But when they looked into the venerable stranger's face, not the most thoughtless among them dared to offer him the least impertinence. Though his features were scarred and distorted with the scrofula, and though his eyes were dim and bleared, yet there was something of authority and wisdom in his look, which impressed them all with awe. So they stood aside to let him pass; and the old gentleman made his way across the market-place, and paused near the corner of the ivy-mantled church. Just as he reached it the clock struck twelve.

On the very spot of ground where the stranger now stood some aged people remembered that old Michael Johnson had formerly kept his book stall. The little children who had once bought picture books of him were grandfathers now.

"Yes; here is the very spot!" muttered the old gentleman to himself.

There this unknown personage took his stand and removed the three-cornered hat from his head. It was the busiest hour of the day. What with the hum of human voices, the lowing of cattle, the squeaking of pigs, and the laughter caused by the merryandrew, the market-place was in very great confusion. But the stranger seemed not to notice it any more than if the silence of a desert were around him. He was rapt in his own thoughts. Sometimes he raised his furrowed brow to heaven, as if in prayer; sometimes he bent his head, as if an insupportable weight of sorrow were upon him. It increased the awfulness of his aspect that there was a motion of his head and an almost continual tremor throughout his frame, with singular twitchings and contortions of his features.

The hot sun blazed upon his unprotected head; but he seemed not to feel its fervor. A dark cloud swept across the sky and raindrops pattered into the market-place; but the stranger heeded not the shower. The people began to gaze at the mysterious old gentleman with superstitious fear and wonder. Who could he be? Whence did he come? Wherefore was he standing bareheaded in the market-place? Even the schoolboys left the merryandrew and came to gaze, with wide-open eyes, at this tall, strange-looking old man.

There was a cattle drover in the village who had recently made a journey to the Smithfield market, in London. No sooner had this man thrust his way through the throng and taken a look at the unknown personage than he whispered to one of his acquaintances,—

"I say, neighbor Hutchins, would ye like to know who this old gentleman is?"

"Ay, that I would," replied neighbor Hutchins; "for a queerer chap I never saw in my life. Somehow it makes me feel small to look at him. He's more than a common man."

"You may well say so," answered the cattle drover. "Why, that's the famous Doctor Samuel Johnson, who they say is the greatest and learnedest man in England. I saw him in London streets, walking with one Mr. Boswell."

Yes; the poor boy, the friendless Sam, with whom we began our story, had become the famous Doctor Samuel Johnson. He was universally acknowledged as the wisest man and greatest writer in all England. He had given shape and permanence to his native language by his Dictionary. Thousands upon thousands of people had read his Idler, his Rambler, and his Rasselas. Noble and wealthy men and beautiful ladies deemed it their highest privilege to be his companions. Even the King of Great Britain had sought his acquaintance, and told him what an honor he considered it that such a man had been born in his dominions. He was now at the summit of literary renown.

But all his fame could not extinguish the bitter remembrance which had tormented him through life. Never, never had he forgotten his father's sorrowful and upbraiding look. Never, though the old man's troubles had been over so many years, had he forgiven himself for inflicting such a pang upon his heart. And now, in his old age, he had come hither to do penance, by standing at noonday, in the market-place of Uttoxeter, on the very spot where Michael Johnson had once kept his book stall. The aged and illustrious man had done what the poor boy refused to do. By thus expressing his deep repentance and humiliation of heart, he hoped to gain peace of 'conscience and the forgiveness of God.

My dear children, if you have grieved (I will not say your parents, but if you have grieved) the heart of any human being who has a claim upon your love, then think of Samuel Johnson's penance. Will it not be better to redeem the error now than to endure the agony of remorse for fifty years? Would you not rather say to a brother, " I have erred; forgive me !" than perhaps to go hereafter and shed bitter tears upon his grave?

Hardly was the story concluded when George hastily arose, and Edward likewise, stretching forth his hands into the darkness that surrounded him to find his brother. Both accused themselves of unkindness; each besought the other's forgiveness; and having done so, the trouble of their hearts vanished away like a dream.

" I am glad! I am so glad!" said Emily, in a low, earnest voice. " Now I shall sleep quietly to-night."

" My sweet child," thought Mrs. Temple as she kissed her, " mayest thou never know how much strife there is on earth! It would cost thee many a night's rest."

CHAPTER VI. .

About this period Mr. Temple found it necessary to take a journey, which interrupted the series of Biographical Stories for several evenings. In the interval, Edward practised various methods of employing and amusing his mind.

Sometimes he meditated upon beautiful objects which he had formerly seen, until the intensity of his recollection seemed to restore him the gift of sight and place every thing anew before his eyes. Sometimes he repeated verses of poetry which he did not know to be in his memory until he found them there just at the time of need. Sometimes he attempted to solve arithmetical questions which had perplexed him while at school.

Then, with his mother's assistance, he learned the letters of the string alphabet, which is used in some of the institutions for the blind in Europe. When one of his friends gave him a leaf of St. Mark's Gospel, printed in embossed characters, he endeavored to read it by passing his fingers over the letters as blind children do.

His brother George was now very kind, and spent so much time in the darkened chamber that Edward often insisted upon his going out to play. George told him all about the affairs at school, and related many amusing incidents that happened among his comrades, and informed him what sports were now in fashion, and whose kite soared the highest, and whose little ship sailed fleetest on the Frog Pond. As for Emily, she repeated stories which she had learned from a new book called THE FLOWER PEOPLE, in which the snowdrops, the violets, the columbines, the roses, and all that lovely tribe are represented as telling their secrets to a little girl. The flowers talked sweetly, as flowers should; and Edward almost fancied that he could behold their bloom and smell their fragrant breath.

Thus, in one way or another, the dark days of Edward's confinement passed not unhappily. In due time his father returned; and the next evening, when the family were assembled, he began a story.

"I must first observe, children," said he, "that some writers deny the truth of the incident which I am about to relate to you. There certainly is but little evidence in favor of it. Other respectable writers, however, tell it for a fact; and, at all events, it is an interesting story, and has an excellent moral."

So Mr. Temple proceeded to talk about the early days of

OLIVER CROMWELL.

Born 1599. Died 1658.

Not long after King James I. took the place of Queen Elizabeth on the throne of England, there lived an English knight at a place called Hinchinbrooke. His name was Sir Oliver Cromwell. He spent his life, I suppose, pretty much like other English knights and squires in those days, hunting hares and foxes and drinking large quantities of ale and wine. The old house in which he dwelt had been occupied by his ancestors before him for a good many years. In it there was a great hall, hung round with coats of arms and helmets, cuirasses and swords, which his forefathers had used in battle, and with horns of deer and tails of foxes which they or Sir Oliver himself had killed in the chase.

This Sir Oliver Cromwell had a nephew, who had been called Oliver, after himself, but who was generally known in the family by the name of little Noll. His father was a younger brother of Sir Oliver. The child was often sent to visit his uncle, who probably found him a troublesome little fellow to take care of. He was forever in mischief, and always running into some danger or other, from which he seemed to escape only by miracle.

Even while he was an infant in the cradle a strange accident had befallen him. A huge ape, which was kept in the family, snatched up little Noll in his fore paws and clambered with him to the roof of the house. There this ugly beast sat grinning at the affrighted spectators, as if it had done the most praiseworthy thing imaginable. Fortunately, however, he brought the child safe down again; and the event was afterwards considered an omen that Noll would reach a very elevated station in the world.

One morning, when Noll was five or six years old, a royal messenger arrived at Hinchinbrooke with tidings that King James was coming to dine with Sir Oliver Cromwell. This was a high honor, to be sure, but a very great trouble; for all the lords and ladies, knights, squires, guards and yeomen, who waited on the king, were to be feasted as well as himself; and more provisions would be eaten and more wine drunk in that one day than generally in a month. However, Sir Oliver expressed much thankfulness for the king's intended visit, and ordered his butler and cook to make the best preparations in their power. So a great fire was kindled in the kitchen; and the neighbors knew by the smoke which poured out of the chimney that boiling, baking, stewing, roasting, and frying were going on merrily.

By and by the sound of trumpets was heard approaching nearer and nearer; and a heavy, old-fashioned coach, surrounded by guards on horseback, drove up to the house. Sir Oliver, with his hat in his hand, stood at the gate to receive the king. His majesty was dressed in a suit of green not very new: he had a feather in his hat and a triple ruff round his neck, and over his shoulder was slung a hunting horn instead of a sword. Altogether he had not the most dignified aspect in the world; but the spectators gazed at him as if there was something superhuman and divine in his person. They even shaded their eyes with their hands, as if they were dazzled by the glory of his countenance.

"How are ye, man?" cried King James, speaking in a Scotch accent; for Scotland was his native country. "By my crown, Sir Oliver, but I am glad to see ye!"

The good knight thanked the king; at the same time kneeling down while his majesty alighted. When King James stood on the ground, he directed Sir Oliver's attention to a little boy who had come with him in the coach. He was six or seven years old, and wore a hat and feather, and was more richly dressed than the king himself. Though by no means an ill-looking child, he seemed shy, or even sulky; and his cheeks were rather pale, as if he had been kept moping within doors, instead of being sent out to play in the sun and wind.

"I have brought my son Charlie to see ye," said

the king. "I hope, Sir Oliver, ye have a son of your own to be his playmate."

Sir Oliver Cromwell made a reverential bow to the little prince, whom one of the attendants had now taken out of the coach. It was wonderful to see how all the spectators, even the aged men with their gray beards, humbled themselves before this child. They bent their bodies till their beards almost swept the dust. They looked as if they were ready to kneel down and worship him.

The poor little prince! From his earliest infancy not a soul had dared to contradict him; every body around him had acted as if he were a superior being; so that, of course, he had imbibed the same opinion of himself. He naturally supposed that the whole kingdom of Great Britain and all its inhabitants had been created solely for his benefit and amusement. This was a sad mistake; and it cost him dear enough after he had ascended his father's throne.

"What a noble little prince he is!" exclaimed Sir Oliver, lifting his hands in admiration. "No, please your majesty, I have no son to be the playmate of his royal highness; but there is a nephew of mine some where about the house. He is near the prince's age, and will be but too happy to wait upon his royal highness."

"Send for him, man! send for him!" said the king.

But, as it happened, there was no need of sending for Master Noll. While King James was speaking, a rugged, boldfaced, sturdy little urchin thrust himself through the throng of courtiers and attendants and greeted the prince with a broad stare. His doublet and hose (which had been put on new and clean in honor of the king's visit) were already soiled and torn with the rough play in which he had spent the morning. He looked no more abashed than if King James were his uncle and the prince one of his customary playfellows.

This was little Noll himself.

" Here, please your majesty, is my nephew," said Sir Oliver, somewhat ashamed of Noll's appearance and demeanor. " Oliver, make your obeisance to the king's majesty."

The boy made a pretty respectful obeisance to the king ; for in those days children were taught to pay reverence to their elders. King James, who prided himself greatly on his scholarship, asked Noll a few questions in the Latin grammar, and then introduced him to his son. The little prince, in a very grave and dignified manner, extended his hand, not for Noll to shake, but that he might kneel down and kiss it.

" Nephew," said Sir Oliver, " pay your duty to the prince."

" I owe him no duty," cried Noll, thrusting aside the prince's hand with a rude laugh. " Why should I kiss that boy's hand ? "

All the courtiers were amazed and confounded, and Sir Oliver the most of all.   But the king laughed heartily, saying, that little Noll had a stubborn English spirit, and that it was well for his son to learn betimes what sort of a people he was to rule over.

So King James and his train entered the house; and the prince, with Noll and some other children, was sent to play in a separate room while his majesty was at dinner.   The young people soon became acquainted; for boys, whether the sons of monarchs or of peasants, all like play, and are pleased with one another's society.   What games they diverted themselves with I cannot tell.   Perhaps they played at ball — perhaps at blindman's buff — perhaps at leap frog — perhaps at prison bars.   Such games have been in use for hundreds of years; and princes as well as poor children have spent some of their happiest hours in playing at them.

Meanwhile King James and his nobles were feasting with Sir Oliver in the great hall.   The king sat in a gilded chair, under a canopy, at the head of a long table.   Whenever any of the company addressed him, it was with the deepest reverence.   If the attendants offered him wine or the various delicacies of the festival, it was upon their bended knees.   You would have thought, by these tokens of worship, that the monarch was a supernatural being; only he seemed to have quite as much need of those vulgar matters, food and drink, as any other person at the table. But fate had ordained that good King James should not finish his dinner in peace.

All of a sudden there arose a terrible uproar in the room where the children were at play. Angry shouts and shrill cries of alarm were mixed up together; while the voices of elder persons were likewise heard, trying to restore order among the children. The king and every body else at table looked aghast; for perhaps the tumult made them think that a general rebellion had broken out.

" Mercy on us!" muttered Sir Oliver; "that graceless nephew of mine is in some mischief or other. The naughty little whelp!"

Getting up from table, he ran to see what was the matter, followed by many of the guests, and the king among them. They all crowded to the door of the play room.

On looking in, they beheld the little Prince Charles, with his rich dress all torn and covered with the dust of the floor. His royal blood was streaming from his nose in great abundance. He gazed at Noll with a mixture of rage and affright, and at the same time a puzzled expression, as if he could not understand how any mortal boy should dare to give him a beating. As for Noll, there stood his sturdy little figure, bold as a lion, looking as if he were ready to fight, not only the prince, but the king and kingdom too.

"You little villain!" cried his uncle. "What have you been about? Down on your knees, this instant, and ask the prince's pardon. How dare you lay your hands on the king's majesty's royal son?"

"He struck me first," grumbled the valiant little Noll; "and I've only given him his due."

Sir Oliver and the guests lifted up their hands in astonishment and horror. No punishment seemed severe enough for this wicked little varlet, who had dared to resent a blow from the king's own son. Some of the courtiers were of opinion that Noll should be sent prisoner to the Tower of London and brought to trial for high treason. Others, in their great zeal for the king's service, were about to lay hands on the boy and chastise him in the royal presence.

But King James, who sometimes showed a good deal of sagacity, ordered them to desist.

"Thou art a bold boy," said he, looking fixedly at little Noll; "and, if thou live to be a man, my son Charlie would do wisely to be friends with thee."

"I never will!" cried the little prince, stamping his foot.

"Peace, Charlie, peace!" said the king; then addressing Sir Oliver and the attendants, "Harm not the urchin; for he has taught my son a good lesson, if Heaven do but give him grace to profit by it. Hereafter, should he be tempted to tyrannize over the stubborn race of Englishmen, let him remember little Noll Cromwell and his own bloody nose."

So the king finished his dinner and departed; and for many a long year the childish quarrel between Prince Charles and Noll Cromwell was forgotten. The prince, indeed, might have lived a happier life, and have met a more peaceful death, had he remembered that quarrel and the moral which his father drew from it. But when old King James was dead, and Charles sat upon his throne, he seemed to forget that he was but a man, and that his meanest subjects were men as well as he. He wished to have the property and lives of the people of England entirely at his own disposal. But the Puritans, and all who loved liberty, rose against him, and beat him in many battles, and pulled him down from his throne.

Throughout this war between the king and nobles on one side and the people of England on the other there was a famous leader, who did more towards the ruin of royal authority than all the rest. The contest seemed like a wrestling match between King Charles and this strong man. And the king was overthrown.

When the discrowned monarch was brought to trial, that warlike leader sat in the judgment hall. Many judges were present besides himself; but he alone had the power to save King Charles or to doom him to the scaffold. After sentence was pronounced, this victorious general was entreated by his own children, on their knees, to rescue his majesty from death.

"No!" said he, sternly. "Better that one man should perish than that the whole country should be ruined for his sake. It is resolved that he shall die!"

When Charles, no longer a king, was led to the scaffold, his great enemy stood at a window of the royal palace of Whitehall. He beheld the poor victim of pride, and an evil education, and misused power, as he laid his head upon the block. He looked on with a steadfast gaze while a black-veiled executioner lifted the fatal axe and smote off that anointed head at a single blow.

"It is a righteous deed," perhaps he said to himself. "Now Englishmen may enjoy their rights."

At night, when the body of Charles was laid in the coffin, in a gloomy chamber, the general entered, lighting himself with a torch. Its gleam showed that he was now growing old; his visage was scarred with the many battles in which he had led the van; his brow was wrinkled with care and with the continual exercise of stern authority. Probably there was not a single trait, either of aspect or manner, that belonged to the little Noll who had battled so stoutly with Prince Charles. Yet this was he!

He lifted the coffin lid, and caused the light of his

torch to fall upon the dead monarch's face. Then, probably, his mind went back over all the marvellous events that had brought the hereditary King of England to this dishonored coffin, and had raised himself, a humble individual, to the possession of kingly power. He was a king, though without the empty title or the glittering crown.

"Why was it," said Cromwell to himself, or might have said, as he gazed at the pale features in the coffin, — "why was it that this great king fell, and that poor Noll Cromwell has gained all the power of the realm?"

And, indeed, why was it?

King Charles had fallen, because, in his manhood the same as when a child, he disdained to feel that every human creature was his brother. He deemed himself a superior being, and fancied that his subjects were created only for a king to rule over. And Cromwell rose, because, in spite of his many faults, he mainly fought for the rights and freedom of his fellow-men ; and therefore the poor and the oppressed all lent their strength to him.

"Dear father, how I should hate to be a king!" exclaimed Edward.

"And would you like to be a Cromwell?" inquired his father.

"I should like it well," replied George; "only I

would not have put the poor old king to death. I would have sent him out of the kingdom, or perhaps have allowed him to live in a small house near the gate of the royal palace. It was too severe to cut off his head."

"Kings are in such an unfortunate position," said Mr. Temple, "that they must either be almost deified by their subjects, or else be dethroned and beheaded. In either case it is a pitiable lot."

"O, I had rather be blind than be a king!" said Edward.

"Well, my dear Edward," observed his mother, with a smile, "I am glad you are convinced that your own lot is not the hardest in the world."

CHAPTER VII.

It was a pleasant sight, for those who had eyes, to see how patiently the blinded little boy now submitted to what he had at first deemed an intolerable calamity. The beneficent Creator has not allowed our comfort to depend on the enjoyment of any single sense. Though he has made the world so very beautiful, yet it is possible to be happy without ever beholding the blue sky, or the green and flowery earth, or the kind faces of those whom we love. Thus it appears that all the external beauty of the universe is a free gift from God over and above what is necessary to our comfort. How grateful, then, should we be to that divine Benevolence, which showers even superfluous bounties upon us!

One truth, therefore, which Edward's blindness had taught him was, that his mind and soul could dispense with the assistance of his eyes. Doubtless, however, he would have found this lesson far more difficult to learn had it not been for the affection of those around him. His parents, and George and Emily, aided him to bear his misfortune; if possible, they would have lent him their own eyes. And this,

(321)

too, was a good lesson for him. It taught him how dependent on one another God has ordained us to be, insomuch that all the necessities of mankind should incite them to mutual love.

So Edward loved his friends, and perhaps all the world, better than he ever did before. And he felt grateful towards his father for spending the evenings in telling him stories — more grateful, probably, than any of my little readers will feel towards me for so carefully writing these same stories down.

"Come, dear father," said he, the next evening, "now tell us about some other little boy who was destined to be a famous man."

"How would you like a story of a Boston boy?" asked his father.

"O, pray let us have it!" cried George, eagerly. "It will be all the better if he has been to our schools, and has coasted on the Common, and sailed boats in the Frog Pond. I shall feel acquainted with him then."

"Well, then," said Mr. Temple, "I will introduce you to a Boston boy whom all the world became acquainted with after he grew to be a man."

The story was as follows : —

BENJAMIN FRANKLIN.

Born 1706. Died 1790.

In the year 1716, or about that period, a boy used to be seen in the streets of Boston who was known among his schoolfellows and playmates by the name of Ben Franklin. Ben was born in 1706; so that he was now about ten years old. His father, who had come over from England, was a soap boiler and tallow chandler, and resided in Milk Street, not far from the Old South Church.

Ben was a bright boy at his book, and even a brighter one when at play with his comrades. He had some remarkable qualities which always seemed to give him the lead, whether at sport or in more serious matters. I might tell you a number of amusing anecdotes about him. You are acquainted, I suppose, with his famous story of the WHISTLE, and how he bought it with a whole pocket full of coppers and afterwards repented of his bargain. But Ben had grown a great boy since those days, and had gained wisdom by experience; for it was one of his peculiarities, that no incident ever happened to him without teaching him some valuable lesson. Thus he generally profited more by his misfortunes than many people do by the most favorable events that could befall them.

Ben's face was already pretty well known to the inhabitants of Boston. The selectmen and other people of note often used to visit his father, for the sake of talking about the affairs of the town or province. Mr. Franklin was considered a person of great wisdom and integrity, and was respected by all who knew him, although he supported his family by the humble trade of boiling soap and making tallow candles.

While his father and the visitors were holding deep consultations about public affairs, little Ben would sit on his stool in a corner, listening with the greatest interest, as if he understood every word. Indeed, his features were so full of intelligence that there could be but little doubt, not only that he understood what was said, but that he could have expressed some very sagacious opinions out of his own mind. But in those days boys were expected to be silent in the presence of their elders. However, Ben Franklin was looked upon as a very promising lad, who would talk and act wisely by and by.

"Neighbor Franklin," his father's friends would sometimes say, "you ought to send this boy to college and make a minister of him."

"I have often thought of it," his father would reply; "and my brother Benjamin promises to give him a great many volumes of manuscript sermons, in case he should be educated for the church. But I have a large family to support, and cannot afford the expense."

In fact, Mr. Franklin found it so difficult to provide bread for his family, that, when the boy was ten years old, it became necessary to take him from school. Ben was then employed in cutting candle wicks into equal lengths and filling the moulds with tallow ; and many families in Boston spent their evenings by the light of the candles which he had helped to make. Thus, you see, in his early days, as well as in his manhood, his labors contributed to throw light upon dark matters.

Busy as his life now was, Ben still found time to keep company with his former schoolfellows. He and the other boys were very fond of fishing, and spent many of their leisure hours on the margin of the mill pond, catching flounders, perch, eels, and tomcod, which came up thither with the tide. The place where they fished is now, probably, covered with stone pavements and brick buildings, and thronged with people and with vehicles of all kinds. But at that period it was a marshy spot on the outskirts of the town, where gulls flitted and screamed overhead and salt meadow grass grew under foot.

On the edge of the water there was a deep bed of clay, in which the boys were forced to stand while they caught their fish. Here they dabbled in mud and mire like a flock of ducks.

"This is very uncomfortable," said Ben Franklin one day to his comrades, while they were standing mid-leg deep in the quagmire.

"So it is," said the other boys. "What a pity we have no better place to stand!"

If it had not been for Ben, nothing more would

have been done or said about the matter.   But it was not in his nature to be sensible of an inconvenience without using his best efforts to find a remedy.   So, as he and his comrades were returning from the water side, Ben suddenly threw down his string of fish with a very determined air.

"Boys," cried he, "I have thought of a scheme which will be greatly for our benefit and for the public benefit."

It was queer enough, to be sure, to hear this little chap — this rosy-cheeked, ten-year-old boy — talking about schemes for the public benefit!   Nevertheless, his companions were ready to listen, being assured that Ben's scheme, whatever it was, would be well worth their attention.   They remembered how sagaciously he had conducted all their enterprises ever since he had been old enough to wear smallclothes.

They remembered, too, his wonderful contrivance of sailing across the mill pond by lying flat on his back in the water and allowing himself to be drawn along by a paper kite.   If Ben could do that, he might certainly do any thing.

"What is your scheme, Ben? — what is it?" cried they all.

It so happened that they had now come to a spot of ground where a new house was to be built.   Scattered round about lay a great many large stones, which were to be used for the cellar and foundation.

Ben mounted upon the highest of these stones, so that he might speak with the more authority.

"You know, lads," said he, "what a plague it is to be forced to stand in the quagmire yonder — over shoes and stockings (if we wear any) in mud and water. See! I am bedaubed to the knees of my smallclothes; and you are all in the same pickle. Unless we can find some remedy for this evil, our fishing business must be entirely given up. And, surely, this would be a terrible misfortune!"

"That it would! that it would!" said his comrades, sorrowfully.

"Now, I propose," continued Master Benjamin, "that we build a wharf, for the purpose of carrying on our fisheries. You see these stones. The workmen mean to use them for the underpinning of a house; but that would be for only one man's advantage. My plan is to take these same stones and carry them to the edge of the water and build a wharf with them. This will not only enable us to carry on the fishing business with comfort and to better advantage, but it will likewise be a great convenience to boats passing up and down the stream. Thus, instead of one man, fifty, or a hundred, or a thousand, besides ourselves, may be benefited by these stones. What say you, lads? Shall we build the wharf?"

Ben's proposal was received with one of those uproarious shouts wherewith boys usually express their delight at whatever completely suits their views.   Nobody thought of questioning the right and justice of building a wharf with stones that belonged to another person.

"Hurrah! hurrah!" shouted they.   "Let's set about it."

It was agreed that they should all be on the spot that evening and commence their grand public enterprise by moonlight.   Accordingly, at the appointed time, the whole gang of youthful laborers assembled, and eagerly began to remove the stones.   They had not calculated how much toil would be requisite in this important part of their undertaking.   The very first stone which they laid hold of proved so heavy that it almost seemed to be fastened to the ground. Nothing but Ben Franklin's cheerful and resolute spirit could have induced them to persevere.

Ben, as might be expected, was the soul of the enterprise.   By his mechanical genius, he contrived methods to lighten the labor of transporting the stones, so that one boy, under his directions, would perform as much as half a dozen if left to themselves.   Whenever their spirits flagged he had some joke ready, which seemed to renew their strength, by setting them all into a roar of laughter.   And when, after an hour or two of hard work, the stones were transported to the water side, Ben Franklin was the engineer to superintend the construction of the wharf.

The boys, like a colony of ants, performed a great deal of labor by their multitude, though the individual strength of each could have accomplished but little. Finally, just as the moon sank below the horizon, the great work was finished.

"Now, boys," cried Ben, "let's give three cheers and go home to bed. To-morrow we may catch fish at our ease."

"Hurrah! hurrah! hurrah!" shouted his comrades.

Then they all went home in such an ecstasy of delight that they could hardly get a wink of sleep.

The story was not yet finished; but George's impatience caused him to interrupt it.

"How I wish that I could have helped to build that wharf!" exclaimed he. "It must have been glorious fun. Ben Franklin forever, say I."

"It was a very pretty piece of work," said Mr. Temple. "But wait till you hear the end of the story."

"Father," inquired Edward, "whereabouts in Boston was the mill pond on which Ben built his wharf?"

"I do not exactly know," answered Mr. Temple; "but I suppose it to have been on the northern verge of the town, in the vicinity of what are now called Merrimack and Charlestown Streets. That thronged portion of the city was once a marsh. Some of it, in fact, was covered with water."

CHAPTER VIII.

As the children had no more questions to ask, Mr. Temple proceeded to relate what consequences ensued from the building of Ben Franklin's wharf.

BENJAMIN FRANKLIN.

Continued.

In the morning, when the early sunbeams were gleaming on the steeples and roofs of the town and gilding the water that surrounded it, the masons came, rubbing their eyes, to begin their work at the foundation of the new house. But, on reaching the spot, they rubbed their eyes so much the harder. What had become of their heap of stones?

"Why, Sam," said one to another, in great perplexity, "here's been some witchcraft at work while we were asleep. The stones must have flown away through the air!"

"More likely they have been stolen!" answered Sam.

"But who on earth would think of stealing a heap of stones?" cried a third. "Could a man carry them away in his pocket?"

The master mason, who was a gruff kind of man, stood scratching his head, and said nothing at first. But, looking carefully on the ground, he discerned innumerable tracks of little feet, some with shoes and some barefoot. Following these tracks with his eye, he saw that they formed a beaten path towards the water side.

"Ah, I see what the mischief is," said he, nodding his head. "Those little rascals, the boys,—they have stolen our stones to build a wharf with!"

The masons immediately went to examine the new structure. And to say the truth, it was well worth looking at, so neatly and with such admirable skill had it been planned and finished. The stones were put together so securely that there was no danger of their being loosened by the tide, however swiftly it might sweep along. There was a broad and safe platform to stand upon, whence the little fishermen might cast their lines into deep water and draw up fish in abundance. Indeed, it almost seemed as if Ben and his comrades might be forgiven for taking the stones, because they had done their job in such a workmanlike manner.

"The chaps that built this wharf understood their business pretty well," said one of the masons. "I should not be ashamed of such a piece of work myself."

But the master mason did not seem to enjoy the joke. He was one of those unreasonable people who care a great deal more for their own rights and privileges than for the convenience of all the rest of the world.

"Sam," said he, more gruffly than usual, "go call a constable."

So Sam called a constable, and inquiries were set on foot to discover the perpetrators of the theft. In the course of the day warrants were issued, with the signature of a justice of the peace, to take the bodies of Benjamin Franklin and other evil-disposed persons who had stolen a heap of stones. If the owner of the stolen property had not been more merciful than the master mason, it might have gone hard with our friend Benjamin and his fellow-laborers. But, luckily for them, the gentleman had a respect for Ben's father, and, moreover, was amused with the spirit of the whole affair. He therefore let the culprits off pretty easily.

But, when the constables were dismissed, the poor boys had to go through another trial, and receive sentence, and suffer execution, too, from their own fathers. Many a rod, I grieve to say, was worn to the stump on that unlucky night.

As for Ben, he was less afraid of a whipping than

of his father's disapprobation. Mr. Franklin, as I have mentioned before, was a sagacious man, and also an inflexibly upright one. He had read much for a person in his rank of life, and had pondered upon the ways of the world, until he had gained more wisdom than a whole library of books could have taught him. Ben had a greater reverence for his father than for any other person in the world, as well on account of his spotless integrity as of his practical sense and deep views of things.

Consequently, after being released from the clutches of the law, Ben came into his father's presence with no small perturbation of mind.

"Benjamin, come hither," began Mr. Franklin, in his customary solemn and weighty tone.

The boy approached and stood before his father's chair, waiting reverently to hear what judgment this good man would pass upon his late offence. He felt that now the right and wrong of the whole matter would be made to appear.

"Benjamin," said his father, "what could induce you to take property which did not belong to you?"

"Why, father," replied Ben, hanging his head at first, but then lifting his eyes to Mr. Franklin's face, "if it had been merely for my own benefit, I never should have dreamed of it. But I knew that the wharf would be a public convenience. If the owner of the stones should build a house with them, no-

body will enjoy any advantage except himself.   Now,
I made use of them in a way that was for the advan-
tage of many persons.   I thought it right to aim at
doing good to the greatest number."

"My son," said Mr. Franklin, solemnly, "so far
as it was in your power, you have done a greater
harm to the public than to the owner of the stones."

"How can that be, father?" asked Ben.

"Because, answered his father, "in building your
wharf with stolen materials, you have committed a
moral wrong.   There is no more terrible mistake
than to violate what is eternally right for the sake of
a seeming expediency.   Those who act upon such a
principle do the utmost in their power to destroy all
that is good in the world."

"Heaven forbid!" said Benjamin.

"No act," continued Mr. Franklin, "can possibly
be for the benefit of the public generally which in-
volves injustice to any individual.   It would be easy
to prove this by examples.   But, indeed, can we
suppose that our all-wise and just Creator would
have so ordered the affairs of the world that a wrong
act should be the true method of attaining a right
end?   It is impious to think so.   And I do verily
believe, Benjamin, that almost all the public and
private misery of mankind arises from a neglect of
this great truth — that evil can produce only evil
— that good ends must be wrought out by good
means."

"I will never forget it again," said Benjamin, bowing his head.

"Remember," concluded his father, "that, whenever we vary from the highest rule of right, just so far we do an injury to the world. It may seem otherwise for the moment; but, both in time and in eternity, it will be found so."

To the close of his life Ben Franklin never forgot this conversation with his father; and we have reason to suppose that, in most of his public and private career, he endeavored to act upon the principles which that good and wise man had then taught him.

After the great event of building the wharf, Ben continued to cut wick yarn and fill candle moulds for about two years. But, as he had no love for that occupation, his father often took him to see various artisans at their work, in order to discover what trade he would prefer. Thus Ben learned the use of a great many tools, the knowledge of which afterwards proved very useful to him. But he seemed much inclined to go to sea. In order to keep him at home, and likewise to gratify his taste for letters, the lad was bound apprentice to his elder brother, who had lately set up a printing office in Boston.

Here he had many opportunities of reading new books and of hearing instructive conversation. He exercised himself so successfully in writing composition, that, when no more than thirteen or fourteen years old, he became a contributor to his brother's newspaper. Ben was also a versifier, if not a poet. He made two doleful ballads — one about the shipwreck of Captain Worthilake; and the other about the pirate Black Beard, who, not long before, infested the American seas.

When Ben's verses were printed, his brother sent him to sell them to the townspeople wet from the press. "Buy my ballads!" shouted Benjamin, as he trudged through the streets with a basket full on his arm. "Who'll buy a ballad about Black Beard? A penny apiece! a penny apiece! Who'll buy my ballads?"

If one of those roughly composed and rudely printed ballads could be discovered now, it would be worth more than its weight in gold.

In this way our friend Benjamin spent his boyhood and youth, until, on account of some disagreement with his brother, he left his native town and went to Philadelphia. He landed in the latter city, a homeless and hungry young man, and bought threepence worth of bread to satisfy his appetite. Not knowing where else to go, he entered a Quaker meeting house, sat down, and fell fast asleep. He has not told us whether his slumbers were visited by any dreams. But it would have been a strange dream, indeed, and an incredible one, that should have foretold how great a man he was destined to become, and how much he would be honored in that very city where he was now friendless and unknown.

So here we finish our story of the childhood of Benjamin Franklin. One of these days, if you would know what he was in his manhood, you must read his own works and the history of American independence.

"Do let us hear a little more of him!" said Edward; "not that I admire him so much as many other characters; but he interests me, because he was a Yankee boy."

"My dear son," replied Mr. Temple, "it would require a whole volume of talk to tell you all that is worth knowing about Benjamin Franklin. There is a very pretty anecdote of his flying a kite in the midst of a thunder storm, and thus drawing down the lightning from the clouds and proving that it was the same thing as electricity. His whole life would be an interesting story, if we had time to tell it."

"But, pray, dear father, tell us what made him so famous," said George. "I have seen his portrait a great many times. There is a wooden bust of him in one of our streets; and marble ones, I suppose, in some other places. And towns, and ships of war, and steamboats, and banks, and academies, and children are often named after Franklin. Why should he have grown so very famous?"

"Your question is a reasonable one, George," answered his father. "I doubt whether Franklin's philosophical discoveries, important as they were, or even his vast political services, would have given him all the fame which he acquired. It appears to me that Poor Richard's Almanac did more than any thing else towards making him familiarly known to the public. As the writer of those proverbs which Poor Richard was supposed to utter, Franklin became the counsellor and household friend of almost every family in America. Thus it was the humblest of all his labors that has done the most for his fame."

"I have read some of those proverbs," remarked Edward; "but I do not like them. They are all about getting money or saving it."

"Well," said his father, "they were suited to the condition of the country; and their effect, upon the whole, has doubtless been good — although they teach men but a very small portion of their duties."

CHAPTER IX.

HITHERTO Mr. Temple's narratives had all been about boys and men. But, the next evening, he bethought himself that the quiet little Emily would perhaps be glad to hear the story of a child of her own sex. He therefore resolved to narrate the youthful adventures of Christina, of Sweden, who began to be a queen at the age of no more than six years. If we have any little girls among our readers, they must not suppose that Christina is set before them as a pattern of what they ought to be. On the contrary, the tale of her life is chiefly profitable as showing the evil effects of a wrong education, which caused this daughter of a king to be both useless and unhappy. Here follows the story.

QUEEN CHRISTINA.

BORN 1626. DIED 1689.

In the royal palace at Stockholm, the capital city of Sweden, there was born, in 1626, a little princess.

The king, her father, gave her the name of Christina, in memory of a Swedish girl with whom he had been in love. His own name was Gustavus Adolphus; and he was also called the Lion of the North, because he had gained greater fame in war than any other prince or general then alive. With this valiant king for their commander, the Swedes had made themselves terrible to the Emperor of Germany and to the King of France, and were looked upon as the chief defence of the Protestant religion.

The little Christina was by no means a beautiful child. To confess the truth, she was remarkably plain. The queen, her mother, did not love her so much as she ought; partly, perhaps, on account of Christina's want of beauty, and also because both the king and queen had wished for a son, who might have gained as great renown in battle as his father had.

The king, however, soon became exceedingly fond of the infant princess. When Christina was very young she was taken violently sick. Gustavus Adolphus, who was several hundred miles from Stockholm, travelled night and day, and never rested until he held the poor child in his arms. On her recovery he made a solemn festival, in order to show his joy to the people of Sweden and express his gratitude to Heaven. After this event he took his daughter with him in all the journeys which he made throughout his kingdom.

Christina soon proved herself a bold and sturdy little girl. When she was two years old, the king and herself, in the course of a journey, came to the strong fortress of Colmar. On the battlements were soldiers clad in steel armor, which glittered in the sunshine. There were likewise great cannons, pointing their black mouths at Gustavus and little Christina, and ready to belch out their smoke and thunder; for, whenever a king enters a fortress, it is customary to receive him with a royal salute of artillery.

But the captain of the fortress met Gustavus and his daughter as they were about to enter the gateway.

"May it please your majesty," said he, taking off his steel cap and bowing profoundly, " I fear that, if we receive you with a salute of cannon, the little princess will be frightened almost to death."

Gustavus looked earnestly at his daughter, and was indeed apprehensive that the thunder of so many cannon might perhaps throw her into convulsions. He had almost a mind to tell the captain to let them enter the fortress quietly, as common people might have done, without all this head-splitting racket. But no; this would not do.

" Let them fire," said he, waving his hand. Christina is a soldier's daughter, and must learn to bear the noise of cannon."

So the captain uttered the word of command, and immediately there was a terrible peal of thunder from the cannon, and such a gush of smoke that it enveloped the whole fortress in its volumes. But, amid all the din and confusion, Christina was seen clapping her little hands and laughing in an ecstasy of delight. Probably nothing ever pleased her father so much as to see that his daughter promised to be fearless as himself. He determined to educate her exactly as if she had been a boy, and to teach her all the knowledge needful to the ruler of a kingdom and the commander of an army.

But Gustavus should have remembered that Providence had created her to be a woman, and that it was not for him to make a man of her.

However, the king derived great happiness from his beloved Christina. It must have been a pleasant sight to see the powerful monarch of Sweden playing in some magnificent hall of the palace with his merry little girl. Then he forgot that the weight of a kingdom rested upon his shoulders. He forgot that the wise Chancellor Oxenstiern was waiting to consult with him how to render Sweden the greatest nation of Europe. He forgot that the Emperor of Germany and the King of France were plotting together how they might pull him down from his throne.

Yes; Gustavus forgot all the perils, and cares, and pompous irksomeness of a royal life; and was as happy, while playing with his child, as the humblest peasant in the realm of Sweden. How gayly did they dance along the marble floor of the palace, this valiant king, with his upright, martial figure, his war-worn visage, and commanding aspect, and the small, round form of Christina, with her rosy face of childish merriment! Her little fingers were clasped in her father's hand, which had held the leading staff in many famous victories. His crown and sceptre were her playthings. She could disarm Gustavus of his sword, which was so terrible to the princes of Europe.

But, alas! the king was not long permitted to enjoy Christina's society. When she was four years old Gustavus was summoned to take command of the allied armies of Germany, which were fighting against the emperor. His greatest affliction was the necessity of parting with his child; but people in such high stations have but little opportunity for domestic happiness. He called an assembly of the senators of Sweden and confided Christina to their care, saying, that each one of them must be a father to her if he himself should fall in battle.

At the moment of his departure Christina ran towards him and began to address him with a speech which somebody had taught her for the occasion. Gustavus was busied with thoughts about the affairs of the kingdom, so that he did not immediately attend to the childish voice of his little girl. Christina, who did not love to be unnoticed, immediately stopped short and pulled him by the coat.

"Father," said she, "why do not you listen to my speech?"

In a moment the king forgot every thing except that he was parting with what he loved best in all the world. He caught the child in his arms, pressed her to his bosom, and burst into tears. Yes; though he was a brave man, and though he wore a steel corselet on his breast, and though armies were waiting for him to lead them to battle, still his heart melted within him, and he wept. Christina, too, was so afflicted that her attendants began to fear that she would actually die of grief. But probably she was soon comforted; for children seldom remember their parents quite so faithfully as their parents remember them.

For two years more Christina remained in the palace at Stockholm. The queen, her mother, had accompanied Gustavus to the wars. The child, therefore, was left to the guardianship of five of the wisest men in the kingdom. But these wise men knew better how to manage the affairs of state than how to govern and educate a little girl so as to render her a good and happy woman.

When two years had passed away, tidings were brought to Stockholm which filled every body with triumph and sorrow at the same time. The Swedes had won a glorious victory at Lutzen. But, alas! the warlike King of Sweden, the Lion of the North, the father of our little Christina, had been slain at the foot of a great stone, which still marks the spot of that hero's death.

Soon after this sad event, a general assembly, or congress, consisting of deputations from the nobles, the clergy, the burghers, and the peasants of Sweden, was summoned to meet at Stockholm. It was for the purpose of declaring little Christina to be Queen of Sweden and giving her the crown and sceptre of her deceased father. Silence being proclaimed, the Chancellor Oxenstiern arose.

"We desire to know," said he, "whether the people of Sweden will take the daughter of our dead king, Gustavus Adolphus, to be their queen."

When the chancellor had spoken, an old man, with white hair and in coarse apparel, stood up in the midst of the assembly. He was a peasant, Lars Larrson by name, and had spent most of his life in laboring on a farm.

"Who is this daughter of Gustavus?" asked the old man. "We do not know her. Let her be shown to us."

Then Christina was brought into the hall and placed before the old peasant. It was strange, no doubt, to see a child — a little girl of six years old — offered to the Swedes as their ruler instead of the brave king, her father, who had led them to victory so many times. Could her baby fingers wield a sword in war? Could her childish mind govern the nation wisely in peace?

But the Swedes do not appear to have asked themselves these questions. Old Lars Larrson took Christina up in his arms and gazed earnestly into her face. He had known the great Gustavus well; and his heart was touched when he saw the likeness which the little girl bore to that heroic monarch.

"Yes," cried he, with the tears gushing down his furrowed cheeks; "this is truly the daughter of our Gustavus! Here is her father's brow!—here is his piercing eye! She is his very picture! This child shall be our queen!"

Then all the proud nobles of Sweden, and the reverend clergy, and the burghers, and the peasants, knelt down at the child's feet and kissed her hand.

"Long live Christina, Queen of Sweden!" shouted they.

Even after she was a woman grown Christina remembered the pleasure which she felt in seeing all these men at her feet and hearing them acknowledge her as their supreme ruler. Poor child! she was yet to learn that power does not insure happiness. As yet, however, she had not any real power. All the public business, it is true, was transacted in her name; but the kingdom was governed by a number of the most experienced statesmen, who were called a regency.

But it was considered necessary that the little queen should be present at the public ceremonies, and should behave just as if she were in reality the ruler of the nation. When she was seven years of age, some ambassadors from the Czar of Muscovy came to the Swedish court. They wore long beards, and were clad in a strange fashion, with furs and other outlandish ornaments; and as they were inhabitants of a half-civilized country, they did not behave like other people. The Chancellor Oxenstiern was afraid that the young queen would burst out a-laughing at the first sight of these queer ambassadors, or else that she would be frightened by their unusual aspect.

"Why should I be frightened?" said the little queen. "And do you suppose that I have no better manners than to laugh? Only tell me how I must behave, and I will do it."

Accordingly, the Muscovite ambassadors were introduced; and Christina received them and answered their speeches with as much dignity and propriety as if she had been a grown woman.

All this time, though Christina was now a queen, you must not suppose that she was left to act as she pleased. She had a preceptor, named John Mathias, who was a very learned man and capable of instructing her in all the branches of science. But there was nobody to teach her the delicate graces and gentle virtues of a woman. She was surrounded almost entirely by men, and had learned to despise the society of her own sex. At the age of nine years she was separated from her mother, whom the Swedes did not consider a proper person to be intrusted with the charge of her. No little girl who sits by a New England fireside has cause to envy Christina in the royal palace at Stockholm.

Yet she made great progress in her studies. She learned to read the classical authors of Greece and Rome, and became a great admirer of the heroes and poets of old times. Then, as for active exercises, she could ride on horseback as well as any man in her kingdom. She was fond of hunting, and could shoot at a mark with wonderful skill. But dancing was the only feminine accomplishment with which she had any acquaintance.

She was so restless in her disposition that none of her attendants were sure of a moment's quiet neither day nor night. She grew up, I am sorry to say, a very unamiable person, ill tempered, proud, stubborn, and, in short, unfit to make those around her happy or to be happy herself. Let every little girl, who has been taught self-control and a due regard for the rights of others, thank Heaven that she has had better instruction than this poor little Queen of Sweden.

At the age of eighteen Christina was declared free to govern the kingdom by herself without the aid of a regency. At this period of her life she was a young woman of striking aspect, a good figure, and intelligent face, but very strangely dressed. She wore a short habit of gray cloth, with a man's vest over it, and a black scarf around her neck; but no jewels nor ornaments of any kind.

Yet, though Christina was so negligent of her appearance, there was something in her air and manner that proclaimed her as the ruler of a kingdom. Her eyes, it is said, had a very fierce and haughty look. Old General Wrangel, who had often caused the enemies of Sweden to tremble in battle, actually trembled himself when he encountered the eyes of the queen. But it would have been better for Christina if she could have made people love her, by means of soft and gentle looks, instead of affrighting them by such terrible glances.

And now I have told you almost all that is amusing or instructive in the childhood of Christina. Only a few more words need be said about her; for it is neither pleasant nor profitable to think of many things that she did after she grew to be a woman.

When she had worn the crown a few years, she began to consider it beneath her dignity to be called a queen, because the name implied that she belonged to the weaker sex. She therefore caused herself to be proclaimed KING; thus declaring to the world that she despised her own sex and was desirous of being ranked among men. But in the twenty-eighth year of her age Christina grew tired of royalty, and resolved to be neither a king nor a queen any longer. She took the crown from her head with her own hands, and ceased to be the ruler of Sweden. The people did not greatly regret her abdication; for she had governed them ill, and had taken much of their property to supply her extravagance.

Having thus given up her hereditary crown, Christina left Sweden and travelled over many of the countries of Europe. Every where she was received with great ceremony, because she was the daughter of the renowned Gustavus and had herself been a powerful queen. Perhaps you would like to know something about her personal appearance in the latter part of her life. She is described as wearing a man's vest, a short gray petticoat, embroidered with gold and silver, and a black wig, which was thrust awry upon her head. She wore no gloves, and so seldom washed her hands that nobody could tell what had been their original color. In this strange dress, and, I suppose, without washing her hands or face, she visited the magnificent court of Louis XIV.

She died in 1689. None loved her while she lived, nor regretted her death, nor planted a single flower upon her grave. Happy are the little girls of America, who are brought up quietly and tenderly at the domestic hearth, and thus become gentle and delicate women! May none of them ever lose the loveliness of their sex by receiving such an education as that of Queen Christina!

Emily, timid, quiet, and sensitive, was the very reverse of little Christina. She seemed shocked at the idea of such a bold and masculine character as has been described in the foregoing story.

"I never could have loved her," whispered she to Mrs. Temple; and then she added, with that love of personal neatness which generally accompanies purity of heart, "It troubles me to think of her unclean hands!"

"Christina was a sad specimen of womankind indeed," said Mrs. Temple. "But it is very possible for a woman to have a strong mind, and to be fitted for the active business of life, without losing any of her natural delicacy. Perhaps some time or other Mr. Temple will tell you a story of such a woman."

It was now time for Edward to be left to repose. His brother George shook him heartily by the hand, and hoped, as he had hoped twenty times before, that to-morrow or the next day Ned's eyes would be strong enough to look the sun right in the face.

"Thank you, George," replied Edward, smiling; "but I am not half so impatient as at first. If my bodily eyesight were as good as yours, perhaps I could not see things so distinctly with my mind's eye. But now there is a light within which shows me the little Quaker artist, Ben West, and Isaac Newton with his windmill, and stubborn Sam Johnson, and stout Noll Cromwell, and shrewd Ben Franklin, and little Queen Christina, with the Swedes kneeling at her feet. It seems as if I really saw these personages face to face. So I can bear the darkness outside of me pretty well."

When Edward ceased speaking, Emily put up her mouth and kissed him as her farewell for the night.

"Ah, I forgot!" said Edward, with a sigh. "I cannot see any of your faces. What would it signify to see all the famous people in the world, if I must be blind to the faces that I love?"

"You must try to see us with your heart, my dear child," said his mother.

Edward went to bed somewhat dispirited; but, quickly falling asleep, was visited with such a pleasant dream of the sunshine and of his dearest friends that he felt the happier for it all the next day. And we hope to find him still happy when we meet again.